I Am a Woman

I Am a Woman

by Ann Bannon

CLEIS
PRESS

Published in the United States by Cleis Press Inc.,
P.O. Box 14684, San Francisco, California 94114.
Printed in the United States.
Cover design: Scott Idleman
Text design: Karen Quigg
Cleis Press logo art: Juana Alicia
10 9 8 7 6 5 4 3 2 1

Introduction

Many years ago, when this book was in its final creative stages, I had a lucky invitation to come to New York and finish it in the home of friends of friends. They were young career women, living in a very small apartment in a very old building on the Upper West Side of Manhattan, near Columbia University. Luckier still, they were on the top floor, and in the hallway outside their front door stood a dubious flight of stairs that took one to the roof. There I repaired when I got stuck, or the typewriter fought back, or the coffee ran out, and gazed out at marvelous Manhattan. I especially liked going up there after dark, when the great city was spread out like a carpet of sparklers, brilliant with promise. I had just invented Beebo Brinker for this book, and with the intensity of youth, I imagined her real-life counterpart out there somewhere, down in the Village going about her business, while I, on my roof, was trying to capture her story. I spent a fair amount of time leaning on the crumbly old parapets, staring deep into the lights and wondering if there were a real Beebo on this planet. If there were, would I ever meet her? Would she be like the woman I had contrived out of sheer need so she would at least exist somewhere in the world, even if only in the pages of my book? Was there anybody like her anywhere? Big, bold, handsome, the quintessential 1950s buccaneer butch, she was a heller and I adored her.

Not once did it occur to me to wonder if other people would ever know or care about Beebo Brinker. Not once did I ask myself if other women would fall under her spell, if readers would be amused and engaged by her, if she would develop a life of her own that would carry her across the decades until I would find myself sharing her with the rest of the world. What I wanted to know was, Would she be there for me, more real than reality? Would she rescue me from the frustration and isolation of a difficult marriage, from the impatience to be my own person before circumstances made it possible, from all the personal needs deferred in the interests of cherishing my children and finding my way in this life? It was a lot to dump on a fictional character. But she was my creature, my fantasy—and once conceived, she stood up and, with her broad shoulders, helped me lift my burdens.

Up there on that long-ago rooftop, I didn't foresee Beebo's future, but I did try to glimpse my own. Looking out at all those bright electric blooms spread at my feet, I pondered, If each one were a reader, how many would remember the name of Ann Bannon? Would I ever come back to Manhattan some day to acclaim? Reluctantly I acknowledged the realities: I was writing paperback pulp fiction. The Beatles had yet to glamorize the "Paperback Writer." The stories were ephemeral; even the physical material of the books was so fragile that it hardly survived a single reading. The glue dried and cracked, the pages fell out, the paper yellowed after mere months, and the ink ate right through it anyway. The covers shouted "Sleaze!" The critics ignored the books in droves, and "serious" writers were going to the hardback publishers. Of course, we did have readers. People were grabbing the pulps off drugstore shelves and bus station kiosks, and reading them almost in a gulp. But then they tossed them in trash cans and forgot them. Given this precarious bit of fleeting notoriety, I had not yet even mustered the courage to acknowledge my authorship to friends and family, much less to the public. No, there was no immortality here for Ann Bannon.

So I worked on *I Am a Woman* under no illusions about the prospects for enduring fame. That I am sitting down to share this with my readers forty-five years and five editions later is a true astonishment. But the perdurable appeal of the butch-femme dichotomy is not. It has, however, undergone some interesting changes.

When I was writing *I Am a Woman,* the unquestioned role choices open to lesbians were two: butch or femme. As Robin Tyler has observed, even if you weren't sure which one you were, you wanted to be butch, because they didn't have to do the dishes. Well, maybe it wasn't that simple for everyone, but women generally were not nearly as experimental with those roles as they later became. Butches were strong, tough, heroic, romantic. They fought battles in back alleys over femmes and were quite capable of ruling the roost. The femmes, by contrast, could be more girly; some were, in a way, early examples of "lipstick lesbians." They might appear seductive, compliant, even pretty. It was almost a mirror image of mainstream society: the guy-gals and the gal-gals. It was exciting, sexy, and dramatic. But it was also confining, and as the Women's Movement unfolded in the '60s and '70s, it began to seem rigid and outdated. This was no way to run a romantic partnership, with one member always on top, one always on the bottom.

As so often happens when the pendulum swings, it swings the old ways right out of the ballpark. The butch-femme dichotomy was rejected altogether for a while, replaced with more egalitarian liaisons. But it always exerted a tug on the heart, propelled by the sheer charisma of the archetypal bulldyke: independent, sensual, provocative, and more than a little dangerous. Today, among young women, it seems to have a place again, as long as it is recognized as a choice. But when Laura met Beebo in that lesbian bar called The Cellar all those years ago, both women were already locked into the paradigm. Laura was feminine in the traditional way. Her defenses, her fear of emotional entanglement, quickly melted under the laser of Beebo's sexual focus. And on her side, Beebo was intrigued by Laura's beguiling femaleness.

I knew of no other way to write about them. Interestingly, I had tried other things. After *Odd Girl Out,* my first book, was published, I completed about a hundred pages of what was to be the second book for Fawcett Publications. They were the publishers of the Gold Medal Series, under whose imprint all my books were originally published. The editor, Dick Carroll, saw those pages and hated them. I was trying to "go straight," thinking it would be easier to face friends and family as an author with at least one conventional romance under my writer's belt. But Dick discerned at once that, whatever the merits of the plot, I didn't even like my characters; it was not possible to care how their lives turned out. They did not, as good characters must, talk to me at all.

Once again, he told me what he had told me at the beginning, when I was trying to bring *Odd Girl Out* to life: "Go back to the people you love and breathe some life into them." Thus was born the idea of developing a series and making some of the characters ongoing. I had left Beth behind in the first book to marry the college man who loved her. But I had put Laura on the train out of her college town with vague aspirations for a new life somewhere where she could be who she really was. After a blow-up with her difficult father, Merrill Landon, she decamped for New York. But whom would she meet there and what would she do?

I had been reading everything I could get my hands on in the two years or so between *Odd Girl Out* and *I Am a Woman,* trying to encompass the whole wonderful, alarming, irresistible idea of women together. I had learned the word *lesbian.* I had learned about butches and femmes. In travel books, I had discovered that mythical hamlet, Manhattan's own Brigadoon, Greenwich Village. I was thoroughly enchanted. But something was missing: I had Laura, my heroine, but I was lacking a hero. The idea of one had been forming out of the mists in my mind during those two years. But it would take the perfect name to bring her to life.

Before that could happen, I had to do some "field work" and get to know my chosen territory. Living first in Philadelphia, where it was easy to get to New York, and later in Southern California, where it was not, I nevertheless made my authorial pilgrimages to Greenwich Village. With the help of friends, most notably Marijane

Meaker and Sandra Scoppetone, wonderful writers themselves, I went exploring and found the haunts of Beebo Brinker: the little brownstones, the specialty shops, the crooked streets, and the wonderful, slightly trashy, and wholly mesmerizing women's bars, replete with their full complement of admiring "johns," tucked into the nooks of the Village.

By the time the Naiad editions were settling into middle age, somewhere in the late '80s and early '90s, I began to realize how many women had taken Beebo and Laura to their hearts. In the most unexpected places, I found references to them: in a poem by Joan Nestle, an essay of Kate Millett's, Audre Lorde's autobiography; in the wrenching life story of Cheryl Crane, Lana Turner's daughter; in college courses, master's theses, articles both scholarly and popular; and ultimately, in communications from women and even some men readers from many parts of the globe. It leaves me wondering what sort of stories I would have produced in the '50s and '60s, had I known then that my work, seemingly so safe from formal scrutiny, would be discussed and analyzed by future generations. The writing might have been better, but it certainly would have been more guarded and self-conscious.

The same critical scorn that deemed the work of us paperback writers unworthy of attention had also seemed to guarantee us privacy, the chance to explore and experiment, to say the unsayable, and to fade away peacefully from the publishing scene when the paperbacks finished their popular run. But some of us didn't fade. After all these years, it is a rare blessing to have the public's attention and support, but a mixed blessing all the same, just because of the disconcerting attention. There are times when I wish I had done enough living back then, when I was doing so much writing, to justify my grand generalizations, my cocksure assertions, my pronouncements on life and love. I was awfully damn young. But maybe it's just as well that I didn't have the advantage of maturity to temper Beebo's outbursts and Laura's emotional extremes. After all, that's how it feels and goes down when you're young.

So here are Beebo and Laura meeting for the first time. Where did the characters come from? The idea for Laura was based on my friendship with a sorority sister during my undergraduate days. She was two years younger than I and had many of the personality traits that make Laura both lovable and exasperating: shyness, lack of self-confidence, and hypersensitivity, but also warmth, sweetness of character, and, once she trusted you, a staunch friendship. She was slightly taller than average, with bright Scandinavian blonde hair and an engaging smile. After we got to be friends, she confided in me about her troubles with her tough-minded and abrupt father, who sounded to me like a man insensitive in reverse proportion to his daughter's delicacy of feeling. The days when his letters arrived were downers for her, and they gave me a sort of scaffolding on which to embroider stories about her interior life. I recognized in "Laura" some of my own shaky sense of self. But unlike me, she rarely dated, seeming content to stay home most weekends and to shine academically. Whether or not she felt stirrings of romantic affection for women, I will never know, although I have my sympathetic suspicions. But I remember her as a sweetheart, with a shy warmth, and a prettiness and appeal she didn't recognize in herself.

Beebo was another story. She was my own unrealized romantic phantom. There was another college friend, it is only fair to concede, who gave me the physical prototype. She was taller than the rest of us and strikingly handsome, with a crop of wavy, dark-blonde hair and an irresistible smile. Her nickname was one of those too-cute tomboy variations on a boy's name. She hated it and made us promise never to use it, but her formal name didn't seem to suit her. I remember running into her in the dorm bathroom—one of those gray marble affairs with rows of icy washbowls and green toilet stalls—in her skivvies, and trying not to admire her unduly. I think I made her a little squirmy, and she did seem to be in love with her serious beau, whom she married upon graduation. Well, we win a few and lose a few.

Actually, I didn't quite know in that early period in my life which glamorous options to hang on the bare architecture of my fantasy hero. I just thought she needed to look like "Tommie" and to have the "heart and stomach of a king," to quote Elizabeth I. It took me a few trips to Greenwich Village, and the reading of some of the then-current pulp paperbacks, to begin to recognize the qualities she required and to flesh them out. By that time, I was into the planning for this book and ruminating hard about my characters.

And so we come back to the roof of that Upper West Side apartment, looking down on the lights of the city. One night, staring across the twinkling horizon and seeing the character in my mind's eye, I thought for the thousandth time, "If I could just find a name for her, she would come into focus for me." For whatever blessed reason, it was at that moment that the childhood nickname of an old friend floated back into my mind: Beebo. I seized upon it and captured my Beebo whole, intact, entire. Never again was I the same, once Beebo began to breathe. The Beebo Brinker Chronicles were off and running, and so was their author. Thus it was that Beebo met Laura, and they began their passionate but rocky odyssey.

There is one other character whose genesis deserves attention for a moment. He is Jack Mann, that cynical, witty, sometimes prickly, but quite lovable gay man who makes his initial bow in this novel. He is shamelessly plucked, right down to his hair and fingernails, from an old hometown friend whom I met through my first serious beau—a "Jack," too, but with a different last name. The original Jack, probably five or six years older than I, loved traditional jazz, and in my family, it was played a lot. My stepfather was a superb jazz piano player, and my mother, a one-woman cheering section. The rest of us were young, feisty, and crazy about the music, which was undergoing a revival of interest in the '40s and '50s. We worshiped Bix Beiderbecke, Louis Armstrong, Jack Teagarden, Sidney Bechet, Muggsy Spanier, and many less well known but excellent musicians playing in the genre. A lot of them came through the Chicago area, where we lived, and our informal weekend jam sessions became well enough recognized to draw some of them out to our suburban bungalow on an occasional Saturday night. We hosted Lil Hardin Armstrong (Louis's first wife and a great jazz pianist herself), Johnny and Baby Dodds (clarinet and drum players par excellence), and others. Jack just gobbled it up. He would settle into an old easy chair in the living room, legs propped up on a hassock and cigarette in mouth, and drum with his fingers on the chair arms. I can't count the beers that disappeared on such an evening, but there are ancient tapes of the music, and it was nothing to apologize for.

The original Jack was always a treat to have in our company. My little brothers adored him, but they didn't learn his name on the first visit. There were so many young musicians around on weekends that we had a standing joke that they were all uncles: Uncle Bob, Uncle Bill, Uncle Harry. So Jack, on his first visit, was greeted with, "Here comes Uncle Somebody." It stuck, even after they mastered his name. He had a funny take on life—ironic, droll, and rather unsparing—and he would sit in that chair and shoot zingers at us between musical numbers. We all loved him. I noticed, however, that unlike the other young men who dropped by so often, he never brought a date with him. Whether or not he was gay is another of those mysteries I never cracked.

I began to lose track of Jack only after I went away to college, when I was able to get news about him only occasionally from the hometown boy I was dating. Finally, shortly after my college graduation, I thought to ask the now-former beau, "Where is Jack these days?" The answer was not reassuring. He had gone to work for the CIA and had been sent to Ho Chi Minh City, then known as Saigon. He had, in fact, made several trips there, and finally, he did not come back from one of those trips. By now, it was the early 1960s, an increasingly dangerous time to be in Southeast Asia. No one from those heedless, happy times in my hometown seems to know how his story ended. It is a source of sorrow to me that he drifted out of my life without leaving a trace—except, I venture to hope, in his incarnation in these stories as Jack Mann, the good-hearted, perpetually frustrated gay man who could never resist taking in lost kids and helping them find jobs and make their way in the Big City. Alas, they always made their way to some other lover and left Jack in the lurch. But he never lost hope, nor do I, that someday, somehow, "Uncle Somebody" will come strolling up the front walk, cracking wise and charming us all.

And oh, the drinking! And oh, the smoking! You follow it all in the narrative, and you really wonder how any of us survived those days. And the truth is, there were casualties. But consider the reason. Where else were we to go? What women's bookstores, what culture clubs, what social safety nets were there for women then? How did they even find one another? They resorted to the one social institution that represented a haven, a place to meet old friends and find new ones, a place to relax and be oneself—a place, in other words, that served an indispensable function in a perilous era. That some of the women from the '50s and '60s were sacrificed to the flow of liquor and smoke, lamentable though it is, is hardly to be wondered at. The options were so few and the need was so great that the bars were always crowded. Still, those women must be remembered with affection and gratitude; they were pioneers, too, and helped to build the foundation of sisterhood we all stand on today.

Last, the title. I had wanted to call the novel *Strangers in This World*. But Dick Carroll wouldn't go for it. I suspect he knew much better than I that my title would not work as a code phrase to alert potential readers to its lesbian content. He was a canny marketer and used every available strategy to promote the books. Indeed, he had come up with the rather clever *Odd Girl Out* as the title for my first book. So what did he invent for this one? *I Am a Woman*. I always thought it was a vacuous sort of name for a book. It has no real referent: Who, for example, is the "I"? The book is not a first-person narrative. The title makes sense only as part of a longer sentence followed by a question, which had to be reproduced in its entirety on the cover of the original edition: *I Am a Woman in Love with a Woman. Must Society Reject Me?* What a mouthful of angst. I thought it was unwieldy and irrelevant to the story line; it could have been slapped on virtually any lesbian pulp paperback. It had no special connection to this one. But *I Am a Woman* the book became and remains. And in that incarnation, it sold like the proverbial hotcakes in 1959. So Dick Carroll was right and I was wrong. It still seems unappealing to me, an almost nameless name. On the other hand, this book, vague title and all, is one of my favorites in the series.

And so the saga of Laura and Beebo begins here, with its somewhat old-fashioned language and a few dated attitudes, but with a fresh and youthful joy in love and lust and all hopeful possibilities that defies the passage of time. It's no great secret that the white-hot romance between them didn't last a lifetime. But that's only the first lifetime. They are still young at heart, still handsome women, still kicking. Who knows what the future holds? My own life is proof positive that none of us knows or perhaps would want to. All the good things seem to come upon us unawares. I leave all doors open.

Ann Bannon
Sacramento, California
December 2001

Chapter One

Tell your father to go to hell. Try it. It's a rotten hard thing to do, even if he deserves it. Merrill Landon did. He was an out-and-out bastard, but like most of the breed, he didn't know it. He said he was a good father: sensible, firm, and just. He said everything he did was for Laura's own good. He took her opposition for a sign that he was right, and the more she opposed him, the righter he swore he was.

But he was a bastard. Laura could have told you that. But she couldn't tell *him,* because he was her father. That was why she ran out on him. Left him high, dry, and sputtering in his plush Chicago apartment with only his job to console him. And never told him where she went. Never told him why.

Never told him of the angry agony of her nights, spent torching for a love gone wrong. Never mentioned his straight-laced bitter version of fatherly affection that hurt her more than his fits of temper. He never kissed her. He never touched her. He only told her, "No, Laura," and "You're wrong, as usual," and "Can't you do it right for once?"

She had taken it all her life, but it was the worst the year after she left school. It was a year of confinement in luxury, of tightly controlled resentment, of soul-searching. And one rainy night when he was out at a press dinner, she packed a small bag and went to Union Station. She bought a ticket to New York City. She could never be free from herself, but she could be free from her father, and at the moment that mattered the most.

So she rode out of the big city, wet and cold with its January gloss, and left behind Merrill Landon, her father. The man in her life. The only man in her life. The only man she ever seriously tried to love.

All she wanted from New York was a job, a place to live, a friend or two. As long as she won them herself, without her father's help, she would be happy. Much happier than when she had been surrounded with comfortable leather chairs, sheathed in sleek fine clothes, smelling like an expensive rose.

In school Laura had studied journalism. She did it to avoid a showdown with Merrill Landon. He had always taken it for granted that she would follow his profession, just as if she were a doting son anxious to imitate a successful father. She accepted his tyranny quietly, but with a corrosive resentment that he was unaware of. There were times when she hated him so actively for making a slave of her that he saw it and said, "Laura, for Chrissake, don't pout at me! Snap out of it. Act your age."

Laura was more afraid of loving Landon than leaving him. She was afraid the yearning in her would flare someday when he gave her one of his rare smiles. When he said, "Klein says you're learning fast. Good girl." And her knees went weak. But he saved her by quickly adding with embarrassed sarcasm, "But you messed up the water tower assignment. Jesus, I can never count on you, can I?"

When things became intolerable she left him at last with no showdown at all. She had considered going in to tell him about it. Walking into the library where he was working, where she was expressly forbidden to go in the evenings, and saying, "Father, I'm leaving you. I'm going to New York. I can't stand it here anymore."

He would have been brilliantly sarcastic. He would have described her to herself in terms so exaggerated that she would see herself as a grotesque mistake of nature, a freak in a fun-house mirror. He was not above such abuse. He had done it to her a few times before. Once when she was very young and hadn't learned to tiptoe around his temper yet, and once when she quit school.

Not all his threats and tantrums could send her back to school, however. There was a ghost lurking there that Laura could never face, that Landon knew nothing about. He was forced to let her stay at home, but he committed her to journalism at once, and made her work on his paper with one of his assistants.

Even Laura was surprised when she was able to resist him about returning to school. She wouldn't have thought she could stick it out. Especially when he roared at her, "Why? Why! Why! Why! Answer me, you stubborn little bitch!" And smashed an ashtray at her feet.

She did not, *could* not, tell him why. It took all her courage to admit it even to herself. She simply said, "I won't go back, Father."

"Why!"

"I won't."

"Why?" It was menacing this time.

"I won't go back."

In the end he swore at her and hurt her with the same ugly irrelevant argument he always used when she resisted him. "You know why you're alive today, don't you? Because I saved you! I dragged you out of the water and let your mother drown. And your brother. I could only save one, and it was *you* I saved! God, what a mistake. My son. My wife!" And he would turn away, groaning.

"You weren't trying to save me, Father," she said once.

"You just grabbed the nearest one and swam for shore. You screamed at Mother to save Rod and then you dragged me to shore. It's a miracle you saved even me. You see, I remember it too. I remember it very well."

He turned a pale furious face to her. "You dare to tell me what *you* remember! You silly little white-faced girl? You don't remember anything? Don't tell me what you remember!"

So she chose a night when he was out and left him without a word, at the start of an unfriendly January, and came to New York. Her first thought was to try to get work on one of the giant dailies. With her experience, surely they could find something for her. But then she realized her father was too well known in journalism circles. She hated the thought of his finding her. He had struck her more than once, and his anger with her sometimes reached such heights that she trembled in terror, expecting him to brutalize her. But it never went that far.

No, newspapers were out. Magazines were out. It would have to be something completely divorced from the world of journalism. She studied the want-ads for weeks. She tried to land a job as a receptionist with a foreign airline, but her French was too poor.

Then, after about two weeks, she found a small ad for a replacement secretary to a prominent radiologist, someone with experience preferred. It appealed to her, without her exactly knowing why. She didn't really suppose she had much of a chance of getting it and it was silly to try. Who wanted a temporary job? Most girls were supposed to want security. But Laura wasn't like most girls. She was like damn few girls, in fact. She was a loner: strange, dream-ridden, mildly neurotic, curiously interesting, like somebody who has a secret.

The next morning she was in the office of Dr. Hollingsworth, talking to his secretary. The secretary, a tremendously tall girl with big bones, a friendly face, and a sort of uncomfortable femininity, liked her right away.

"I'm Jean Bergman," she said. "Come on in and sit down. Dr. Hollingsworth isn't here yet; he gets in at nine."

Laura introduced herself and said she'd like to have the job. She was a hard worker. Jean was disposed to believe her on a hunch. It was one of those lucky breaks.

"I've talked to some other girls," she said, "but nobody seems to have had any experience. The girls with training want permanent jobs. So I guess I'll just have to find a bright beginner."

Laura smiled at her. She spoke as if it was settled. "The job will last till June first, Laura," Jean went on. "I'll be gone two months. We'll spend the time till then teaching you the routine. Sarah will be coming in in a minute—she's the other secretary. There'll be plenty for the three of us." She paused, eying Laura critically. "Well? Do you think you'd like a crack at it?"

"Yes, I would." Laura felt her heart lighten.

"Okay." Jean smiled. "I'm a trusting soul. You strike me as the efficient type. Of course, I'll have to introduce you to Dr. Hollingsworth. You understand. Now don't let me down, Laura."

"I won't. Thanks, Jean."

"You might make yourself indispensable, you know," Jean said. "I mean, they really need three girls around here. If they like you well enough—well, maybe they'll keep you on in June. It's just a chance; don't count on it."

Laura felt really worthwhile for the first time since she left home. She had never considered turning back, but there had been moments when the barren want-ads discouraged her and the wet biting weather dragged her spirits down. Now, the sun was shining through the rain.

It turned out to be a fine office to work in. Doctors have a crazy sense of humor and they are often tolerant. Dr. Hollingsworth was small and quiet, quite dignified, but tender-hearted. He had two young assistants, Dr. Carstens and Dr. Hagstrom. They were both fresh from medical school—pleasant young men. Carstens was married, but with a wildly roving eye. Every female patient fascinated him, even if he saw no more than her lungs. Hagstrom had a permanent girlfriend named Rosie with whom he conducted endless conversations on the phone. Both were devoted to Dr. Hollingsworth and considered themselves lucky to be with him.

Laura fell into the routine rapidly. She was much slower than the other girls at translating the mumbo-jumbo on the dictaphone at first. She spent nearly half the time looking up terms in the medical dictionary and the rest beating the typewriter.

The problem of finding a place to live before the hotel bills broke her was urgent. She discovered in a hurry, like most newcomers to New York, that it was a real struggle to find a decent apartment at a decent price. She asked Jean about it.

"I'm stuck," she said. "Where do people *live* in this town?"

"What's the matter with me?" Jean said. "I should have asked you if you had a place. I know a girl who's looking for a roommate. The one she had just got hitched. I'll call her."

Later she told Laura, "I talked to her. She says a couple of gals have already asked her, but to call if you want to.

"She hasn't made up her mind yet. She's a doll, you'll like her. Here's her number."

"What's her name?"

"Marcie Proffitt. *Mrs.* Proffitt." She laughed at Laura's consternation. "She's divorced," she said.

Laura called at once.

"I'm at West End and a hundred and first," Marcie said when Laura got her. Her voice was low and appealing. Laura hoped she looked like she sounded. "The penthouse," Marcie said. "It's not locked. You have to walk up the last flight."

"A penthouse?" Laura said, taken aback. "Jean said—"

"It's not as fancy as it sounds," Marcie laughed. "In fact it's falling apart. That's how I can afford it. But it has a wonderful view. Come over tonight. I'll give you some dinner. I may be late, though, so I'll leave a key for you under the doormat."

"Thanks, Marcie, I'd like to." Laura wondered, when she hung up, if Marcie's hospitality was always so impulsive.

It was dark and getting windy when Laura got off the subway at 99th Street. She walked the two blocks up Broadway to 101st, holding her coat collar close around her throat.

The apartment building was a block off Broadway, up a hill at the corner of West End Avenue. It had been a chic address once, some years ago, when West End was an exclusive neighborhood. But it was deteriorating now, quietly, almost inconspicuously, slipping into the hands of ordinary people—families with lots of kids and not much money, students, working girls. And the haut monde was quietly slipping out and heading for the other side of town.

Laura entered the vestibule. It looked like the reception hall in a medieval fort. The only light came from a small bare bulb on a desk in one corner. The whole hall was full of heavy shadows.

Laura found the elevator tucked into a corner and pressed the button. She swung slowly around on her heels to look at the hall while she waited. It gave her the shivers.

She climbed into the elevator with misgivings. It looked well used and little cleaned. There was a paper sticker plastered on the wall above the button panel saying that it had passed inspection until June of that year. Laura looked it up and down and wondered if it would last till June. She reached the twelfth and last floor and walked out into a hall. To the right of the elevator she found a pair of swinging doors, and beyond them a steel staircase. She climbed the stairs, her heels ringing, and found herself in a short dark hall with two doors in it: one to the penthouse, one to the roof. Laura went out on the roof for a look.

She walked over the red tiling toward a stone griffin carved on the railing and looked over it to the city. Below her, around her on all sides, sparkled New York. It honked and shouted down there, it murmured and sighed, it blinked and glittered like a gorgeous whore waiting to be conquered. Laura breathed deeply and smiled secretly at it. She could live with a dank front hall and patched-up elevator for a view like this.

It was ten minutes before she went into the dark corridor again and found the penthouse door. She rang twice, and when there was no answer she fumbled in the darkness for the key under the mat and unlocked the door. It opened into an unlit living room. Laura went in, shut the door behind her, and stumbled around looking for a light switch. She knocked something off a table and heard it break before she discovered a lamp in a far corner and pulled the cord.

The room was small and furnished with bamboo furniture—a couch, an easy chair, a round cocktail table. There was a console radio against one wall, and books were lying around on the floor and furniture. There were a couple of loaded ashtrays and one lay shattered on the floor—Laura's fault.

Laura found the switch in the kitchen. It was long and narrow, painted a garish yellow. Beyond that was the bedroom, with two beds and two dressers jammed into it, and some shoes and underwear scattered around. It was bright blue, with two big windows opening onto the roof. The bathroom was enormous, almost as big as the bedroom, and the same noisy yellow as the kitchen. All the pipes were exposed and the plumbing looked as if it were full of bugs.

Laura walked back into the living room and sat down stiffly. She began to have serious misgivings. This was no place for a civilized girl to live. Surely in this tremendous city there was an apartment for a girl that didn't have an astronomical rent. And where she could eat in private out of cans.

Suddenly the door burst open and Marcie came in. And Laura forgot her discomfort.

Marcie smiled. "I'm Marcie. Hi."

Laura cursed the shyness that tied knots in her tongue.

"How do you like this crazy little palace?" Marcie said, gesturing grandly around her.

"It's very nice."

Marcie laughed, and Laura was struck with the sweet perfection of her features. Her lips were full and finely balanced; her nose was of medium length and dainty. Hair with a true gold hue that no peroxide can imitate framed her face and hung nearly to her shoulders. She had the lucky black lashes and eyebrows that sometimes happen to blondes, and high color in her cheeks. She was, in short, a lovely looking girl. Laura smiled at her.

"It's a hole," said Marcie. "Don't be polite. The rent is one thirty a month."

Laura gasped.

"I know. It sounds awful. But that's only sixty-five apiece. And it includes maid service—so-called. The maid doesn't pick up a damn thing. Did you see the rest of the place?"

Laura nodded.

"Discouraged?"

"A little." Laura followed Marcie awkwardly into the kitchen.

"You'd better know the worst right off," Marcie went on. "Three other girls have called wanting to share this place with me." Laura's incredulous face made her laugh. "It's not that the place is irresistible," she explained. "It's just that apartments are hard to get in this town. Sit down, Laura." Laura obeyed her, finding a chair at the kitchen table while Marcie fussed at the stove. "Have you been here long?"

"Three weeks."

"Where did you come from?"

"Chicago."

"Oh, *that* place. I was there once with Burr. He was my husband."

"Oh," Laura said softly, almost sympathetically, as if Marcie had announced his demise.

"Well, don't put on a long face," Marcie said with a sudden laugh. "He's divorced, not dead. It was final last November." Her face became serious again and she gave Laura a plate of vegetables and hamburger. "He's very nice to know," Marcie mused. "But hell to live with. Laura, do you cook?"

"I can't boil water."

"Well, I can do that much."

Marcie lapsed into silence then, her burst of charming vitality spent. She ate quietly, as if unaware of Laura's presence, gazing at the tablecloth and forking her food up mechanically. She had withdrawn suddenly and soundlessly into a private corner where fatigue and secret thoughts absorbed her.

Laura felt more awkward than ever. She was afraid to interrupt Marcie's reverie, but like all shy people she was convinced that if you can just keep the other person talking, everything will be all right. It was an urge she couldn't resist After a few false starts she said, "Have you been in New York long, Marcie?"

Marcie looked at her, mildly surprised to find her still there. "Yes. Since we were married." She spoke absently, turning to her plate.

"When was that?"

"Three years ago." She came suddenly back to the present. "Laura, did you ever love a man and hate him at the same time?"

Laura was nonplussed. This was more than she counted on. "Well—I don't know exactly." She wasn't sure if she had ever loved Merrill Landon. She knew well enough how she hated him.

"I shouldn't throw my problems in your face like that, before you get your dinner down," Marcie smiled. She reached out and gave Laura's arm a pat that made Laura jump a little. "It's just that that damn character proposed to me again today. I don't know what to do with him. I thought maybe you could give me some advice. Have you ever been married?"

"Me? No," said Laura emphatically, as if it were a slightly lewd suggestion. "Who is 'that character'?"

"Burr. My ex-husband."

"He wants to marry you again?" It seemed unnatural to Laura. If the marriage was legally over, physically over, emotionally over, why beat the carcass?

"Yes. The fool." Marcie smiled ruefully. "He's a very persuasive fool, though."

Marcie was one of those people with the rare gift of intimacy. You knew her a few minutes, an hour, a couple of days, and you discovered to your surprise that you felt close to her. It wasn't the personal revelations she couldn't help making, as much as it was her look, her questions that asked for Laura's help. Laura felt curiously like an expert on marital affairs, and it was so ridiculous that she smiled.

"What's funny?" Marcie asked.

"You make me feel like Miss Lonelyhearts or something," Laura said.

Marcie laughed. "You don't have to give me advice, Laura, just because I ask for it. I guess you can't anyway if you're single. But just for the hell of it, what would you do if a decent honorable sort of ex-husband chased you like a demon and swore he'd kill you if you went out with anybody else?"

"I'd send him to a clinic."

Marcie shook her head. "He's healthy. If I didn't know we'd quarrel twenty-four hours a day, I'd marry him tomorrow." She sighed. "I almost said yes to him today. What's the matter with me? I'm not a dope. Or am I?"

"You don't look like one," Laura said uncomfortably.

"Poor Laura!" Marcie laughed. "I'm embarrassing you to tears. You make a good listening post. Come on, finish your hamburger. It didn't kill me."

When they cleared up the dishes, Marcie turned on the tap in the sink. A thin hesitant stream of water was called up after some pitiful groaning from the pipes. Marcie kicked a pipe under the sink.

"It's enough to drive you wild!" she exclaimed. "Some nights you have to wait around till the cows come home before there's enough to wash anything in. Oh, here it comes!"

With a scream the pipes vomited steaming water. Marcie looked at Laura and the little smile on her face widened.

Suddenly they were laughing hilariously. Laura felt the laughter soothing and tickling her tight muscles, making her relax.

"It hates me," Marcie said to the sink, grasping the faucets and rattling them furiously. The stream came to an abrupt halt. She turned to Laura again. "Do you think you can stand it?" she said.

"I think I can." Laura knew now why she wanted to move in, but she was ready to ignore the reason. She would bury it, forget it. It had no place in her world any more. She would say to herself, and half believe, that she was moving in simply because apartments were hard to find; because she could pay the rent on this one; because she and Marcie were congenial. Period. "What's your job like?" she asked Marcie casually.

"I'm supposed to be a typist-receptionist," Marcie said. "But I could never type very well. Mr. Marquardt doesn't care, though.

He just told me to make a good impression on his customers and don't chew gum on the job. I told him that would be a cinch, and he said, 'You're hired.'" She laughed. "He's nuts. But it's a great job. I just sit around most of the day."

With a face like that, I'm not surprised, Laura thought. It gave her a bad feeling. Laura worked hard, she tried hard at anything she did. It was part of her nature. Either you did a thing the whole way or you didn't do it at all. It was part of Merrill Landon's code that had rubbed off on her. It made her a little jealous to hear this lovely girl brushing idly over a comfortable job that asked almost nothing of her. Marcie would not have understood Laura's feelings at all.

"You'll get along fine with Burr," Marcie said, drying her hands on a towel. "He's always reading something. Those are his books in there." She waved a hand toward the living room. "He brings them over in hopes that I'll improve my mind." She made a face and Laura smiled at her.

"Does he come over a lot?" Laura asked.

"Yes, but don't worry. He's harmless. He talks like Hamlet sometimes—gloomy, I mean—but he's nice to dogs and children. He has a parakeet, too. I always think a man who has a parakeet can't be very vicious. Besides, I lived with him for two years, and the worst he ever did to me was spank me one time. We shouted at each other constantly, but we didn't hit each other."

"Sounds restful," Laura said.

Marcie laughed and went into the bedroom. "See if you think you'll have enough room in here," she called to Laura, who followed her slowly. "It's pretty crowded, but the bathroom makes up for it. We could fence it off and make an extra room of it if we wanted to."

Laura sat down on one of the beds. "I like it fine, Marcie," she said. "I'd like to move in. If you think we'd get along." She looked at her lap, confused. She never said these things right. Marcie laughed good-naturedly and flopped on the bed beside Laura, on her stomach. Laura had to twist around to see her. "Oh, I can get along with anybody," she said. "Even you. I'll bet you're terribly hard to get along with."

"I don't think so. I mean—" She never knew when she was being teased until she had put on a solemn face and felt like an ass. "I'm impossible," she said with a smile.

"That settles it!" Marcie exclaimed, sitting up with the pillow crushed against her bosom.

Chapter Two

They got along unusually well together, as the weeks passed into months. April came, and Jean left on her European tour, Laura and Sarah were alone in the office with the doctors, and Laura worked with a will to make up for what she still had to learn. With each day, each fact acquired and skill polished, the job meant more to her.

At home, there were no scenes or suspicions, such as female roommates have a talent for. Laura was quiet, shyly friendly, thoughtful. Marcie gave her a cram course in cooking, saw an occasional movie with her, and asked her how to spell things. Most of her free time was spent with Burr.

Laura liked Marcie very much. She tried to keep it that way. She was relieved, as time went on, that her friendship didn't get complicated by stronger feelings.

I like Marcie, and that's all, she mused to herself one time. It gave her a certain satisfaction that most women would not have understood.

As for Marcie, she was somewhat amused with Laura; with her modesty, which seemed so old-fashioned; with her shyness; with her books. But she felt a real affection for her. Laura wasn't much for gossip, but she always listened to Marcie's compulsive confessions. She was gentle and sympathetic. Her ideas were different, and Marcie listened to her with respect.

Laura wasn't pretty, but at certain angles, with certain expressions, she was striking and even memorable. Not everyone saw this quality; not everyone took the trouble to study her features. But they made a curious appeal to those who did. Her face was long and slim, and her coloring pale. But her eyes were deep and cornflower blue. If Marcie had studied them she might have seen more worldly wisdom than she dreamed of in her bookish roommate.

Laura had a good grasp on what it meant to be a woman; on what it meant to live deeply, completely, even when it didn't last; on what it meant to be a loser. And everyone must lose at least once before he can understand what it is to win.

Burr had come over the night after Laura moved in. He was of medium height but powerfully built, with a pleasant face. His brown hair was crew cut, his brown eyes sparkled zealously, like those of a man with a mission. His mission, apparently, was Marcie. He seemed to adore her; it was so plain, in fact, that it made you wonder if it was real.

He walked into the kitchen where Laura and Marcie were finishing the dishes, grabbed Marcie without a word to Laura—he didn't even seem to see her—and kissed her passionately. Laura self-consciously wiped a dish, put it on the cupboard shelf, and started to back out of the room.

"Burr! You could have said hello!" Marcie gasped when he released her. "Laura, don't go. This is—" But he kissed her again. This time when he let go she was mad. It was beautiful to see. Laura was exhilarated with the force of it. Marcie, who was always full of laughter, was walloping Burr with a wet dishcloth and calling him "You bastard!" Her eyes flashed, and she swiped at his face with long meticulously pointed nails. Laura headed for the bedroom, but Marcie turned and caught her.

"Oh, no!" she said, pulling Laura back. "I want you to see what I married. I want you to tell me if I wasn't smart to get a divorce. Look at him."

Burr, his face damp with dishwater, was gently exploring a nail-inflicted wound with one finger.

Laura tried to back out, but Burr saw her then and smiled. "Hello, Laura," he said. "You'll have to forgive my charming wife. She's very emotional."

"I'm not your wife!" Marcie flared.

Laura couldn't help thinking it was all a joke. They both seemed to be enjoying it too much.

Burr ignored Marcie. "You've probably never seen this side of her," he remarked to Laura. "I used to get it once or twice a day, like medicine. Finally drove me to divorce." Marcie threw a towel at him and he smiled pleasantly at Laura. "But don't let it bother you. You'll never have to marry her, so you'll avoid the problem."

There was a stormy pause. "Have some coffee?" Laura said suddenly to Burr.

"I'll fix him a highball," Marcie sighed. "He hates coffee."

"I don't hate it. Why do you exaggerate, honey?"

"Well, you drink that horrible Postum crap, like all the grandfathers."

"It's not crap. It's a hell of a lot better for you than coffee, I can tell you that."

"Then why don't you live on it, darling?"

"If I wanted sarcasm tonight, I would have gone over to Chita's."

"That whore!"

"I—I think I'll turn in," Laura said softly and hurried toward the door.

"Don't be silly!" Marcie looked at her, chagrined. "You haven't said two words to Burr."

"She couldn't say two words, honey. You've been talking too fast. I couldn't either, for that matter." He went over to Laura and led her by the hand to a chair. "Let's talk about you," he said. "Sit down."

Laura felt ridiculous, but she obeyed him.

"Where're you from?" he demanded.

"She's from Chicago." Marcie handed him his drink and perched on the drainboard of the sink.

"Say something from Chicago, Laura." He grinned at her.

She shrugged and laughed, embarrassed.

"What does your old man do?"

Laura was startled to think of him. He had been out of her mind in the bustle of moving in with Marcie. "He's a writer—a newspaperman," she said. She looked so uncomfortable that Burr let it drop.

After a slight quiet he said, "What do you think of my girl?"

"Burr, please!" Marcie exclaimed, but he waved at her to shut up.

"You know you won't be rooming with her for long, don't you?" He smiled at Laura, and it looked like a warning sort of smile. It made Laura faintly queasy, as if she had already done something wrong.

Laura hated to compliment a woman. It was always hypocritical because she could never tell the truth without blushing. The more she admired a girl, the harder it was to talk about her. She began to blush. "She's a very nice girl," she said hesitantly.

"Say it like you mean it!" Burr said. "She's a wonderful girl. Even if she is a shrew."

"Damn! Stop humiliating us, Burr. You aren't funny."

Burr stared at Laura, until she had to say something. "We get along just fine," she said.

"Sure. The first two days." He laughed a little.

"Burr!" Marcie exploded. "She's a girl, not an ornery bastard male like you."

"Well, I hope you two will be ecstatically happy," he said, and downed his drink.

"I won't be talked about like this!" Marcie said. She dropped down from the drainboard and started out of the room, but Burr caught her around the waist. He was sitting next to Laura, and he buried his face in Marcie's stomach. Marcie tried to grasp his short hair and push him back. Laura felt the old revulsion rising in her. Burr was doing nothing very shocking or immoral. He was just embracing the girl he loved, the girl who had been his wife. Laura knew that intellectually but her spirit retreated from the sight, repulsed.

"You know something, Laura?" Burr turned his head to look at her, still pressed against Marcie. "She acts like a damn virgin with me. She acts like she didn't have any idea what it's all about. Like we'd never been married at all, and I'd never—well, never mind what I did. She won't let me do it anymore."

"Burr, you're really repulsive," Marcie said, shaking her head at him.

"Am I?" He smiled at her.

"You know you are. Laura doesn't want to hear about that. Do you, Laura?"

"I think I'd better get to bed," Laura said.

"That's a good girl," Burr said approvingly. "Always knows when to cut out. Laura, we're going to get along fine."

"Don't go, Laura!" Marcie ordered her.

Laura, halfway to the bedroom, stopped.

"Scram!" said Burr. As she shut the door behind her he added, "Sweet dreams, Laura. You're a doll."

Laura shut the door on them as he took Marcie, still resisting, in his arms. She walked uncertainly around the bedroom for a few minutes. It occurred to her that Burr would be grateful for the use of the bedroom, but Marcie would never forgive her for suggesting it. Laura ran a bath—it took fifteen minutes to get enough water to sit in—and sat contemplatively in it, wondering what her roommate was doing in the kitchen. She tried not to think of it. But when a thing revolted her it stuck stubbornly in her head and tormented her deeply.

Laura climbed out of the tub and dried herself, looking in the mirror as she did so. She had never liked the looks of herself very well. It still amazed her to think that this slim white body of hers, this tall, slightly awkward, firm-fleshed body, had been desirable to someone once. She studied herself. She was not remarkable. She was not lush and ripe and sweet-scented. On the contrary, she was firm and flat everywhere, with long limbs and fine bones. Her pale hair hung long over her shoulders, and bangs framed her brow.

I am certainly not beautiful, she thought consciously to herself. *And yet I have been loved. I have loved.*

She gazed at herself for a moment more and the ghosts of old kisses sent shivers down her limbs. Then she rubbed herself briskly with the towel and put her pajamas on.

That's over now, she said to herself. *That happened a million years ago. I'm not the same Laura anymore. I can't—I won't love like that again. I'll work, I'll read, I'll travel. Some people aren't made for love. Even when they find it, it's wrong. I'm one of those.*

She picked up a book she had been reading—one of Burr's—and climbed into bed. There was a small lamp between the beds and she switched it on, drawing her knees up for a book rest. The covers formed a tent over her legs.

For a long while she sat and read about the mixups of other people, the people in the book. Then she closed it and put it on the bedside table. She turned the light off, but still she didn't lie down. She simply sat there in the dark, listening...listening...and heard nothing. She put her head back, resting, thinking about them in the other room, hating her thoughts but unable to shake them. After a while she slept, still sitting half-upright.

Much later, muscle cramps woke her up and forced her to lie down. She noticed that the light under the kitchen door was out. She pulled the covers over her shoulders, wondering what time it was. In a moment, all was silence again.

"Laura?" It was Marcie, whispering.

Laura sat up with a start. "Yes? Marcie, are you all right?"

"I'm all right."

"Is he gone?"

"Yes. For the time being."

"Oh. What time is it?"

"About three."

"You shouldn't stay up so late. You have to go to work in the morning."

There was a little silence.

"Laura?"

"Yes?"

"Were you ever in love?"

Laura felt a terrible wave of emotion come up in her throat. What a damnable time, what a damnable way, to ask such a question! She was defenseless against her feeling in the soft black night, with the soft voice of a lovely girl asking her, "Were you ever in love?" For a while she tried to keep her mouth clamped shut. But Marcie asked her again and she was undone.

"Were you, Laura?"

"Yes," she whispered.

"What was it like?"

"Oh, God, Marcie—it was so long ago—it was so complicated. I don't know what it was like."

"Was it good?"

"It was awful."

Marcie turned over in bed at this, raising herself on her elbows. "Wasn't it good sometimes? Now and then?"

"Now and then—" Laura whispered, "it was paradise. But most of the time it was hell."

"Did—did he love you? As much, I mean?"

Laura pressed her hands to her mouth, not trusting herself for a minute. Then she whispered, "No."

"Oh, I'm sorry." Marcie's voice was warm with sympathy. "Men are such bastards, aren't they?"

"Yes. They are."

After a moment of thought Marcie said, "Burr likes you."

"I'm glad." She couldn't stand to talk anymore. "Good night, Marcie."

"Good night, Laura." Marcie sounded a little disappointed. But she said nothing more and in a minute Laura heard her roll over and fall asleep. Laura did not sleep again that night.

Chapter Three

If Laura and Marcie went along together on greased wheels, Marcie and Burr did nothing of the kind. There was never anything real to argue about. But Burr couldn't pick up a book or clear his throat or make a suggestion without causing a disagreement. And he was as quick to snap at his ex-wife. The only times they weren't shouting at each other, they were kissing each other.

"You probably wonder why we keep seeing each other when we fight like this," Marcie said to her one night.

"Do you love each other?"

"I don't know—Yes."

"Then I guess it doesn't matter if you fight."

"I hope it doesn't drive you nuts."

"No, not at all." Laura wouldn't even look up from her book. Marcie embarrassed her with these confidences. But she couldn't go on reading. She stared at the page and waited for Marcie to continue.

Marcie couldn't keep a secret. Things poured out of her, even intimate things, even things that belonged to her private soul and should have stayed there. Laura squirmed to hear her sometimes.

"We see each other," Marcie went on, "because we can't keep our hands off each other. We fight because we're ashamed of what we want from each other. At least, I am. I guess Burr doesn't have any shame. No, that's not fair. I guess he's the one who's sure he's in love. Sometimes I think I am, because I want to keep seeing him. And other times, I think it's just his big broad shoulders."

"Don't see him for a while," Laura said. "Or try talking less when you do. See what happens. Or do you just want to keep torturing yourself?"

"I guess I do," said Marcie with such a disarming smile that Laura had to smile back.

"Well, it's not my business. I can't pass out any helpful hints," Laura said. *I won't care about your personal life, I can't,* she thought.

Marcie laughed, walking around the room, peeling off her clothes. "Laura, you're a funny girl," she said. "You're not like other girls I know."

"I'm not?" Laura felt an old near-forgotten sick feeling come up in her chest.

"No. Other girls love to talk about things. They love to gossip. Why, I know some who would get started on Burr and keep going until they had to be gagged. But you're different. You just sit there and read and think. Don't you get worn out doing so much thinking?"

"What makes you think I do so much?"

"Oh, I don't know. Don't you?"

"Everybody thinks."

"Not as much as you do."

"There's nothing wrong with it."

"I don't mean that. I mean—I guess I mean, why don't you ever go out?"

"I do. I saw that musical last week."

"I don't mean with me. Or other girls. I mean with boys."

Laura loathed conversations like these. She felt as if she had spent her whole life justifying herself to somebody—mostly Merrill Landon, but others too. As if everything she did or didn't do had to be inspected and approved. If it wasn't approved it stuck in her craw somewhere and came up now and then to make her sick. "I'm new in New York," she said. "I don't know anyone yet."

"How about Dr. Carstens? You said he was good-looking."

"He's married."

"Well, the other one, then?"

"He's practically married."

"Well, how about the big shot?"

"He's a grandfather." She said it sarcastically.

Marcie threw her hands up and laughed. "Laura, I'm going to have to do something about you."

"Don't do anything about me, please, Marcie." Something in the tone of her voice sobered Marcie up.

"Why not?" she said.

"I—I just don't want to be a bother, that's all."

"A bother!" Marcie came and sat beside her on the bed, wearing only the bottoms of a pair of blue jersey pajamas, cut like slim harem pants. Her breasts were high and full and unbearably sweet. "Laura, I like you. We're living together. We're friends. I guess I've made a bad impression on you with Burr and everything, but I want you to know I really like you. You're no bother." She smiled. "I'll get Burr to fix you up with Jack Mann. We'll go somewhere together. We need to get out. Maybe we'd quit quarreling if we didn't sit around this apartment all the time."

She paused, and Laura tried not to look at her.

"How about it?" Marcie said.

Laura was in a familiar situation. She'd been in it before, she'd be in it again, there was no escaping it. This is a heterosexual society and everybody plays the game one way or another. Or pretends to play it for appearances' sake.

"I'd love to," Laura said.

"Good! What night?"

"Any night." Laura wanted to shove her off the bed, to throw the covers at her; anything to cover up her gleaming bosom. She felt herself go hot and cold by turns and it exasperated her. She wondered how obvious it was. But even in her discomfort she knew it didn't show as much as it felt. She finally climbed past Marcie and out of the bed, making a hasty way to the bathroom.

"I'll call Burr," Marcie called after her.

Laura closed the bathroom door and leaned heavily against it, panting, her arms clasped tight around herself, rocking back and forth, her eyes shut. Spasms went through her and she shook herself angrily. Her hands stole downward in spite of herself and suddenly all her feeling was fixed in one place, clarified, shattering. There was a moment of suppressed violence when she clapped one hand over her mouth, helpless in her own grasp, and her imprisoned mouth murmured, "Marcie, Marcie, Marcie," into her hand. And then came relief, quiet. The trembling ceased, the heaving breath slowed down. She relaxed utterly, with only just enough strength in her legs to hold her up, depending on the door to do the rest. "Damn her," she said in a faint whisper. "Damn her." It was the first time she realized how strong her "friendly" feelings for Marcie really were and she was dismayed.

Laura went quickly to the washbowl and turned on the tap. She ought to be making some noise. People don't disappear into bathrooms for ten minutes in utter silence. At least not in this bathroom where every pipe had its own distinct and recognizable scream. In a few seconds Marcie was calling at her through the door.

"Laura? Can I come in?"

"Of course."

"We're going to make it for Friday. We'll see a show."

"That sounds fine."

"It'll be fun."

I will not look at her, Laura told herself, and buried her face in a washcloth. She scrubbed herself assiduously while Marcie chattered. *Damn her anyway, I won't look at her. She has no claim on me, that was a silly fool thing I did. I'll pretend it didn't happen. It didn't happen, it didn't happen.* She was afraid that if she did look it might happen again. She rinsed her face slowly and carefully in water from the groaning tap, and still Marcie stood there talking.

Laura reached for a towel and dried her face. She hung the towel up again and turned to walk out of the bathroom, ready to ignore Marcie. But Marcie had slipped into pajama tops and looked quite demure. Except for her extraordinarily pretty face. Laura stared at her, as she had known she would, as she did more and more lately.

"We'll take in a show in Greenwich Village, because it's easier to get tickets—at least to this one—and besides, Burr knows— what's the matter, Laura?"

"What? Oh, nothing. Nothing."

"You looked kind of funny."

"Did I? I didn't mean to. That sounds fine, the show I mean." She hurried past Marcie into the bedroom.

In bed she cursed herself for an idiot. *I'm just an animal,* she berated herself. *I hardly know Marcie. I won't start feeling this way, I won't!*

Out of the past rose the image of another face, a face serenely lovely, a face whose owner she had loved so desperately that she had finally been forced to leave school because of her.

Why, they look alike! she thought, startled. *Why didn't I see it before? I must be blind. They look alike, they really do.* In the dark she pictured Marcie's face beside the other, matching, comparing, regretting. It tore at her heart to see them together. She wished the morning would never come when she would have to get up, bright and cheerful and ordinary, like every other morning, and look at Marcie's face again. And Marcie's breasts.

Morning came, as mornings will, and it went the same way. It was not intolerable. Laura was secretly on guard against Marcie now. Or rather, on guard against herself. She wasn't going to fall. Marcie loved a man—men, anyway—and Laura wasn't in any hurry to go through hell with her.

A curious change had come over Laura since the days of the terrible, and wonderful, college romance with a girl named Beth. She had been so frightened then, so lost, so completely dependent on Beth. She had no courage, except what Beth gave her; no strength except through Beth; no will but Beth's. She had loved her slavishly; adored her. And when Beth left her for a man, when she told Laura it had never been real love for her at all, Laura was wounded clear through her heart.

All these things were unknown to Merrill Landon; unknown and unsuspected. They would remain forever in the dark corners of Laura's mind, where she heaped her old hurts and fears.

She had thought of killing herself when she left school and went home to face her father. But she was young and her youth worked against such thoughts. Perhaps the very fact that she had loved so deeply and so well prevented her. She had learned to need love too much to think seriously about death.

Beth had left scars on Laura. But she had been a good teacher too, and some of the things she taught her lover were beginning to assert themselves, now that Laura was on her own and time was softening the pain. Laura walked tall. She felt tall. It wasn't the simple physical fact of her height. It was a curious self-respect born of the humiliation of her love. Beth had taught Laura to look within herself, and what she found was a revelation.

Chapter Four

The following evening Laura got home rather early after seeing a show with Sarah. She rode home on the subway with a dirty gray little man, repulsively anxious to be friendly. He kept saying, "I see you're not married. You must be very careful in the big city." And laughed nervously. Laura turned away. "You mustn't ignore me, I'm only trying to help," he whined. He babbled at her about young lambs in a den of wolves until she got off. He got off with her, still talking.

Laura wasn't afraid—just mad. She turned suddenly on the little gray man at the subway entrance and said, "Leave me alone or I'll call the police."

He smiled apologetically and began to mumble. Laura's eyes narrowed and she turned away contemptuously, walking with a sure swift gait that soon discouraged him. Something proud and cold in her unmanned him. At last he stopped following and stood gaping after her. She never looked back.

Laura arrived home, her cheeks warm with the quick walk and with the victory over the little man. *God, if I could do that to my father!* she thought wistfully. She walked up the flight of stairs from the twelfth floor to the penthouse and swung open the front door. The living room was lighted and so was the kitchen. The bedroom door was open, the room showing a cool blue beyond the loud yellow kitchen. Laura walked in, swinging her purse, thinking of the ugly little man and proud of the way she had trounced him.

She stopped short with a gasp at the sight of Burr and Marcie naked together in Marcie's bed. "I'm sorry!" she exclaimed, and backed out, closing the door behind her. She collapsed on a kitchen chair and cried in furious disgust for half a minute. Then she stood up and went to the refrigerator, pretending to want a glass of milk just for an excuse to move, to ignore the hot silence in the next room.

For a while no sounds issued from the bedroom. Laura poured the milk busily and carried it into the living room. She was just putting a record on when the bedroom door opened and Marcie slipped out in her bathrobe. Laura had put her milk down. Just the sight of it was enough to make her feel green. She turned to Marcie.

"Hi," she said, too brightly. "Sorry I had to go and break in."

Marcie burst out laughing. "That's okay. Damn him, I *told* him to go home. I knew you'd get home early. I just had a feeling." She went up to Laura, still laughing, and Laura turned petulantly away. Marcie didn't notice. "We took your advice, Laura," she said. "We haven't said a word to each other tonight. Well—I said when he came in—'All right, we're not going to argue. Don't open your mouth. Not one word.' And he didn't. He didn't even say hello!" And her musical laughter tickled Laura insufferably.

Burr came out of the bedroom, looking rather sheepish, rather sleepy, very satisfied. He smiled at Laura, who had to force herself to wear a pleasant face. He was buttoning his shirt, carrying his coat over his arm, and all he said was, "Thanks, Laura." He grinned, thumbing at Marcie. "We're not speaking. I hear it was your idea." He swatted Laura's behind. "Good girl," he said. He kissed Marcie once more, hard, drew on his coat, and backed out the door, still smiling.

Marcie whirled around and around in the middle of the living room, hugging herself and laughing hilariously. "If it could always be like that," she said, "I'd marry him again tomorrow."

Laura brushed past her without a word, into the kitchen, where she poured the milk carefully back into the bottle, closed the refrigerator door, went into the bedroom, and got ready for bed.

Marcie followed her, laughing and talking until Laura got into bed and turned out the light. She wouldn't even look at Marcie's rumpled bed. But it haunted her, and she didn't fall asleep until long after Marcie had stopped whispering.

Jack Mann was small, physically tough, and very intelligent. He was a sort of cocktail-hour cynic, disillusioned enough with things to be cuttingly funny. If you like that kind of wit. Some people don't. The attitude carried over into his everyday life, but he saved his best wit especially for the after work hours, when the first fine careless flush of alcohol gave it impetus. Unfortunately he usually gave himself too much impetus and went staggering home to his bachelor apartment under the arm of a grumbling friend. He was a draftsman in the office where Burr worked as an apprentice architect and he called his work "highly skilled labor." He didn't like it. But he did like the pay.

"Why do you do it, then?" Burr asked him once.

"It's the only thing I know. But I'd much rather dig ditches."

"Well, hell, go dig ditches then. Nobody's stopping you."

Jack could turn his wit on himself as well as on others. "I can't," he told Burr. "I'm so used to sitting on my can all day I'd be lucky to get one lousy ditch dug. And then they'd probably have to bury me in it. End of a beautiful career."

Burr smiled and shook his head. But he liked him; they got along. Jack went out with Burr and Marcie before and after they got married. And after they got divorced. He was the trouble-shooter until he got too drunk, which was often.

When he arrived with Burr on Friday night Laura was irked to find that she was taller than he was. She had made up her mind that she wasn't going to enjoy the evening—just live through it. She'd have to spend the time mediating for Marcie and Burr and trying to entertain a man she didn't know or care about. So she was put out to discover that she did like Jack, after all. It ruined her fine gloomy mood.

Marcie introduced them and Jack looked up at her quizzically. "What's the matter, Landon?" he said. "You standing in a hole?"

Laura laughed and took her shoes off. It brought her down an inch. "Better?" she said.

"Better for me. Very bad for your stockings." He grinned. "Have you read Freud?"

"No."

"Well, thank God. I won't have to talk about my nightmares."

"Do you have nightmares?"

"You *have* read Freud!"

"No, I swear. You said—"

"Okay, I confess. I have nightmares. And you remind me of my mother."

"Do you have a mother?" said Burr. "Didn't you just happen?"

"That's what I keep asking my analyst. Do I have to have a mother?"

"Jack, are you seeing an analyst?" Marcie was fascinated with the idea. "Imagine being able to tell somebody *everything*. Like a sacred duty. Burr, don't you think I should be analyzed?"

"What will you use for a neurosis?" Jack asked.

"Do I need one?"

"How about Burr?"

"I'm taken," Burr said. "Besides, you talk like a nitwit, honey. You don't go to an analyst like you go to the hairdresser."

Marcie's eyes flashed. "Thanks for the compliment," she said. "I'm not as dumb as I look."

"Come on, Mother." Jack took Laura's arm and steered her out the door. "I see a storm coming up."

But it was dissipated when Marcie grabbed her coat and hurried after them.

After the play they walked down Fourth Street in the Village, meandering rather aimlessly, looking into shop windows. Laura was lost. She had never been in the Village before. She had been afraid to come down here; afraid she would see someone, and do something, and suddenly find herself caught in the strange world she had renounced. It seemed so safe, so remote from temptation to choose an uptown apartment. And yet here she was with her nerves in knots, her emotions tangled around a roommate again.

Laura pondered these things, walking slowly beside Jack in the light from the shop windows. She was unaware of where she walked or who passed by. It startled her when Jack said, "What are you thinking about, Mother?"

"Nothing." A shade of irritation crossed her face.

"Ah," he said. "I interrupted something."

"No." She turned to look at him, uncomfortable. He made her feel as if he was reading her thoughts.

"Don't lie to me. You're daydreaming."

"I am not! I'm just thinking."

He shrugged. "Same thing."

She found him very irritating then. "You don't say," she said, and looked away from him.

"You hate me," he said with a little smile.

"Now and then."

"I messed up your daydream," he said. "I'm rarely this offensive. Only when I'm sober. The rest of the time, I'm charming. Someday I suppose you'll daydream about me."

Laura stared at him and he laughed.

"At least, you'll tell me about your daydreams."

"Never."

"People do. I have a nice face. Ugly, but nice. People think, 'Jesus, that guy has a nice face. I ought to tell him my daydreams.' They do, too." He smiled. "What's the matter, Mother, you look skeptical."

"What makes you think you have a nice face?"

"Don't I?" He looked genuinely alarmed.

"It wouldn't appeal to just anyone."

"Ah, smart girl. You're right, as usual. A boy's best friend is his mother. Only the *discriminating* ones, my girl, think it's a nice face. Only the sensitive, the talented, the intelligent. Now tell me—isn't it a nice face?"

"It's a face," said Laura. "Everybody has one."

He laughed. "You're goofy," he said. "You need help. My analyst is very reasonable. He'll stick you for all you've got, but he's very reasonable."

Burr, who was walking ahead of them with Marcie, turned around to demand, "Somebody tell me where I'm going."

"Turn right at the next corner," said Jack. "You're doing fine, boy. Don't lose your nerve."

"I just want to know where the hell I'm going."

"That's a bad sign. Very bad."

"Cut it out, Jack," said Marcie. "Where are we going?"

"A little bar I know. Very gay. I go there alone when I want to be depressed."

It sounded sinister, not gay, to Laura. "What's it called?" she said.

"The Cellar. Don't worry, it's a legitimate joint." He laughed at her long face.

Marcie laughed too, and Laura's heart jumped at the sweetness of the sound. It made her hate the back of Burr, moving with big masculine easiness ahead of her in a tweed topcoat, his bristling crew cut shining.

A few minutes later Jack led them down a few steps to a pair of doors which he pushed in, letting Laura and Marcie pass.

Laura heard Burr say, behind her, in an undertone, "It *is* gay," and he laughed. "You bastard." She was mystified. It looked pretty average and ordinary. They headed for a table with four chairs, one of the few available, and Laura looked around.

The Cellar was quite dark, with the only lights placed over the bar and glowing a faint pinky orange. There were candles on the tables, and people crowded together from one end of the room to the other. Everybody seemed reasonably cheerful, but it didn't look any gayer than any other bar she had been in. She looked curiously at Burr, but he was helping Marcie out of her coat.

"No table service," Jack said. "What does everybody want?"

They gave him their orders and Laura tried to catch his eye, hoping for more information about the place. She was curious now. There were checkered tablecloths, fish nets on the wall, a lot of people—all rather young—at the tables and bar. The jukebox was going and somebody was trying to pick up a few bucks doing pencil portraits, but no one seemed very interested. The customers looked like students. There were girls in cotton pants, young men in sweaters and open-collared shirts.

"They all look like students," she said to Burr.

He grinned. "I never thought of it that way," he said. "I guess they do, all right."

She stared at him. And then she looked around the room again, and suddenly she saw a girl with her arm around another girl at a table not far away. Her heart jumped. A pair of boys at the bar were whispering urgently to each other.

Gay, Laura thought to herself. *Is that what they call it? Gay?* She was acutely uncomfortable now. It was as if she were a child of civilization, reared among the savages, who suddenly found herself among the civilized. She recognized them as her own. And yet she had adopted the habits of another race and she was embarrassed and lost with her own kind.

They looked at her—her own kind—from the bar and from the tables, and didn't recognize her. And Laura looked around at them and thought, *I'm one of you. Help me.* But if anyone had approached her she would have turned away.

Jack came back with the drinks and sat down, passing them around. He drank a shot of whisky and said to Laura, "Well? How do you like tonight's collection?"

"Tonight's collection of what?" Laura said.

"Of nuts." He looked around The Cellar. "Doesn't anyone tell you anything, Mother? Burr, what's the matter with you? She's a tourist. Make with the old travelogue, boy."

Burr laughed. "I thought you didn't get it, Laura." He smiled. "They're all queer."

Laura's face went scarlet, but the candlelight hid it. She felt an awful tide of anger and fear come up in her at that word. She felt trapped, almost frantic, and she vented it on Jack. "Why didn't you tell me?" she said. Her voice trembled with indignation.

"Take it easy, Mother," he said.

"Tonight's collection!" she mimicked bitterly. "You talk about them as if they were a bunch of animals."

"They are," he said quietly. "So are we."

"We're human beings," she said. "We have no right to sit here and laugh at them for something they can't help."

"Can't help, hell," Burr said, leaning over the table toward her. "All those gals need is a real man. That'd put them on the right track in a hurry."

Laura could have belted him. She wanted to shout, "How do you know, you big ape?" But she said instead, "You're not irresistible, Burr."

"I don't mean that!" he said, frowning at her. "Christ! I only mean a man who knows the first thing about women could lay any one of these dames—even a butch—and make her like it."

"What's the first thing about women?" Jack asked, smiling, but they ignored him.

"If men revolt her and somebody tried to—to lay her—he'd only make her sick. No matter how much he knew about women," Laura said sharply.

"Any girl who doesn't like men is either a virgin or else some bastard scared the hell out of her. She needs gentling."

"You talk about us as if we were horses!" Laura flared.

"Us?" Burr stared at her.

"Us—us women." Laura's face was burning.

Burr watched her as he talked. "Some girls get a bastard the first time," he said. "It's too bad. They end up in joints like this swapping horror stories with the other ones."

Laura hated the way he talked. She couldn't take it. "What if the bastard is her father?" she said. "And he scares the hell out of her when she's five years old? And twenty years later some ass who thinks he's a great lover comes along and throws her down and humiliates and horrifies her?"

Jack remarked, with amusement, and probably more enlightenment than the others, "Jesus, we have a moralist in our midst." He looked at her as if she were a new species of fish.

"Damn it, Laura, that's the point," Burr said. "He *wouldn't* humiliate her. I don't mean some God-damn truck driver with nothing but a quick lay on his mind. I mean a considerate decent sort of guy—a sort of Good Samaritan—" He grinned and Marcie said, "God!" and rolled her eyes to the ceiling.

"—who really wants to help the girl," Burr finished.

"Why don't you try it?" Jack said.

Marcie's face darkened. "Yes, darling, why don't you prove your little theory? I'm sure we'd all be fascinated."

"Now damn it, don't you go yammering at me. I'm talking to Laura."

"Excuse *me!*" Marcie said.

Laura leaned toward her. "I didn't mean to start anything," she said.

"Nobody ever does," Jack remarked to himself.

"He said he could lay any girl and make her like it," Marcie said.

"I said," Burr said, turning to her and intoning sarcastically, "That any guy with any—"

"We know what you said, boy," Jack interrupted. "Let's keep it purely theoretical. Nobody has to prove anything. Burr loves Marcie and Marcie loves Burr. Jack loves whisky and whisky hates Jack. Laura loves animals. Everybody happy?"

Thinking over what she had said while Jack talked, Laura began to feel sick. She wished she had been perceptive enough to see where she was when they first came into The Cellar. But she took things at face value. They had entered a little bar and they were going to have a nightcap. Okay. What was so sinister about that? Why did it have to turn out to be a damn gay bar? And why did she have to react like an angry virgin when she found out?

They stayed long enough to get pretty high. They were stared at by the regular customers, but Laura was afraid to stare back.

When she did, once or twice, she couldn't catch anyone's eye. She was ashamed of herself for trying to, but she couldn't help it.

There was a girl at the bar, standing at one end, in black pants and a white shirt open at the collar. Her hair was short and dark, and there once again was that troubling resemblance to Beth. There were some other people with her and they were all talking, but the short-haired girl seemed somehow apart from them. Now and then she would turn and smile at one of them and say a word or two. Then she turned her gaze back to the bar or into her drink, or just stared into the mirror behind the bar without seeing anything.

Laura glanced at her now and then. She had an interesting face. It made Laura want to talk to her. *It must be the drinks,* she thought, and refused another.

"I see by the look in your eye," Jack said, "that you've had enough of this place. It's nearly midnight. Are you going to turn into a pumpkin?"

"God, I hope not," said Laura.

"It's *after* midnight," said Marcie. "Let's go. After all, poor Burr had to get up at six this morning to get to work. He's probably exhausted. Maybe we should leave him here and let him organize a night school for the ladies."

"Wouldn't be any takers in here," Jack observed, looking around. "They aren't ladies, they're lessies."

"Do you have to talk about them as if they were exhibits in a zoo?" Laura exclaimed.

"God, now *we're* quarreling" said Jack, laughing. But they weren't really, for it takes two to make a quarrel and he was feeling powerfully good-natured with all that booze in him. "Leave us not forget our dignity," he told Laura. He enunciated with meticulous care, not to let the liquor trip his tongue.

Marcie laughed at him, and pulled Laura aside as they got up. "Let's go," she said, and Laura walked with her to the ladies' room. It was a glaring change from the softly lighted Cellar. They were nearly blinded with a big bare bulb which hung by a frayed wire far down into the room and watched all the proceedings with an unblinking eye.

"You go first," Laura said to Marcie. There were few things less appealing to her than a public rest room—especially a one-horse job like this with its staring light, cracked mirror, and mounds of used paper towels on the cement floor. She wet her comb slightly in the tap and ran it through her hair. The door opened and the girl with the short dark hair and black pants came in. She lounged indolently against the wall, studying Laura. Laura recognized her from the bar, but ignored her royally. Marcie was talking to her through the john door.

"How do you like Jack?" she said.

"A lot," Laura said, for the benefit of the girl in the black pants. Her voice was warm enough to surprise Marcie.

"I'm glad," she said. "I thought once or twice you were mad at him."

Laura's cheeks went red again. God, how she hated that! And there was nothing she could do about it. She pulled the comb hard through her hair, afraid to look into the mirror. She knew she would meet the eyes of the girl in the black pants. "He's very intelligent," she said to Marcie.

"He's funny," Marcie said, coming out of the john. She nearly walked into the strange girl and said, "Oh! Excuse me."

"My pleasure," the girl murmured with a grin.

Laura felt suddenly jealous. It was maddening. She didn't know who she was jealous of. She wanted the other girl to notice *her,* not Marcie. And she wanted Marcie to notice her, too. She stood a moment in confusion and then she said to the girl in the black pants, "Go ahead." And nodded at the john. She said it to make her look up, which she did, slowly, and smiled. She looked shockingly boyish. Laura stared slightly.

"Thanks," said the girl.

She shut the door behind her and Marcie laughed silently, covering her mouth with her hand. But Laura turned away, excitement tight in her throat. "Let's go," she said impatiently, dragging Marcie away from the mirror. She was afraid the strange girl would come out and talk to them. She was anxious to get out of The Cellar, out of the Village. She felt a pressing sense of danger.

Marcie turned to her as they went back to the table, and said, "I'll bet Burr couldn't have gotten anywhere with *that* one!" And she laughed. "She'd throw a hammer lock on him and tell him to pick on somebody his own size."

Laura smiled faintly at her.

"Did you see how she stared at you?" Marcie said.

"Did she stare at me?"

"Yes, but she stared at me too. That's the awful thing about Lesbians, they have no discrimination."

Laura suddenly wanted to scream at her. It was so wrong, so false; so agonizing to have your lips sealed when you wanted to shout the truth.

They left the smoky Cellar and walked a few blocks, talking. Jack took a weaving course, and Laura had to steer him with one arm.

"Let's take a taxi," Marcie said.

"It's only two blocks to the subway," Burr reminded her.

"Can't you ever spend a little extra on me?" she exclaimed. "Don't you think I'm good enough to ride in a taxi? Don't you think I'm worth another buck once in a while? You did when we got married."

"Yeah, and I went broke. Subway's cheap."

"Well, I'm not!"

"Here, here," said Jack. He took a quarter from his pocket and held it up to Marcie's face.

"Heads," she said.

He flipped while Laura thought to herself what child's play it all was. Jack seemed unsophisticated now and Marcie and Burr had lost the beauty and excitement they seemed to generate together, even in the midst of their quarrels, perhaps because of them. *We all look tired and silly,* Laura thought, *and I wish we were anywhere but the middle of Greenwich Village flipping over a taxi ride.*

"Heads!" said Marcie. She poked Burr in the stomach.

"No show next week," he said.

"You don't think I care, do you?"

"Never mind, children, this is my treat," said Jack. He smiled foxily. "I'm no fool with money," he said. "I grow it in my window box. I give it all to Mother, here, and she invests it for me. Don't you, Mother?"

"Don't be an ass," said Laura, but she laughed at him. "She loves me," Jack explained to Burr and Marcie. Suddenly he left them all to dash into the middle of the street, waving his arms wildly at a pair of headlights that were bearing down on him. They screeched to a halt with an irate taxi driver behind them. Marcie gave a little scream and the driver leaned out and said, "You damn fool!"

"You'd better get that punk home and give him some black coffee, lady," he told Laura as they started uptown. "If you don't mind a little advice."

"He's going to hate himself tomorrow," Marcie said.

"He's damn lucky he's gonna be *around* tomorrow," said the cabbie. They all talked about him as if he were deaf.

And in fact, he was, for he had fallen asleep almost as soon as he got into the cab.

"Does he do this all the time?" Laura asked Burr.

"He's a great guy, Laura," Burr said, as if trying to bolster Jack in Laura's eyes. "He just flies off the handle now and then. I guess he's got problems."

At the apartment Laura got out first. Burr said, "I'll wake him up, Laura," but she protested. "Just let him sleep," she said. "I'd hate to interrupt his dreams."

"I heard that," said a ragged voice from the shadow inside the car. "You're a doll, Mother. Sleep well."

"Good night," Laura said, smiling.

Chapter Five

She was under the covers and almost asleep when Marcie tiptoed in after bidding Burr goodnight. She moved around the room for a few minutes, getting ready for bed. Laura was just barely aware of her. After a little while she heard her turn the light off and cuddle the covers around herself. The silence, up above the city late at night, was deep, lulling, almost country-like. Only an occasional stray horn filtered up to their level. It sounded like a far-off echo.

"Laura? Are you asleep?" Marcie whispered.

"Yes."

"Oh." She was quiet for a minute. Then she whispered, "I have to ask you something."

"Don't marry him. It'll never work."

"No, I don't mean that. I mean—does it make you feel funny to see those people?"

"What people?"

"Queers?"

"They aren't queer, Marcie. That's a cruel word." Her eyes were wide open now in the dark.

"What are they, then?"

"Homosexuals." She said it shyly.

"That's too long. Well, *does* it make you feel funny?"

"I don't know what you mean, Marcie."

"Well, I mean like the butch in the ladies' room. Didn't she make you feel queer—I mean funny—" She laughed. "—looking at us like she was a man, or something?"

"I guess so."

"She was looking at us when she was at the bar, too."

"She was?" Laura was amazed that Marcie would notice such a thing. "How do you know?"

Marcie laughed again. "I was looking at her," she said.

"You what?"

"Oh, not the way you think. I was just sort of looking around and she was looking at our table. I think she wanted to come up and talk to us but she didn't dare with the boys there. She knew we weren't gay."

"Is that what they call it—gay?"

"Yes. You know, it gave me the funniest feeling, her staring at us like that."

Laura turned over in her bed, very wide awake. She said to herself, *I won't ask her about it,* but she couldn't help asking. "What sort of feeling?" she whispered.

"Well, it was like…if I tell you you won't think I'm like *them,* will you?"

"Oh, no! Of course not." Laura felt the blood beating in her throat.

"It was like I wanted to know what she'd do to me. If we were alone, I mean. I was sort of curious. I wondered what it would feel like. Not that I'd ever let a girl—I mean—Laura, did you ever kiss a girl?"

"No," Laura said. In the dark she could lie pretty well. Her blushing cheeks didn't show.

"I did, once."

Laura put her hands to her throat and tried to still her breathing. "Did you like it?" she whispered.

"Not much. But I didn't dislike it. I was at that age. She was a friend of mine in Junior High. Maybe she turned out queer. I mean homosexual. She probably thinks *I* turned out queer," and she laughed. "She was always wanting to touch tongues."

Laura shivered. "Did you?"

"A couple of times. It gave me the creeps. With a man it's so lovely." Laura heard her turn in her bed to face her. "Didn't you ever do that when you were little? We used to do it a lot, just because it felt so awful. But Lenore was always wanting to do it with me when we got older. We were sort of best friends for a while."

Laura was sitting up, shivering, on the edge of her bed. She thought, *Dear God, if there is a God, help me now. Don't let me touch her. Please don't let me.*

Suddenly Marcie got up and crossed the small aisle between the beds. She felt Laura and sat beside her. "Stick out your tongue," she commanded, giggling.

"No!"

"Come on. I want to feel twelve years old again. I feel silly. Stick your tongue out." She was teasing and Laura could see the flash of gold hair in the moonlight that struck them from the window by the bed.

"Marcie, don't do this! Don't! You're playing with fire. Please, this is crazy." But her voice dwindled to a whisper as Marcie took her face in her hands, and she was powerless to resist. She let herself be pulled toward Marcie, felt Marcie's soft wet tongue searching for her own. Laura opened her mouth with a slight gasp. Her arms went out to grasp Marcie's slender body as a groan escaped her.

Suddenly the phone rang. Laura gave a little scream of shock. They were both utterly silent and motionless until it rang again. Then Marcie began to laugh. "Oh, wouldn't you know!" she said. "Saved by the bell. Saved from a life of sin." The phone rang again. "I'll get it," Marcie said. She sprang up from the bed. Laura sat frozen where she was, hugging herself, trembling and miserable. "It's probably Burr wanting to apologize for being such a skunk," Marcie said. She threw herself across her bed and lifted the receiver. "Hello?...Laura, it's for you." She put her hand over the mouthpiece and said, "It's Jack."

"I don't want to talk to him."

"Don't be silly. Talk to him."

Unwillingly Laura took the phone, sitting on the bed beside Marcie. She was so conscious of Marcie's body stretched out there beside her that she had trouble concentrating on Jack.

He said, "Mother, I've been an ass."

"I know."

"Forgive me."

"You're forgiven," she said. "Now go to bed. Good night."

"But I am in bed," he said. He was still pronouncing each word with elaborate care. "My question is this—did you really mean it?"

"Mean what?" said Laura, looking at the faint moonlit curve of Marcie's leg.

"I'd swear you said you loved me," he said.

"You were dreaming."

"Do you?"

"No. Jack, please go to bed. Let me go."

"If I went any more to bed than I already am, Mother—and don't think that was easy to say, because it wasn't—I don't know where I'd be. Say you love me."

"No. Jack, it's late. I'm tired."

"Tomorrow is Saturday. You can sleep."

"I don't care what tomorrow is, I'm tired right now. Now good night."

"Do something for me, Mother."

Marcie turned over, lying across her pillow on her stomach.

"What?" Laura said softly, losing contact with him.

"Promise."

"Okay." She whispered it.

"Kiss Marcie for me."

"What?" Laura was shocked into total awareness.

"Good night, Mother," Jack said. And hung up.

Laura replaced the receiver and sat uncertainly on the bed next to Marcie for a minute. She didn't dare to wonder what Jack meant. She had enough to do just keeping her hands off Marcie's smooth behind. She felt afraid of her.

What would Beth have done if it had been me lying there? she wondered, and knew at once. Beth would have laid down on top of her, her front to Marcie's back. Beth would have kissed her neck, her ears, her shoulders. Beth would have—

"Laura," Marcie murmured.

"Yes?" Her throat was dry, making it hard to answer.

"We'd better get to sleep."

It was all over, then. Laura had waited too long. Maybe Marcie would have repulsed her anyway. Maybe her hesitation had saved her. On the other hand, maybe—Laura burned to know. But Marcie had lost the playful, childish, experimental mood, and was already half asleep. There might never be another chance.

Chapter Six

At work on Monday Laura's phone rang halfway through the morning. "Doctors Hollingsworth, Carstens, and Hagstrom," she said, business like. What a mouthful! she thought to herself.

Her listener apparently had the same idea. "Jesus, what a tongue-twister," he said. "What happened to Smith?"

"There is no Dr. Smith," she said, taken aback.

"Oh, don't be so damn formal, Mother. It's not like you. I thought I'd better apologize while I'm sober. I was drunk the last time."

"I know. How are you, Jack?" She smiled at the thought of his face.

"Bored. But healthy. I didn't mean to fall asleep in your face Friday night."

"It's okay. Forget it."

"Just for that I'll give you a free ticket to see my analyst. He's a great guy. He needs you."

"He needs me?"

"Have you got fifty bucks a week to spend on your salvation?"

"I haven't got fifty bucks a week to spend on my *groceries,*" she said.

"Well, I guess he doesn't need you as much as I thought. But I'd be glad to stake you to your first session. After that it becomes habitual. You crave it. You'll find the money somehow."

Laura was laughing. "Give it to Marcie, not me," she said. "She's the one who loves to talk."

"You do some pretty good talking yourself."

"I do?"

"You got lyrical in defense of oddballs Friday night."

"I did not! Let's not go into that again anyway," she said. "Look, Jack, I'd like to talk to you, but—"

"I know, you're at work. So am I. Don't you ever get tired of work?"

"I'm on probation here. If I don't do well they'll fire me in June."

"So your poor virtuous hardworking little life revolves around that office."

"Now you're being an ass again."

"I'm telling you, Laura, you'd make a good soap opera. So would the rest of us. We're all a bunch of nuts in a million nutsy little soap operas. Will Burr marry Marcie? Will Jack take the pledge? Will Laura stick it out till June? Tune in tomorrow. We won't have the answer for you, but we'll sell you soap like all hell. Do you know why people buy soap?"

"To wash themselves."

"No. They like to play with themselves in the bathtub."

Laura had to laugh at him. "You fool," she said. "Jack, I can't talk to you, honestly."

"Okay. I'll call back."

"No, no, call tonight."

"But I want to see you tonight."

She was unaware that she might have impressed him on their date, and he took her by surprise. "You do?"

"Well, don't sound so damn shocked. You're a nice girl even if you are ten feet tall. I'll pick you up at seven-thirty."

"No, I can't, Jack."

"Okay, eight."

"I'm busy."

"The hell you are."

"I am."

"You lie! I have an instinct about these things. Eight sharp."

All at once Laura became aware of another voice calling her. "Laura?" It was Dr. Hollingsworth. He was standing over her desk and she looked up suddenly like a scared little kid.

"Yes, sir?" she said. She hung up without even saying good-bye to Jack.

Jack Mann was not a pushy type. On the contrary, he was rather shy, although it rarely showed. He went to parties and hid behind a stream of wisecracks. He did the same thing on dates. He did it with anyone and everyone. It was a sort of defense mechanism, a way of hiding his real self, and he had done it for so many years that by now it was second nature. Even people who knew him fairly well, like Burr and Marcie, never saw beneath this facade of witticism. They thought that *was* Jack: all funny asides and not much serious straight talk. It was hard to take him seriously. He didn't want that. He wanted to be laughed at, to be amusing, and he usually contrived to be. He was content to let people take him for a wag.

But once in a while he ran across somebody who made him feel sick of the mask he hid behind. Somebody who made him yearn to talk, quietly and seriously, about the things that mattered to him. It happened when he was unlucky enough to fall in love. Or when he met a loner like himself and felt an unspoken sympathy. It happened with Laura.

It wasn't easy for him to call her back. It would have been, if she hadn't appealed to his emotions. There were a lot of girls he called just for the sake of their mutual amusement, or just to amuse himself. But if he bantered lightly with Laura it was more because he couldn't help it than because he wanted to, more because he had found it almost impossible to talk straight anymore.

At eight o'clock he showed up at the apartment. He walked into the living room without knocking and said, "It's me." When nobody answered he wandered through to the bedroom and found Laura giving Marcie a home permanent. "God, what a stink!" he said.

Laura looked up in surprise. "I thought you were kidding," she said. "About the date."

He smiled at her. She was dressed in tight chinos and a boy's shirt. It was her favorite after-work outfit. "You weren't planning on the Stork Club, I see," he cracked.

"I wasn't planning on anything."

"That's a dangerous attitude, Mother. Always plan on something. Avoid accidents."

"Jack, you can't have her," Marcie said. "I'll never get this thing right without her." She waved a plastic curler at him helplessly.

"You're better off without it, doll. Take it from me. Come on, we'll go as you are."

"Jack, I can't. I had no idea—"

"Come on, I want to talk to you."

"We can talk here."

"No we can't. Marcie's here."

"I won't listen," Marcie said with a smile.

"Besides, I can't talk," he said, and Laura caught a glimpse of the shyness hidden in him. "I'm sober as a post." He shrugged. "Let's go."

"I can't go like this."

"Never mind the pants, they're becoming."

For some deep buried and curious reason she was flattered. She stood there hesitating and Jack took advantage of her. He grabbed her arm and pulled her toward the door.

"Kidnaper!" Marcie wailed.

"My coat—" Laura said.

"You don't need one. It's balmy."

"So are you."

"Thanks." He guided her down the steps.

This was a switch for Laura. She had never been especially attractive to men before, starting at the beginning with her father and going right on up through college. She didn't look warm and soft and yielding. She was remote and involved in herself, aloof from everybody, men included. She didn't like them very much and they sensed it.

Now, here was a well-educated intelligent male giving her the rush. She didn't understand it. Jack didn't appeal to her physically any more than any other man; in fact, a little less. He was small, wiry, rather owlish in his horn rims. He looked like an Ivy League undergrad. She guessed he was about twenty-five. Laura was twenty. But she supposed that in five or six years she might be as cynical as Jack was. She liked to hear him say things she never dared to say herself.

They went to a little bar a few blocks away where Laura had gone once with Marcie for a beer. It was a quiet spot with a steady clientele.

They walked in and took a booth in the back. "I usually prefer the bar," said Jack, "but I always end up telling my troubles to the bartender. So we'll sit back here."

Laura felt a little strange walking into a bar in a pair of pants, but she was with a man and she hoped that made it all right.

"Just a beer," she said to Jack. A year ago she would have said,"Just a coke." And said it in a way to make him think she disapproved of liquor. But lately she had picked up a taste for beer. Beth liked it and so did Marcie. That was too much for Laura. There must be something to it. So she had gotten into the habit of having one now and then in the evening when she got home from work. It relaxed her. It made her feel that she could think of Merrill Landon without exploding, or of Marcie without crawling out of her skin. She felt like maybe she could stand it, living this way with Marcie, and everything would turn out all right.

The waitress brought their drinks, and Jack poured her beer for her. Then he downed his shot and drank some water. He seemed to be looking for a way to talk to her. "How long have you and Marcie been together?" he said finally.

That's an odd way to put it, Laura thought warily. "Since January," she said.

"Oh, yeah. I guess Burr mentioned it. He likes you." He smiled at her and she relaxed a little.

"Why don't Burr and Marcie get along?" she asked.

Jack shrugged and hailed the waitress. Then he looked at Laura. "They don't want to," he said. "It would spoil the fun."

"They love each other," said Laura.

"Physically, yes, they do."

Laura didn't like his definition. "Marcie says they might get married again."

"Yeah. They're just blind enough to do it, too."

"Marcie's not blind!"

"Sorry. A slip of the tongue." He grinned and drank the fresh drink the waitress had just delivered.

"Well, she's not," Laura said, disconcerted by his manner. "She really loves Burr—at least, she thinks she does."

He put his glass down. "Marcie hasn't learned to love yet," he said.

"You mean she doesn't love Burr?" She asked the question eagerly.

"No," he said quietly, studying her. "She loves physical excitement. She loves a big virile passionate sonofabitch to make a fuss over her."

"You're wrong," she said, disappointed. "She doesn't fight just for the sake of fighting. It's just with Burr. She never fights with me."

Jack laughed a little, privately. "That's because you're a girl, Mother," he said. "I can tell 'cause you got long hair."

Laura began to sweat under his searching eyes. "That's not the point," she said, exasperated. "Marcie has a sweet disposition. She's very quiet. It must be Burr."

"Quiet?" Jack laughed. "The way that girl talks she's about as quiet as Grand Central during rush hour."

"All right, she talks a lot" Laura was getting mad. "That doesn't mean she likes fights. Or men who thrive on them."

"That's just what it does mean. Believe it. It's true."

"You're screwy."

"You're in love."

"What?" She said it in a shocked whisper, staring at him, feeling her cheeks go scarlet. "What does that mean?" she said. Her voice was dry and small and her hands were wet.

Jack drank another shot. Then he put the glass down and leaned toward her over the table, his face serious. "You're gay, Laura."

Laura was speechless for a moment, surprised beyond her capacity to think or feel. Then an awful sick trembling came up in her throat. For a minute she hung between flight and a fight. She was furious, scared, and humiliated. It never occurred to her to deny the truth. Jack had hit the bull's eye. She clenched her fists on the table top and violent things came to her lips. But before she could utter them Jack spoke again.

"Oh, don't look so damn mad. You're not the only one." He sighed, crushing his cigarette in a scorched ashtray. "I am too. So don't give me a martyr act." And he nodded again to the waitress.

Laura put her hands over her face suddenly, pressing one hand over her mouth to catch the sobs. She heard the waitress come up and turned her head to the wall.

"Same for me," Jack said.

"How about the lady?"

"Bring her a double whisky."

Laura could feel the woman looking at her curiously. She wanted to evaporate. She hated the impersonal curiosity of this stranger. After a minute Jack said, "She's gone."

Laura put her hands down, but she couldn't look at him. She just said, rather hopelessly, "How did you know?"

"Takes one to know one," he said with light sarcasm.

"How?" Laura demanded. "You're a man."

"So I'm a man. You're a girl. We're both queer."

"How did you know?" she said sharply, looking at him now.

"You've got a crush on Marcie. That's how."

Laura gasped a little. "Is it so obvious?" she asked, frightened.

Jack shook his head. "To me, maybe, but only because I was looking for it."

"You were? Why?"

51

"I'm always looking for it." He was bantering again. She realized now that he had called her Laura when he said it: *You're gay, Laura.* He was dead serious then.

"Do you look for it even in girls?" she said.

"In anybody. You might say it's a hobby with me. I spot one and I think to myself, 'Another poor bastard like me.' It boosts my morale. I guess it's a case of misery loves company."

"I'd rather suffer alone," she said, not without pride.

"You'll get over that. When you learn your way around." Laura was still trembling all over. "Listen to me, Jack," she said, leaning over the table and brushing the last tear impatiently from her cheeks. "I never heard that word—gay—like you use it until our date Friday. Nobody ever called me 'gay' before. I didn't even know what it meant. But I'll tell you this: I never touched Marcie. I've never tried to get away with anything with her. Never. She doesn't know and she never will." She said this almost fiercely, but Jack only smiled at her.

"Okay," he said. "Don't preach at me. I believe you. I believe you haven't been climbing into Marcie's bed after hours, anyway. But don't let Marcie fool you. She can be wild sometimes. She gets in crazy moods and she'll do anything. I saw her go up to a bum in Central Park and kiss him once on a dare. A big ugly slob of a guy. It was enough to get her killed, but she loved it."

Laura was revolted. But not surprised. Not after what Marcie had done to her last Friday night.

"She couldn't possibly suspect me," she said stubbornly. "I never do a thing."

"You did plenty in The Cellar Friday night."

"I—I did?" She felt that old sick feeling come over her again.

"You looked at her like you had ideas. You held the door for her. You argued with Burr."

"But all I said was—"

"All you said was you were gay. To anybody who bothered to figure it out. Well, I did, that's all."

Laura's face was hot and she tried to defend herself. "All I did was defend them—homosexuals, I mean. just said they were human beings, not animals. Is that against the law?"

"Not 'they,' Mother," Jack said softly. "'We.' You're one of us."

"But Burr and Marcie don't know that," she said, almost pleading with him to agree.

Jack raised a finger to his lips. "Everybody will know it if you don't keep your voice down," he said. "Okay, Burr doesn't know it. As for Marcie, you live with the girl. You should know."

"She couldn't," Laura said, but she felt shaky.

"You aren't sure, are you? Why don't you find out?"

"How?" She looked at him eagerly.

"Ask her." He laughed to see her face fall.

"Damn you!"

"Okay. Don't ask her. Make a pass at her."

"You're mad!" Laura stared at him, shocked. "I'd never do such a thing! She might—why, my God, she might call the police. Or Burr. She'd hate me. I couldn't stand it. Jack, don't tell me to make a fool of myself. Do you want to get me into a tragic mess?"

"I want to keep you *out* of one, Mother. That's why I'm talking this way."

"Well, act like you did, then. You drag me down here, when I didn't want to come in the first place, and tell me—" She swallowed convulsively. "—tell me I'm *gay.*" She spat the word at him. "And then you have the gall to sit there and tell me to make love to Marcie—" She almost choked on the words. "—when you know damn well she'd probably be revolted by it, she'd—"

"Calm down, Mother, have a drink." And he held her glass up to her until she took it from him. It burned her throat but she was too worked up to care.

"Now," said Jack. "I asked you down here to tell you I know you're gay. And so am I. I want to be friends with you, Laura." She glanced up at him, and found that he was embarrassed, for all the liquid courage he was consuming, and it was hard for him to talk. "Damn it," he said. "I'm so used to talking like an idiot, I can't say what I mean anymore. I—I wanted to tell you—to warn you, Laura—I was in the situation you're in now. Once. Long ago. I fell for a roommate of mine, I didn't think he knew anything either. I didn't see how it was possible. I was so damn careful. I never said anything, I never *did* anything. Jesus Christ, I even avoided the guy. I went out of my way to avoid him. But I was nuts about him, Laura. I wanted him so bad it hurt. I'd lie there in the dark and tell myself, 'You can't have him, you can't have him' over and over. I'd say, 'Who the hell do you think you are? If you were the prettiest boy on earth he wouldn't look twice. And, Mann, you aren't the prettiest boy on earth. You're the ugliest.' Whenever we talked late at night, whenever we went anywhere together, whenever we touched I used to burn up inside, I used to die of it. I wanted to kiss him, feel him all over, just hold him. God, it killed me! But I never let on. Never. And one day—this'll give you an idea of what to expect, Mother—one day after all this noble chastity and virtue and self-denial crap I was going through, he came up to me and said, 'Jack, I hate to say this, but I'm moving out.'"

"Why?" Laura asked softly, her forehead wrinkled with sympathy.

"Because I was gay. He didn't say it that way, of course. He didn't say, 'Because you're queer, you poor bastard. I'm sorry for you but I can't take it anymore.' I could have stood that. But he just handed me a lot of bull."

Laura felt like crying again. But she only said, "Isn't that something to be grateful for? He tried, anyway."

"Yeah. He tried." He said it so acidly that Laura was afraid to say any more.

"There've been a lot since Joe," he said, after awhile. "Just like there'll be a lot for you after Marcie." Laura tried to protest but he waved her down. "I know, I know, you're going to keep your hands off. You're going to spend your whole life ignoring sex, ignoring what you are. Denying that you want it, running away from it. I was going to, too. That was twenty-five years ago."

"Twenty-five years ago!" Laura stared at him. "How old are you, Jack?"

"Forty-two. Surprised?" He smiled at her gaping astonishment.

"I thought you were maybe five years older than I am. Twenty-five or so. You *can't* be forty-two."

"That's what I keep telling myself. I can't be. But I sure as hell am."

"I don't believe it."

He grinned. "Good," he said. "I like to fool people."

"Why?" It seemed crazy. "What does a man care how young he looks? I thought that was for women," Laura said.

"Women and gay boys. Do you think some pretty twenty-year-old is going to fall for a fat, bald, middle-aged bastard with not even a bankroll to offer? I'm ugly, Mother. That's enough of a hand-icap. When I start looking old, I'll quit."

"You're not ugly, Jack," she said gently, trying to console him.

But he took it with a sardonic laugh. "Only a Mother could love me," he said.

"Don't talk like this. You make me so sad."

"Ahhh, Christ," he said, and drank. He looked up at Laura, and she could see he wasn't focusing very well now. "I came here to talk about you anyway, not me. What did your father do to you when you were five years old?"

Laura started. "When did I say that? Did I mention my father?" she asked.

"Yes, in The Cellar. Probably as good a place as any."

"I—I didn't mean *my* father," she said.

"Don't fib to me, Laura. Let's be friends."

After a few moments, she said, "I can't talk about it, Jack."

"What did he do?"

"We—we were at a summer resort." It began to spill out of her. Jack had bared his anguish, and she felt suddenly safe with him, and needed. "We were there for a vacation one summer. We went

55

fishing on the lake—Father and Mother and my brother and me."
Her voice grew soft as she spoke. "The boat capsized. I was the
only one he could save. I was the closest to him. Mother and Rod
drowned." She shut her eyes with a little gasp against the old
horror, still so sharp in her heart, like a big ugly needle, stuck
there to remind her she had no right to be alive. "All my life I've felt
as if I killed them. He says I did. He hates me because I'm not his
son. He hates me because I'm not my own mother, his wife." Jack
seemed completely sober for a minute, staring at her with his
brows knit. She put her head down and cried quietly. "That's all,"
she said. "I can't tell you any more."

"You don't need to," he said softly. "Jesus."

She took a deep breath and sat up, feeling as if she had lightened
the weight of that leaden secret by sharing it. She was somewhat
surprised to find that she was able to share it. She felt very close
to Jack, as if they were now truly friends. Each of them had risked
a little of himself to the other. And neither, now, was sorry.

With a sigh, she looked at her watch. It was getting late. "I have
to get up early," she said, her voice still unsteady. "So do you. I
know, Burr's always yelling about the hours. Let's go."

"One more," he said, holding up his glass. "I'm not quite
through with you yet."

"I don't get it," Laura said to him. "We don't even know each
other. This is the second time we've seen each other. And here we
are talking like old friends."

"You're wrong, Laura. We know each other a lot better than
some people who've been acquainted for years. Like Burr and
Marcie. We know each other instinctively, don't you feel that? I
wouldn't have called you otherwise. You wouldn't have let me
drag you out tonight otherwise."

"Don't talk about Marcie as if she didn't have a brain in her
head," Laura said.

Jack smiled. "You *are* in love," he said. "This is serious. She has
a few brains, Mother, she just doesn't use them."

"She's not stupid," Laura defended her eagerly.

"She's not sacred either."

"I didn't mean that."

"Oh, yes you did. I thought Burr was once."

"Burr?" Laura stared at him. "Did you—were you—"

"Nuts for Burr? Yes. Once. When I first met him."

"What happened?"

"Nothing. Thank God. I got over it. I go for big virile sons of bitches, just like Marcie. But I take care not to room with them anymore."

Laura shook her head, a wry little smile on her face. "Don't you ever fall for the gay ones?"

"I try to make a point of it." He grinned sadly. "Unfortunately I sometimes miss the point. If you know what I mean."

"I'm not sure."

"It's just as well. I met Burr at work when he was hired about four years ago. I knew he was straight."

"What's 'straight'?"

"Everything that's not 'gay'—so I pussyfooted around the issue. I made him like me. I did his homework for him. I made him laugh. I told him what to tell the boss. I double-dated with him and Marcie and I was an usher at the wedding. I was Number One troubleshooter *after* the wedding. He thinks I'm indispensable."

"But you—you don't still—"

"No, I don't. Not anymore. But I still like to be with him. I like to watch them fight." He smiled at her. "You do too."

She felt embarrassed, as if he were looking through her clothes to her naked feelings.

"However," he went on, "I'm not under any lovely illusions about him being an intellectual giant. Or Marcie either. And I know damn well he won't give me a tumble if I just stick around long enough." He gave her a piercing look. "Those are your illusions, Mother," he said. "I suggest you drown them."

"What does that mean?"

"You can set Marcie's hair till the moon turns blue and she's not going to crawl into your bed to thank you for it."

"I don't expect her to."

"Sure you do. It's a mark of our breed. We're hopeless optimists. Otherwise we'd all commit suicide. We get a crush on somebody, and if he's straight we figure we'll just love him so much he'll *have* to turn gay. It doesn't work that way. Marcie isn't going to start kissing you just because you want her to."

Laura was incensed. "She already has," she snapped.

Jack's eyebrows went up. "When?" he said.

"The night we got back from The Cellar. She said she felt funny, in there with all those girls staring at her. She said she used to touch tongues with a girl when she was in her teens, and she wanted to do it again. And she did. You—you—" She didn't know what to call him. "You had to call me up right in the middle, just when I thought—" She stopped herself. "Oh, this isn't like me," she moaned. "I never talk like this."

"Only to yourself, hm?" He laughed. "I mess up your day-dreams and your affair. God! What more can I do? I'm becoming the Man in your Life, Mother." His laughter fizzled slowly, and Laura could tell he was quite drunk from the way he let his head hang for a minute. "You know," he said and wagged a finger at her, articulating cautiously, "I never have trouble thinking when I'm drunk. But my tongue gets sloppy." He laughed a little. "I say what I want to say, that's one good thing. But it sounds sloppy as hell." He finished the drink in front of him. Laura started to get up, but he caught her wrist and said, suddenly very serious again, "You're in trouble, Laura. Marcie's straight. Accept that. It's a fact. If she's playing games with you, she's doing it for private kicks, not to give you a thrill. And her kicks have nothing to do with being gay. They have to do with going out on a limb, with acting nuts once in a while. Maybe she's just pushing *you* out on a limb to see if you'll fall off. And you'll fall all right. Flat on your can." He stopped for a minute to focus his gaze on her.

"Marcie's about as queer as Post Toasties, Laura. Take my advice: move out."

"But I can't! I won't!" she exclaimed defensively. "Why should I? I've done nothing wrong!"

"I hadn't either when Joe gave me the glad news."

"I'm not you. I've done nothing I'm ashamed of."

"No, but you will. If you hang around, feeling like you feel. You were saved by a phone call Friday night. What if my timing isn't so good next time?"

"I don't want to move out." She said it stubbornly like a thwarted child.

"All the more reason why you should."

Laura got indignant. "I've got more will power than you give me credit for and I'm not going to be scared out."

"What are you going to do for will power if she gets cold some night and crawls into your bed to keep warm? Or you take a shower together? Or she feels like pulling your nerves out by the roots one by one again, and makes you play let's-touch-tongues just for the hell of it? Just to see if she can get you sent up for sodomy? Be thankful you're female, Mother. At least your passion won't stand up and salute her."

"I've had enough from you tonight!"

"Okay, okay. But I advise you to find a nice butch somewhere and set up housekeeping in the Village. Or at least, cultivate a few lovelies down there so you'll have a place to let off steam when Marcie feels like playing games."

"You're drunk and repulsive."

"I know what I am, Laura. Don't change the subject."

"I'm going home."

"I'm coming with you." He got up unsteadily and followed her toward the door. Outside he stopped her. "Don't hate me, Laura," he said. And she couldn't, looking at him there in the pink glare of neon, short and plain, brilliant and miserable, offering her his curious stinging sympathy.

"I wish I could," she said and shook her head.

He smiled at her. "I'll walk you home," he said.

"You don't need to. Why don't you get a taxi and get yourself home?"

"Are you suggesting I can't walk?"

"No." She laughed.

"You are. Just for that I'm going to walk you home whether you like it or not. To prove I can."

"All right." But she had to lead him most of the way. Jack could talk better than he could navigate when he was high. When they reached the apartment she hailed a cab for him and put him in it. She stood there watching it pull away down West End Avenue, watching it till it was indistinguishable from the sea of red tail lights traveling with it. And she felt an awakening affection for him.

Chapter Seven

It was hard to get up the next day. Not impossible, just hard. Discouraging. Her head ached, and she was dissatisfied with herself. For the first time she wanted to cut work. But she went and she did her job. It wasn't until the middle of the afternoon that she jumped to hear Sarah ask, "What's the matter, Laura? A little under the weather?"

Laura looked up at her. *Do I look that bad?* she wondered. "I'm a little tired. Why?"

"The reports are piling up," Sarah said, nodding at them.

Laura rubbed her forehead. "I'm sorry, Sarah. I'll catch up. I'll work late."

"Don't be silly!" Sarah laughed good-naturedly. "Catch up tomorrow. There's not that much of a rush."

But the next day she didn't quite catch up; she got farther behind, in fact. Burr and Marcie had kept her up. It was partly the quarrel and partly the torturing silence that followed it. She went to work still more tired than the day before. Dr. Carstens came in to tell her a story about one of his woman patients, and she was frankly irritated. He picked himself up from her desk, where he was sitting, and huffed out, offended. "Okay, don't laugh," he said. "The others thought it was funny."

Laura drove herself almost crazy with her errors that afternoon. When her phone rang she jumped half out of her chair. It was Jack.

"Good afternoon, Mother," he said. "I'm selling used toothbrushes. Interested?"

"No. I'm very busy. Good-bye."

"I'll see you at eight."

"No."

"Eight-fifteen."

"No."

"Eight-thirty."

"All right! All right! All right! Good-bye!" She slammed the receiver down and Sarah stared at her.

Laura decided to work late, and it was close to eight-thirty when she got up to go. The reports, though fewer, were still not done.

At the elevator the boy said, "Nice evening."

"Is it?" She answered him apathetically, involved in her own world.

"Yes, ma'am. It's really spring tonight." He smiled at her.

He was right. The air was soft and gentle, lavender and clear. It even smelled good, right there in mid-Manhattan, although that was probably a hallucination. Laura smiled a little. She hated to go underground to the subway, but it was late, and she wanted to get home in a hurry. It would really be gorgeous out on the roof tonight.

She walked in to find Jack and Burr playing checkers. Marcie was cross-legged on the floor, in velvet lounging pants and a silk shirt, humming while she covered the top of the round cocktail table with a plastic veneer treated to look like marble.

She smiled up at Laura, who paused to admire her. "Alcohol-proof," Marcie said, rattling the table cover. "Mr. Marquardt gave it to me. We're advertising it for a new client, and they passed some around today. It sticks by itself. How do you like it?"

"It looks wonderful," Laura said. So did Marcie, her cheeks pink with enthusiasm.

"You've had it, Mann," Burr said, and Laura heard a checker smacking triumphantly over the board in a devastating series of jumps. "Touché, boy."

"Why don't you take up tiddly winks? I could beat you at tiddly winks." Jack sat with his elbows on his knees and his chin in his hand. He looked up at Laura without raising his head and smiled. She looked at him, absorbed in the idea that he had once been infatuated with the man beside him, and Burr had never known it. Burr thought he was as normal as himself. But of course, they had never roomed together. Suddenly Laura recalled that she had agreed to go out with Jack.

"Jack—" she began, but he cut her off.

"I see I have less allure than your typewriter," he said. He cocked an eye at her. "Well, never mind, I don't have so many friends I can afford to be jealous of their typewriters."

"Thanks, Jack," she said with a little smile. She turned to go into the kitchen, but he jumped up and followed her.

"Where the hell do you think you're going?"

"Straight to the icebox. I'm starved."

"We have a date. I'm taking you out to dinner."

"Why don't we just stay here?" she pleaded.

But all he said was, "No," and she understood that he had made his mind up and had something planned.

She was reluctant to leave Marcie, who looked so pretty. But the prettier Marcie looked, the worse Laura suffered. Maybe it would be better just to talk about her tonight. Talk to Jack about her. It sounded good.

"Okay, but let's get home early. I'm beat, I really am," she said.

"Whatever you say, Mother." He smiled, and she felt suddenly that it was terribly good to have him for a friend.

When they got outside she said, "Let's go over to Hempel's. It's only a block."

"No. We're going to The Cellar."

"Oh, God no! It's miles away. We wouldn't get home till midnight."

"A friend of mine wants to meet you."

"Who?"

"The name wouldn't mean anything. It would just scare you away, probably. She saw you when we were there last week. She likes your face."

"Oh, that's ridiculous. Come on, I'm starving. I've got to eat or I'll faint."

"This is a very interesting girl. She could teach you a lot."

"I know everything I want to know." He laughed, but she went on, "Jack, I'm not going to the Village with you."

But when they reached Broadway he hailed a cab and she let him put her in it, as she knew she would. "I can't. I won't. I'm tired and hungry," she said. But she got in. "I'll fall asleep over my typewriter tomorrow," she moaned.

When they reached The Cellar she felt a lift of excitement in spite of herself. They arrived after the kitchen had closed, but Jack was a regular customer, and they were willing to fix him up.

They followed a waitress to a table. Laura walked with a strange light queasiness in her stomach and sat down with Jack feeling terribly self-conscious and looked-at, as if every pair of eyes in the room was inspecting her. Jack laughed, waving at somebody. "All my friends'll think I've gone straight," he said. He gave the waitress an order and she scuttled off. He leaned back in his chair to look at Laura then. "Sorry you're here?" he asked.

"No. But I wish it was Friday night."

"Relax. We'll leave when you say the word."

She began to feel adventurous and crazy. Jack went up to get them both a drink. She eyed it with suspicion but then she picked it up and drank half of it down, and it hit her like a bomb, a big soft lovely explosion of warmth in the pit of her stomach. She blinked at Jack, who only smiled, knowing the feeling.

"How would you like to be in here some night," he said slowly, "with Marcie beside you? And sit alone together at that little table over there? And tell her you love her?" Laura took another gulp of the drink and almost finished it. "And hear her say the same thing?"

Laura put the glass down with trembling hands. "Oh, Jack, you bastard," she said, her insides aflame. "Cut it out."

"You want it so badly," he said, "that it's tearing your guts out. And it's never going to happen. So open your eyes. Look around. There are some beautiful women here tonight. There's one as pretty as Marcie." He squinted over her shoulder. Laura turned around indignantly to look, and saw a charming face framed in short brown curls smiling at a table partner. She looked up at the sudden sight of Laura's own face, pale and compelling.

"Nobody's as pretty as Marcie," Laura told him.

"Somebody was," Jack said, with his peculiar intuition taking him straight to the point.

"What do you mean?" Laura said defensively, and finished her drink.

"Whenever you know damn well what I mean," he said with a smile, "you ask 'what do I mean.' As if I were nuts. Well, I'm not. Give me your glass." He took it and got up. "Never thought you'd beat me to the bottom, Mother." He peered into it with one eye and then left to get it refilled.

Laura leaned back in her seat and shut her eyes. After all, what did it matter if she were here? She felt wonderful. She had put in a terrific day's work, she had a right to a little fling. Her body glowed through its whole length. Marcie loomed in her mind like a lovely apparition, not quite real.

I'll have her someday, Laura thought. *No matter what he says.*

She looked around her, half consciously searching for someone. But the girl in the black pants wasn't there. The crowd was much the same as before, but thinner. The artist was walking around with his sketch pad, stopping to talk to tablesful of friends. The bar was crowded, more than the tables.

Jack came back, put a fresh glass in front of her, and sat down. "Now. What was her name?" he said.

Laura opened her eyes slowly. "Who?"

"Number one."

She wrinkled her nose in some disgust. "Jack, she wasn't a number. Or an animal. Or part of a collection."

"What was she?"

"She was a wonderful girl."

"Beautiful like Marcie?"

"No. Beautiful—but not like Marcie. They have some features in common. But Beth was taller. She was quite boyish." She felt a little embarrassed suddenly, putting it this way. "Marcie's very feminine."

"What are you?"

Laura stared at him over the rim of her glass. "What am I?" she repeated, confusedly. "Do I have to be something? I don't know."

"You'll find out fast enough," he said. "Beth probably taught you a lot. The one who brings you out always does."

"Yes, she did," she said dreamily. Beth had loosened her up wonderfully when they were together. She had taken her by the hand and led her to herself. She had also abandoned her there. But Laura couldn't hold anything against her. That had been a sacred love and always would be in her memory, like all loves that are broken off in full passion. If they had been together till it had worn off a little, Laura might have left her without any desperate regrets and loneliness. She might have been able to see Beth as a whole person, not as an ideal. But it hadn't happened that way, and Beth still looked like a goddess to her.

Now, in a new world, with new people, she wasn't sure what she was. With Marcie she felt aggressive and violent. Here, in The Cellar, with so many eyes on her, she felt timid.

Jack grinned at her. "You're a boy," he said. "With Marcie, anyway. My friend won't like that."

Laura put her glass down. "I'm a girl," she said. "Don't look at me that way."

Jack put his head back and laughed. "Correction," he said. "You're a girl. Why don't you move down here where you don't have to be either?"

"Everybody has to be one or the other."

"You're too literal, Laura. Cut off your hair. Wear those pants you look so nice in. Get some desert boots, a car coat and some men's shirts, and you're in business."

"Jack," she said, "You are positively revolting."

"That's the uniform," he said. "Can't join the club without it."

"I don't want to join."

"Yes you do. You feel good in pants. You swagger."

"I do not!" But she was laughing at him. At herself.

"Shhh!" he said softly. "Or they'll cut you off. Here comes dinner."

The presence of the waitress made it impossible to talk. She set a delectable dinner in front of Laura. But somehow, after the first few bites, it lost its appeal. She sat gazing at the plate, wondering where her enormous appetite had gone, pushing a mushroom dreamily from one side to the other. Jack smiled, watching her. He leaned over the table on his elbows and picked up her knife.

"Laura," he said, pointing at her mushroom. Then he pushed another one slowly across the plate from the other side. "Marcie," he said, nodding at it. The two mushrooms made contact south of the fried potatoes, and Laura felt crazy, watching it. It made her smile; she thought it was ridiculous. It made her want to laugh, and it brought a warm, unwanted, urgent feeling up in her legs at the same time. She pushed "Laura" behind the steak.

"Ah," said Jack. "Laura's afraid of Marcie. But Marcie's not afraid of anything. Marcie's a little heller. Here she comes." And he pushed his mushroom after hers. Laura felt her cheeks get hot.

"I'm not going to run away," she said, and took a swallow from her drink, letting "Laura" stay put.

"Okay, be a hero," said Jack. "Make it easy for her. Look at that little bitch!" and he scooped "Marcie" over "Laura," back and forth, the passage facilitated by the gravy. "She's nuts. She's on a kick. She wants you to make a fool of yourself."

Laura wouldn't watch. She finished her drink for an excuse not to look.

"But look at Laura," Jack went on. "She can't stand it. Where Marcie goes, Laura goes." And he pushed "Marcie" and "Laura" around the plate together.

"Stop it, Jack. Get me another drink."

"Here's where Laura goes crazy."

"Now stop it!"

He crammed the two mushrooms into the potatoes, helter skelter, one over the other. "Laura got what she wanted," he said, after a minute, looking up at her briefly. "But see what happens to her." And with one sudden cruel stroke he sliced "Laura" in half. Laura gave a little start. "Marcie got bored with the game," he explained.

Laura laughed nervously. "Now cut it out and get me a drink," she said.

He got up smiling, without a word, and went to the bar. Laura couldn't look at the plate. She signaled the waitress, who came over with a water pitcher.

"Will you take this out please?"

"Something wrong with it?"

"I can't eat mushrooms."

"Well, why dincha say so!" She took the plate with an angry "Jeez!" muttered under her breath.

Jack came back to find her laughing. "Couldn't take it, hm?" He nodded at the vacant space where the plate was, and then looked at Laura. "Want to leave?"

"No. I don't want to go anywhere, Jack. Let's just sit here a while and talk."

"About Marcie?"

"About Marcie." She laughed again.

"By Jesus, you're a pretty girl," he said quietly. "I didn't realize it till now. You ought to get soused more often."

"I'm not soused, I'm in love."

He gave a snort of disbelief. "Okay not-soused and in-love. You're headed straight blind for misery. You know that."

"My eyes are wide open. She'll never love me."

"Don't tell me. Tell yourself. Believe yourself."

"I do."

He shook his head and laughed a little. "I see it coming and I tell you 'Look out, she's murder' and you say 'You're absolutely right' and then off you go to slit your own throat." He leaned over the table seriously. "Leave her, Laura," he pleaded, and took her by surprise with his earnestness. "It's no good falling for a straight one. Believe me."

"I won't leave her," she said stubbornly. "I know what I'm doing."

He leaned back with a sigh. "Then at least look at somebody else," he said. "Look at Beebo. She's cruising you like mad."

"Who's Beebo? I wouldn't look at anybody with such a ridiculous name. What's cruising?"

"Beebo's a friend of mine. And cruising—well—you'll catch on." He grinned.

Laura turned warily around. At the bar sat the handsome boyish girl she had admired the week before. She was gazing boldly, but without great interest, at Laura. When Laura turned to see her she smiled, very slightly.

Laura turned back to Jack. "Is that Beebo?" she asked. "In the black pants?"

Jack laughed at her. "You mean tan shorts?"

Laura looked again. "Well, she had on black pants last time."

"Did she?" He grinned. "She says you had on a blue dress with a white collar. You did, too. I remember it. She liked it."

Laura stared at him and then got indignant. "What's she doing, remembering my clothes like that? That's silly."

"So are you. You noticed hers."

"I just—oh, damn! She followed us into the john."

"I know. She talked to me before she went after you. I told you, Mother. She likes your face."

"She likes Marcie's. That's why she followed us," she snapped.

He shook his head "no."

"How do you know?" Laura flared, the jealousy working in her.

"I know Beebo," he chuckled.

Laura was getting curious. She finished her drink in three big swallows, which made Jack laugh. "Is she a friend of yours?" she said.

He shrugged. "More or less. I keep running into her at parties. For years we ran into each other before we got acquainted. I like her. She's a hellion, but I like her. She's a cynic like me."

"What a pity." Laura feigned unconcern, running a wet finger around the edge of her glass. "She looks like Beth," she said. "A little."

Jack blew smoke through his nostrils from a freshly lighted cigarette. "That means you like her," he said.

Laura refused to honor such nonsense with an answer. She was rather drunk now. She turned again to look at Beebo. Beebo was still gazing at her, and she winked, with that faint private smile still on her face. Laura turned quickly back to Jack. "Is she coming over?" she said, feeling slightly elated.

Jack was grinning past her at Beebo and nodding. At her words he glanced at her. "No," he said. "She's an uppity bitch."

Laura was disappointed.

"Another drink?"

"One more. That's all. What time is it?"

"Eleven-thirty."

"No!" She tried to collect her thoughts, to right her time sense, while Jack fetched the drinks. When he came back, she said, "How many drinks have I had?"

"Jesus, Mother, what a thing to ask a man. I can't even keep track of my own."

"I'm lost," she said. "I've lost count."

"Shall we take off, Mother mine?" Jack said, very carefully.

Laura tried to clear her head by shaking it and pressing her eyes shut. "I guess we'd better," she said.

"I guess we *have* to. It's four o'clock. They're closing."

"Four!" Laura came half awake at this.

"Four o'clock," he repeated elaborately.

"Oh, God. Oh, my head."

"Never mind, Mother, you can stay with me tonight. I'll try to keep my hands off you." He laughed to himself.

Laura saw Jack looking up at somebody with a grin and heard him say, "Hi, doll. I want you to meet my mother. Mother, look alive." He squinted at her doubtfully. "If possible," he added.

Laura looked up and saw a startlingly handsome face gazing down at her: black hair, pure blue eyes, a slight smile that widened a little when Laura turned her face up.

"Hello," Beebo said. "Laura." Her smile gave emphasis to the way she said Laura's name.

Laura put her hands to her head dizzily. "You look just like Beth," she murmured.

At which Beebo grinned, turning to Jack. "Three aspirins and some warm tomato juice," she said. "First thing when she gets up. She'll live."

Laura watched her, fascinated, half smiling.

Beebo turned back to her and returned the smile. Then she reached into her pocket and pulled out a dime. She flipped it in the air and then dropped it insolently in front of Laura. "Here's a dime, sweetheart," she said. "Call me sometime." And with a little grin at Jack, she turned and left them.

Laura stuck her chin out indignantly. She was not too drunk to be insulted. "Well, thanks a bunch, your majesty!" she said sarcastically to Beebo's back. She could hear Beebo laughing but she wouldn't turn around. She was already headed for the door.

Laura let Jack drag her to his apartment, three blocks away. He took her up a few stone steps into a long dim hall, and opened the first door on the left. He steered her to his bed and pushed her till she collapsed backwards on it. She fell asleep at once. Jack pulled her shoes off and her skirt, with total unconcern for her femininity, and got her under the covers.

Laura slept like a stone, a deep almost motionless sleep that could have lasted far into the next day. But Jack got her up at seven-thirty. She had three and a half hours' sleep, on virtually no dinner and eight or ten stiff drinks. She felt strange new pains all over. Jack was used to excesses, though he tried to ration himself to one or two a week. He took it pretty well in stride, but Laura felt awful. Her first words when Jack shook her were, "Oh, God! What time is it?"

"Seven-thirty."

She turned over on her stomach and put her head down on the pillow. "Where's Marcie?"

"At home. Where else?"

"What time is it? Oh, I asked you that. My head hurts."

"Take these, Mother," he said, handing her some aspirin and a glass of water.

"I don't think I can swallow."

"That's a chance you'll have to take. Here we go." He popped the pills into her mouth and gave her the water. She gulped them convulsively. "That'll see you through till—" He looked at his watch. "—about noon. After that, take three more and a No-Doz tablet. And hit the sack tonight about six. It's Friday. You can sleep for two days."

"I will, too." She rolled gingerly to a sitting position, and looked at Jack with aching eyes. "You did this to me," she said mournfully.

"Be fair, Mother. I said I'd go whenever you wanted to. I kept asking and you kept saying no."

She stared at him, disbelieving. "Jack, you louse. You should have dragged me out, you knew I—what's that?" There was a dime on the bed table.

Jack grinned at her. "Beebo's calling card," he said.

Laura remembered it in a flash, although the rest of the evening was little more than a blur. She picked it up and threw it angrily across the room. "Give it back to her for me," she said. "All I remember about last night is that awful girl and those awful mushrooms! God!"

Jack went out of the room laughing.

Chapter Eight

The first thing Laura did when she got to work was to call Marcie.

"Where were you?" Marcie demanded. "I was just going to call you. I was worried sick."

"You were?" She felt a momentary relief from her headache. "Are you all right?"

"I think so. It got so late. We were talking. I finally spent the night—" It suddenly occurred to her, as if a brick had dropped on her tender head, that she had spent the night in a man's apartment. For the first time in her life. Never mind that it was an innocent stay, or a short one. Or that the man had no designs on her. It was the idea of the thing.

"I spent the night with Jack," she blurted. Marcie was silent, having suspected as much, but not sure what to say. And it was then Laura realized that she had said the best possible thing. Even if it hadn't happened it would have been the best thing to say. Marcie didn't know either of them was gay. She only knew they were man and girl and they had spent a night together. What could sound more normal, more straight? Immoral, maybe, slightly immoral. But straight.

Marcie laughed finally.

"Is it funny?" Laura said.

"I'm sorry," Marcie said through her giggles. "I never dreamed you and Jack would hit it off like this. He must really like you, Laur." She sobered suddenly. "He never took much to the other girls we fixed him up with."

Laura squirmed a little.

"But he talked you up for half an hour before you got home last night. He thinks you're very pretty."

Laura felt grateful to him. He must have done it to enhance her in Marcie's eyes, even if he did disapprove of her infatuation.

"Did he say that?" she said, pleased.

"He did. And he's right."

Laura was taken aback. Then she said quickly, "You're both crazy."

"No, you are. We're right. You never looked at yourself, you silly girl. You don't *know* what you look like."

"Do you?" It sounded stupid, but it came out in spite of her.

"Sure. I've looked at you when you weren't noticing."

When could that have been?

"I think you have a fascinating face."

"But not pretty."

"Lovely."

"Marcie, listen to me, I—" She was shaky, mixed up from the hangover and the unexpected flattery. She would have said something terrible, something intimate, if Dr. Hollingsworth hadn't come in early. He nodded at her as he walked through the office. Sarah was still in the wash room putting on her face.

"'Morning, my dear," said the doctor with a sort of modified bow as he sailed past.

She returned the greeting and Marcie said, "I'll get you in dutch. You'd better hang up. Will you be home tonight?"

"Yes. I'll be home."

"Good girl. See you at six."

Laura hung up bewildered. She felt good and she felt lousy. Her head was throbbing but her heart was high. She wanted to talk to Jack. She didn't care who caught her. She picked up the phone and dialed his office.

"I just talked to Marcie," she said, unable to keep the pleasure out of her voice.

He sensed her excitement. "Did she propose?" he said, wryly amused.

"No, you idiot!" Laura burst out laughing. "She said I was beautiful." Unconsciously she exaggerated.

"Jesus, she has a screw loose," he said.

"She said you were talking about me before I got home. Thanks, Jack."

"Listen, Mother," he said. "Let's get this straight. I want her to think we're nuts for each other. I also think you're a pretty girl, and I said so. But I didn't say it to get Marcie all steamed up."

"Well, I don't care why you did it. She is steamed up."

"You're making a mountain out of a molehill."

"Oh, Jack, be nice to me! I'm in love, for God's sake."

"Okay, you're in love. I believe you. Worse things have happened. I'll have to work a drastic cure on you."

She laughed at him. "Too late," she said.

"You're not going to get stabbed like I was, Laura."

She recalled the defenseless mushroom with a little shiver of distaste. "Don't be morbid," she said.

"I'm a realist."

"You're blind. She's falling for me. I can tell. She must be, or she wouldn't—" Here Sarah walked in. "Jack, I'll call you back," she said.

"I dare you to. Call me back this afternoon, when you're hung over to your knees, and tell me how much you're in love."

"I'm telling you now!"

"You talk like a fish. Go on, type your damn reports. Send some poor bastard up for TB. Or enlarged heart. At least it'll be a normal disease."

She hung up with a smack. *He's a morbid miserable old man,* she thought. *I'm not that cynical yet.*

"Was that your friend?" Sarah said. "Jack?"

"Yes." She put paper and carbons into her machine.

"He's giving you the rush, hm?"

"I guess so."

"That's one of us, anyway."

Laura looked at her, and caught an expression of frustration on her face that made Laura's problems seem smaller. Sarah was plain. She was unremarkable. But so nice. It was depressing. Laura put a hand on her arm. It would cheer her up if she could cheer someone else. "Maybe Jack could fix you up with a friend of his," she said. "We could make it a foursome."

Sarah shook her head. "They all want to know 'Is she pretty?' Never mind if she's nice or wants a man so badly she could... excuse me, Laura, I sound like an old maid already. I haven't given up yet."

Laura studied her on the way down in the elevator. She ached to say the things she thought, but she didn't know Sarah well enough. They were walled up in themselves. *Poor plain Sarah,* she thought. *I'm not beautiful either. But I've been loved. I know love and I can tell you, you don't have to be a beauty to feel passion. Sometimes it helps if you're not. I wonder if you know that already.*

"I'll talk to Jack," she said as they walked out.

"That'd be awfully nice, Laura." She laughed diffidently. "At twenty-eight you begin to feel kind of frantic," she said.

Outside she left Sarah and walked toward the subway station. All the way she noticed the women, as she never had before. She was at a loss to explain it. Before, she had always hurried, on her way somewhere, with a deadline to beat, somebody to meet, things on her mind. Now—perhaps it was the fatigue that made her slow—she sauntered, looking at the women.

Looking at their faces: sweet, fine-featured, delicate, some of them; others coarse, sensual, heavily female. They all appealed to her, with their soft skirts, their clicking heels, their floating hair. It caught in her throat, this aberration of hers, in a way it never had until that moment. It suffused her. She surrendered quietly to her feelings, walking slowly, looking without staring but with a warm pleasure that made her want to smile. She had trouble controlling her mouth.

God, I love them, she thought to herself, vaguely surprised. *I just love them. I love them all. I know I'm nuts, but I love them.* She stopped by a jewelry window where an exquisite girl was admiring a group of rings. She was all in gray, as fine and soft as twilight. Gray silk graced her slim legs, gray suede pumps with the highest heels were on her feet. A gray suit, impeccably tailored, terribly expensive—gray gloves—a tiny gray hat. Laura had never liked gray much before, but suddenly it was ideal on this cool dainty little creature, with her small nose and moist pink lips. She was extremely pretty. She looked up to find Laura gazing at her, collected herself with pretty confusion, and went off, pulling a recalcitrant gray poodle after her. Laura had not even noticed it till it moved. She looked after the girl for a minute with a foolish smile.

When she finally reached the subway she collapsed on a seat, exhausted. She wanted to get home and in bed so badly that she could hardly wait.

She was late getting home but even so, Marcie had not arrived. She wanted very much to see her, but there was no help for it. She would have to wait. She fell on her bed, meaning to rest for a minute before she took her bath. But so tired was she that before five minutes had passed she was asleep. She woke up to hear small sounds in the bedroom, and it seemed like perhaps half an hour had passed.

She opened her eyes and found herself all tangled up in her clothes, her shoes still on, her dress wrinkled. There was a light on, the small table lamp between the beds. She pulled herself up and turned around. Marcie was standing in the bathroom door, with a frame of light around her, holding her toothbrush and smiling at Laura. She was all in white lace, in a short gown that barely reached her thighs. Laura smiled at her and blinked, shaking her head slightly.

"Know what time it is?" Marcie said.

"About seven."

"Quarter of twelve." Marcie laughed at her surprise. She walked over to her bed and stood beside her for a moment. She smelled gorgeous—intoxicating, sweet and clean, faintly powdered, warm and damp from her bath. She looked sleepy, soft, very feminine. Laura began to tremble, desperate to touch her, afraid even to look.

"You must have been awfully tired, Laur. You've been asleep for hours."

"I could sleep till Monday and never wake up," Laura murmured. She spoke without looking at Marcie. She couldn't. The scent of her was trouble enough.

"Burr and I went out for dinner. We didn't want to bother you."

"Did you have a nice big fight?" Irresistibly Laura's eyes traveled up Marcie to her face.

Marcie sighed. "We always have a nice big fight."

"You must enjoy them."

Marcie sat down beside her. "Don't talk that way, Laur," she said. "I wish I could get interested in books, like you."

Laura smiled at her, so close, so distant.

"Help me, Laura," she said.

"How?" Laura felt herself on very shaky ground.

"I don't know how," Marcie said impatiently. "If I knew I could help myself. There must be something in life besides fights, Laur."

"Don't call me Laur."

Marcie looked at her in surprise. "Why not?"

"Somebody else used to call me that. It still hurts a little."

"I'm sorry. I remember, you told me about him."

Laura felt confession working itself urgently into her thoughts. She wanted to clasp Marcie to her and say, "Not 'him.' Her. *Her.* It was a girl I loved. As I love you." *No, not as I love you. I can't love you that way, not even you.* To her sudden disgust the face of a handsome arrogant girl named Beebo came up in her mind. She frowned at her, trying not to see.

"What's the matter, Laur? Laura?" Marcie smoothed Laura's hair off her hot forehead. "You must have loved him a lot."

In a sudden convulsion of desire, Laura threw her arms around Marcie, pressing her hard, tight, in her arms. Her need was terrible, and a sort of sob, half ache and half passion, came out of her. Marcie was frightened.

"Laura!" she said, pushing at her. Laura was always so docile; now suddenly she was strange and violent. "Laura, are you all right?" Laura only clung to her the harder, wrestling against herself with all her strength.

For a moment, Marcie tried to calm her, whispering soothingly and rubbing her back a little. But this only aggravated Laura.

"Marcie, don't!" she said sharply. Panic began to well up in her. "Oh, God!" she cried, and stood up abruptly, shaking all over. She covered her face with her hands, trying to force the tears back with them. Marcie watched her, astonished, from the bed.

With a little gasp Laura turned and ran out. Marcie rose to her feet and called after her, but it was too late. She heard the front door slam as she ran toward it. She pulled it open but Laura was in the elevator a floor below her and on her way out. Marcie stared into the black stairwell, feeling shocked and confused.

She slipped back into the apartment and into her bed, but she couldn't sleep. She simply sat there, her eyes wide and staring, oscillating between a fear of something she couldn't name and bewildered sympathy for Laura. For whatever it was that tortured her. She shivered every time she thought of Laura's near-hysterical embrace, returning to it again and again. It gave her a reckless kick, a hint of shameless fun, like the night she kissed the bum in the park. She didn't know why it recalled that to her mind. But it did. Laura had scared her; yet now she felt like giggling.

Laura ran all the way to the subway station, three blocks off. She fell into a seat gasping, trembling violently. People stared at her but she ignored them, covering her face with her hands and sobbing quietly. She rode down to the Village and got off at Tenth Street. She had managed to control herself by this time, but she felt bewildered and lost, as if she didn't quite know what she was doing there. She stood for a moment on the platform, shivering with the chilly air. It was nearly the end of April, but it was still cold at night. She had run out in nothing but a blouse and skirt, with a light topper over them—the clothes she had fallen asleep in. She was aware of the cold, yet somehow didn't feel it.

Resolutely she began to walk, climbing the stairs and then starting down Seventh Avenue. She walked as if she had a goal, precisely because she had none and it frightened her. It was Friday night, and busy. People were everywhere. Young men turned to stare at her.

Within five minutes she was standing in front of The Cellar, rather surprised at herself for having found it so quickly. There was a strange tingling up and down her back and her eyes began to shine with a feverish luster. She walked down the steps and pulled the door open.

Almost nobody noticed her. It was too crowded, at this peak hour of one of the best nights of the week. She made her way through the crowd to the nearest end of the bar. She had to squeeze into a corner next to the jukebox and it was work to get her jacket off. It was sweaty and close after the chill air outside.

Laura stood quietly in her corner, looking at all the faces strung down the bar like beads on a necklace. They were animated, young for the most part, attractive... There were a few that were sad, or old, or soured on life—or all three. Across the room the artist, with his sketch pad, was drinking with some friends.

Laura felt alone and apart from them all somehow. There were one or two faces she might have recognized from the night before, people Jack might have introduced her to, but she couldn't be sure. She had been too drunk to be sure of anything last night.

God, was it only last night? she wondered. It seemed like a thousand nights ago. She didn't really want to be noticed now. She only wanted to watch, to be absorbed in these gay faces, in the idioms, the milieu.

"What'll you have?" She realized the bartender was leaning stiff-armed on the bar, looking at her.

"Whisky and water," she said, wondering suddenly how much it would be. She pulled out a dollar and put it on the counter self-consciously. When he brought her the drink she gulped it anxiously. Marcie kept coming into her thoughts; Marcie's face, her shocked voice saying, "Laura—don't!"

The bartender took her dollar and brought some change. It meant she could have another drink. Drinking your dinner. Where had she heard that? One of her father's friends, no doubt. She gazed at the ceiling. She wanted to talk to Jack, but she was ashamed to call him. She thought of her father again, and it gave her a sort of bitter satisfaction to imagine his face if he could see her now, alone and unhappy, disgracing him by drinking by herself, in a bar—a gay bar. Gay—that would strike him dead. She was sure of it. She smiled a little, but it was a mirthless smile.

After a moment, she ordered another drink. She counted her change fuzzily. There might be enough for a third. She slipped it back in her pocket and looked up to find a young man forcing himself into a place beside her.

Damn! she exclaimed to herself. *As if I didn't have enough on my mind.* Her slim arresting face registered subtle contempt and she turned away. It would have frozen another man, but this one only seemed amused.

"Hello, Laura," he said.

At this, she looked at him. Her mind was a blank; she couldn't place him. "Do I know you?" she said.

"No." He grinned. "I'm Dutton. This is for you. He held out a piece of paper and she took it, curious. On it was a devilish reproduction of her own features mocking her from the white page.

"You're the artist," she accused him suddenly.

"Thanks for the compliment."

"I don't want it."

"Keep it"

"I won't pay for it."

"You don't have to." He laughed at her consternation. "It's paid for, doll. Take it home. Frame it. Enjoy it."

Laura stared at him. "Who paid for it?"

"She said not to tell." He laughed. "You're a bitch to caricature. You know? Look me up sometime, I'll do a good one. I like your face." And he turned and wriggled out of the crowd.

Laura was left standing at the bar with the cartoon of herself. She was suddenly humiliated and angry. She felt ridiculous standing there holding the silly thing, not knowing who paid for it. Her glance swept down the bar, looking for a face to accuse, but she recognized no one. No one paid her any attention.

She studied the sketch once more. It was clever, insolent; it made a carnival curiosity of her face. Quietly, deliberately, with a feeling of satisfaction, she tore the sketch in half. And in half again. And threw it down behind the bar where the bartender would grind it in the wet floor. Then she picked up her glass and finished her drink.

"What did you do that for?" said a low voice, so close to her ear that she jumped and a drop of whisky ran down her chin. "It was a damn good likeness."

Laura looked up, gazing straight ahead of her, knowing who it was now and mad. She pulled a dime out of her pocket and smacked it on the bar in front of her. "I owe you a dime, Beebo. There it is. Thanks for the picture. Next time don't waste your money."

Beebo laughed. "I always get what I pay for, lover," she said. Laura refused to look at her, and after a pause Beebo said, "What's the matter, Laura, 'fraid to look at me?"

Laura had to look then. She turned her head slowly, reluctantly. Her face was cold and composed. Beebo chuckled at her. She was handsome, like a young boy of fourteen, with her smooth skin and deep blue eyes. She was leaning on her elbows on the bar, and she looked sly and amused. "Laura's afraid of me," she said with a quick grin.

"Laura's not afraid of you or anybody else. Laura thinks you're a bitch. That's all."

"That makes two of us."

Under her masklike face Laura found herself troubled by the smile so close to her; the snapping blue eyes.

"Where's your guardian angel tonight?" Beebo said.

"I suppose you mean Jack. I don't know where he is, he doesn't have to tell me where he goes." She turned back to the bar. "He's not my guardian angel. I don't need one. I'm a big girl now."

"Oh, excuse me. I should have noticed."

Laura's cheeks prickled with embarrassment. "You only see what you want to see," she said.

"I see what I want to see right now," Beebo said, and Laura felt her hand on the small of her back. She straightened suddenly.

"Go away," she said sharply. "Leave me alone."

"I can't."

"Then shut up."

Beebo laughed softly. "What's the matter, little girl? Hate the world tonight?" Laura wouldn't answer. "Think that's going to make it any prettier?" Beebo pushed Laura's whisky glass toward her with one finger.

"I'm having a drink for the hell of it," Laura said briefly. "If it bothers you, go away. You weren't invited, anyway."

"Don't tell me you're drinking just because you like the taste."

"I don't mind it."

"You're unlucky in love, then. Or you just found out you're gay and you can't take it. That it?"

Laura pursed her lips angrily. "I'm not in love. I never was."

"You mean love is filth and all that crap? Love is dirty?"

"I didn't say that!" Laura turned on her.

Beebo shrugged. "You're a big girl, lover. You said it yourself. Big girls know all about love. So don't lie to me."

"I didn't ask you to bother me, Beebo. I don't want to talk to you. Now scram!"

"There she stands at the bar, drinking whisky because it tastes good," Beebo drawled, gazing toward the ceiling and letting the smoke from a cigarette drift from her mouth. "Sweet sixteen and never been kissed."

"Twenty," Laura snapped.

"Excuse me, twenty. Your innocence is getting tedious, lover." She smiled.

"Beebo, I don't like you," Laura said. "I don't like the way you dress or the way you talk or the way you wear your hair. I don't like the things you say and the money you throw around. I don't want your dimes and I don't want you. I hope that's plain because I don't know how to make it any plainer." Her voice broke as she talked and toward the end she felt her own crazy tears coming up again. Beebo saw them before they spilled over and they changed her. They touched her. She ignored the hard words Laura spoke, for she knew enough to know they meant nothing.

"Tell me, baby," she said gently. "Tell me all about it. Tell me you hate me if it'll help."

For a moment Laura sat there, not trusting her, not wanting to risk a word with her, letting the stray tears roll over her cheeks without even brushing them away. Then she straightened up and swept them off her face with her long slim fingers, turning away from Beebo. "I can't tell you, or anybody."

Beebo shrugged. "All right. Have it your way." She dinched her cigarette and leaned on the bar again, her face close to Laura's. "Try, baby," she said softly. "Try to tell me."

"It's stupid, it's ridiculous. We're complete strangers."

"We aren't strangers." She put an arm around Laura and squeezed her a little. Laura was embarrassed and grateful at the same time. It felt good, so good. Beebo sighed at her silence. "I'm a bitch, you're right about that," she admitted. "But I didn't want to be. It's an attitude. You develop it after a while, like a turtle grows a shell. You need it. Pretty soon you live it, you don't know any other way."

Laura finished her drink without answering. She put it down on the bar and looked for the bartender. She wouldn't care what Beebo said, she wouldn't look at her, she wouldn't answer her. She didn't dare.

"You don't need to tell me about it," Beebo went on. "Because I already know. I've lived through it, too. You fall in love. You're young, inexperienced. What the hell, maybe you're a virgin, even. You fall, up to your ears, and there's nobody to talk to, nobody to lean on. You're all alone with that great big miserable feeling and she's driving you out of your mind. Every time you look at her, every time you're near her. Finally you give in to it—and she's straight." She said the last word with such acid sharpness that Laura jumped. "End of story," Beebo added. "End of soap opera. Beginning of soap opera. That's all the Village is, honey, just one crazy little soap opera after another, like Jack says. All tangled up with each other, one piled on top of the next, ad infinitum. Mary loves Jane loves Joan loves Jean loves Beebo loves Laura." She stopped and grinned at Laura.

"Doesn't mean a thing," she said. "It goes on forever. Where one stops another begins." She looked around The Cellar with Laura following her gaze. "I know most of the girls in here," she said. "I've probably slept with half of them. I've lived with half of the half I've slept with. I've loved half of the half I've lived with. What does it all come to?"

She turned to Laura, who was caught with her fascinated face very close to Beebo's. She started to back away but Beebo's arm around her waist tightened and kept her close. "You know something, baby? It doesn't matter. Nothing matters. You don't like me, and that doesn't matter. Someday maybe you'll love me, and that won't matter either. Because it won't last. Not down here. Not anywhere in the world, if you're gay. You'll never find peace, you'll never find Love. With a capital L."

She took a drag on her cigarette and let it flow out of her nostrils. "L for Love," she said, looking into space. "L for Laura." She turned and smiled at her, a little sadly. "L for Lust and L for the L of it. L for

Lesbian. L for Let's—let's," she said, and blew smoke softly into Laura's ear. Laura was startled to feel the strength of the feeling inside her.

It's the whisky, she thought. *It's because I'm tired. It's because I want Marcie so much. No, that doesn't make sense.* She caught the bartender's eye and he fixed her another drink.

Beebo's arm pressed her again. "Let's," she said. "How about it?" She was smiling, not pushy, not demanding, just asking. As if it didn't really matter whether Laura said yes or no.

"Where did you get that ridiculous name?" Laura hedged.

"My family."

"They named you *Beebo?*"

"They named me Betty Jean," she said, smiling. "Which is even worse."

"It's a pretty name."

"It's a lousy name. Even Mother couldn't stand it. And she could stand damn near anything. But they had to call me something. So they called me Beebo."

"That's too bad."

Beebo laughed. "I get along," she said.

The bartender set Laura's glass down and she reached for her change. "What's your last name?" she said to Beebo.

"Brinker. Like the silver skates."

Laura counted her change. She had sixty-five cents. The bartender was telling a joke to some people a few seats down, resting one hand on the bar in front of Laura, waiting for his money. She was a dime short. She counted it again, her cheeks turning hot.

Beebo watched and began to laugh. "Want your dime back?" she said.

"It's your dime," Laura said haughtily.

"You must have left home in a hurry, baby. Poor Laura. Hasn't got a dime for a lousy drink."

Laura wanted to strangle her. The bartender turned back to her suddenly and she felt her face burning. Beebo leaned toward him, laughing. "I've got it, Mort," she said.

"No!" Laura said. "If you could just lend me a dime."

Beebo laughed and waved Mort away.

"I don't want to owe you a thing," Laura told her.

"Too bad, doll. You can't help yourself." She laughed again. Laura tried to give her the change she had left, but Beebo wouldn't take it. "Sure, I'll take it," she said. "And you'll be flat busted. How'll you get home?"

Laura went pale then. She couldn't go home. Even if she had a hundred dollars in her pocket. She couldn't stand to face Marcie, to explain her crazy behavior, to try to make herself sound normal and ordinary when her whole body was begging for strange passion, for forbidden release.

Beebo watched her face change and then she shook her head. "It must have been a bad fight," she said.

"You've got it all wrong, Beebo. It wasn't a fight. It was—I don't know what it was."

"She straight?"

"I don't know." Laura put her forehead down on the heel of her right hand. "Yes, she's straight," she whispered.

"Well, did you tell her? About yourself?"

"I don't know if I did or not. I didn't say it but I acted like a fool. I don't know what she thinks."

"Then things could be worse," Beebo said. "But if she's straight, they're probably hopeless."

"That's what Jack said."

"Jack's right."

"He's not in love with her!"

"Makes him even righter. He sees what you can't see. If he says she's straight, believe him. Get out while you can."

"I can't." Laura felt an awful twist of tenderness for Marcie in her throat.

"Okay, baby, go home and get your heart broken. It's the only way to learn, I guess."

"I can't go home. Not tonight."

"Come home with me."

"No."

"Well…" Beebo smiled. "I know a nice bench in Washington Square. If you're lucky the bums'll leave you alone. And the cops."

"I'll—I'll go to Jack's," she said, suddenly brightening with the idea. "He won't mind."

"He might," Beebo said, and raised her glass to her lips. "Call him first."

Laura started to leave the bar and then recalled that all her change was sitting on the counter in front of Beebo. She turned back in confusion, her face flushing again. Beebo turned and looked at her. "What's the matter, baby?" And then she laughed. "Need a dime?" She handed her one.

For a moment, in the relative quiet of the phone booth, Laura leaned against a wall and wondered if she might faint. But she didn't. She deposited the dime and dialed Jack's number. The phone rang nine times before he answered, and she was on the verge of panic when she heard him lift the receiver at last and say sleepily, "Hello?"

"Hello, Jack? Jack, this is Laura." She was vastly relieved to find him at home.

"Sorry, we don't want any."

"Jack, I've got to see you."

"My husband contributes to that stuff at the office."

"Jack, please! It's terribly important."

"I love you, Mother, but you call me at the God-damnedest times."

"Can I come over?"

"Jesus, no!" he exclaimed, suddenly coming wide awake.

"Oh, Jack, what'll I do?" She sounded desperate.

"All right now, let's get straightened out here. Let's make an effort." He sounded as if he had drunk a lot and just gotten to sleep, still drunk, when Laura's call woke him up. "Now start at the beginning. And make it quick. What's the problem?"

She felt hurt, slighted. Of all people, Jack was the one she had to count on. "I—I acted like a fool with Marcie. I don't know what she thinks," she half-sobbed. "Jack, help me."

"What did you do?"

"Nothing—everything. I don't know."

"God, Mother. Why did you pick tonight? Of all nights?"

"I didn't pick it, it just happened."

"What happened, damn it?"

"I—I sort of embraced her."

There was a silence on the other end for a minute. Laura heard him say away from the receiver, "Okay, it's okay. No, she's a friend of mine. A friend, damn it, a girl." Then his voice became clear and close again. "Mother, I don't know what to say. I'm not sure I understand what happened, and if I did I still wouldn't know what the hell to say. Where are you?"

"At The Cellar. Jack, you've just got to help me. Please."

"Are you alone?"

"Yes. No. I've been talking to Beebo, but—"

"Oh! Well, God, that's it, that's the answer. Go home with Beebo."

"No! I can't, Jack. I want to come to your place."

"Laura, honey—" He was wide awake now, sympathetic, but caught in his own domestic moils. "Laura, I'm—well, I'm entertaining." He laughed a little at his own silliness. "I'm involved. I'm fraternizing. Oh, hell, I'm making love. You can't come over here." His voice went suddenly in the other direction as he said, "No, calm down, she's not coming over."

Then he said, "Laura, I wish I could help, honest to God. I just can't, not now. You've got to believe me." He spoke softly, confidentially, as if he didn't want the other to hear what he said. "I'll tell you what I'll do, I'll call Marcie and get it straightened out. Don't worry, Marcie believes in me. She thinks I'm Jack Armstrong, the all-American boy. The four-square troubleshooter. I'll fix it up for you."

"Jack, please," she whimpered, like a plaintive child.

"I'll do everything I can. You just picked the wrong night and that's the God's truth, honey. Where's Beebo? Let me talk to Beebo."

Laura went out of the booth to get her, feeling half dazed, and found her way back to the bar. "He wants to talk to you," she said to Beebo, without looking at her.

Beebo frowned at her and then swung herself off her seat and headed for the phone. Laura sat down in her place, disturbed by the warmth Beebo left behind, twirling her glass slowly in her hand. She was crushed that Jack had turned her down.

Perhaps he had a lover, perhaps this night was so important to him that he couldn't give it up, even though she had all his sympathy. These things might be—in fact, were—true. But Laura could hardly discern them through her private pains.

Beebo came back in a minute and leaned over Laura, one hand on the bar, the other on Laura's shoulder. "He says I'm to take you home," she said, "feed you aspirins, dry your tears, and put you to bed. And no monkey business." She smiled as Laura looked slowly up into her face. It was a strong interesting face. With a little softness, a little innocence, it might have been lovely. But it was too hard and cynical, too restless and disillusioned. "Come on, sweetie pie," Beebo said. "I'm a nice kid, I won't eat you."

They walked until they came to a small dark street, and the second door up—dark green—faced right on the sidewalk. Beebo opened it and they walked down a couple of steps into a small square court surrounded by the windowed walls of apartment buildings. On the far side was another door with benches and play areas grouped in between on the court. Beebo unlocked the other door and led Laura up two flights of unlighted stairs to her apartment.

When they went inside a brown dachshund rushed to meet them and tried to climb up their legs. Beebo laughed and talked to him, reaching down to push him away.

Laura stood inside the door, her hands over her eyes, somewhat unsteady on her feet.

"Here, baby, let's get you fixed up," Beebo said. "Okay, Nix, down. Down!" she said sharply to the excited little dog, and shoved him away with her foot. He slunk off to a chair where he studied her reproachfully.

Beebo led Laura through the small living room to an even smaller bedroom and sat her down on the bed. She knelt in front of her and took her shoes off. Then, gently, she leaned against her, forcing her legs slightly apart, and put her arms around Laura's waist. She rubbed her head against Laura's breasts and said, "Don't be afraid, baby." Laura tried weakly to hold her off but she said, "I won't hurt you Laura," and looked up at her. She squeezed her gently, rhythmically, her arms tightening and loosening around Laura's body. She made a little sound in her throat and, lifting her face, kissed Laura's neck. And then she stood up slowly, releasing her.

"Okay," she said. "Fini. No monkey business. Make yourself comfortable, honey. There's the john—old, but serviceable. You sleep here. I'll take the couch. Here! Here, Nix!" She grabbed the little dog, which had bounded onto the bed and was trying to lick Laura's face, and picked him up in her arms like a baby. She grinned at Laura. "I'll take him to bed, he won't bother you," she said. "Call me if there's anything you need." She looked at Laura closely while Laura tried to answer her. The younger girl sat on the bed, pale with fatigue and hunger, feeling completely lost and helpless. "Thanks," she murmured.

Beebo sat down beside her. "You look beat, honey," she said.
"I am."
"Want to tell me about it now?"
Laura shook her head.
"Well..." she said. "Good night, Little Bo-peep. Sleep tight." And she kissed her forehead, then turned around and went out of the bedroom, turning out the light on her way.

Laura had gotten off the bed without looking at her, but feeling Beebo's eyes on her. She shut the door slowly, until she heard the catch snap. Then she turned, leaning on the door, and looked at the room. It was small and full of stuff, with yellowed walls. Everything looked clean, although the room was in a state of complete confusion, with clothes draped over chairs and drawers half shut.

All of a sudden, Laura felt stronger. She undressed quickly, taking off everything but her nylon slip, and pulled down the bedclothes. She climbed in gratefully.

She didn't even try to forget Marcie or what had happened. It would have been impossible. Mere trying would have made it worse. She relaxed on her back in the dark, her arms outflung, and waited for the awful scene to come up in her mind and torture her.

Her mind wandered. The awful embrace was awful no longer—only wrong and silly and far away. The damage was irreparable. She stared at the ceiling, invisible in the dark, and felt a soft lassitude come over her. She felt as if she were melting into the bed; as if she could not have moved if she tried.

Time flowed by and she waited for sleep. It was some time before she realized she was actually waiting for it. It didn't come. She turned on her side, and still it eluded her. Finally she snapped the light on to squint at her watch. It said five of four. She switched it off again, her eyes dazzled, and wondered what the matter was. And then she heard Beebo turn over in the next room, and she knew.

An old creeping need began to writhe in Laura, coming up suddenly out of the past and twisting itself around her innards. The pressure increased while she lay there trying to ignore it, becoming more insistent. It began to swell and fade with a rhythm of its own; a rhythm she knew too well and feared. Slowly the heat mounted to her face, the sweat came out on her body. She began to turn back and forth in bed, hating herself and trying to stop it, but helpless with it.

Laura was a sensual girl. Her whole being cried out for love and loving. It had been denied her for over a year, and the effects were a severe strain on her that often brought her nerves to the breaking point. She pretended she had learned to live with it, or rather, without it. She even pretended she could live her whole life without it. But in her secret self she knew she couldn't.

Beebo turned over again in the living room and Laura knew she was awake, too. The sudden realization made her gasp, and she could fool herself no longer. She wanted Beebo. She wanted a woman; she wanted a woman so terribly that she had to put her hand tight over her mouth to stop the groan that would have issued from it.

For a few moments more she tossed feverishly on her bed, trying to find solitary release, but it wouldn't come. The thought of Beebo tortured her now, and not the thought of Marcie. Beebo— with her lithe body, her fascinating face, her cynical shell. There was so much of Beth there. At that thought, Laura found herself swinging her legs out of bed.

Moonlight glowed in two bright squares on the living room floor. Laura could see the couch, draped in blankets. She wondered whether Beebo had heard her and waited breathlessly for some sign. Nix lifted his head but made no sound, only watching her as she advanced across the room on her tiptoes, her white slip gleaming as she passed through the light.

Laura stood and hovered over the couch, uncertain what to do, her heart pounding hugely against her ribs. Beebo was on her side, turned toward Laura, apparently asleep. Nix was snuggled into the ditch between the back of Beebo and the back of the couch.

Beebo stirred slightly, but she didn't open her eyes. "Beebo," Laura whispered, dropping to her knees and supporting herself against the couch with her hands. "Beebo?" she whispered again, a little louder. And then, sensing that Beebo had heard her she bent down and kissed her cheek, her hands reaching for her. Beebo was suddenly completely roused, coming up on her elbow and then falling back and pulling Laura with her.

"Laura?" she said huskily. "Are you all right?" And then she felt Laura's lips on her face again and a shock of passion gripped her. "Oh, God—Oh, baby," she said, and her arms went around Laura hard.

"Hold me," Laura begged, clinging to her. "Oh, Beebo, hold me."

Beebo rolled off the couch onto Laura and the abrupt weight of her body fired Laura into a frenzy. They rolled over each other on the floor, pressing each other tight, almost as if they wanted to fuse their bodies, and kissed each other wildly.

Laura felt such a wave of passion come up in her that it almost smothered her. She thought she couldn't stand it. And then she didn't think at all. She only clung to Beebo, half tearing her pajamas off her back, groaning wordlessly, almost sobbing. Her hands explored, caressed, felt Beebo all over, while her own body responded with violent spasms—joyous, crazy, deep as her soul. She could no more have prevented her response than she could the tyrannic need that drove her to find it. She felt Beebo's tongue slip into her mouth and Beebo's firm arms squeezing her and she went half out of her mind with it. Her hands were in Beebo's hair, tickling her ears, slipping down her back, over her hips and thighs. Her body heaved against Beebo's in a lovely mad duet. She felt like a column of fire, all heat and light, impossibly sensual, impossibly sexual. She was all feeling, warm and melting, strong and sweet.

It was a long time before either of them came to their senses. They had fallen half asleep when it was over, still lying on the floor, where Nix, after some trepidation, came to join them. When Laura opened her eyes the gray dawn had replaced the white moonlight. She was looking out the window at a mass of telephone and electric wires. She gazed slowly downward until she found Beebo's face. Beebo was awake, watching her—no telling for how long. She smiled slightly, frowning at the same time. But she didn't say anything and neither did Laura. They only pulled closer together, until their lips touched. Beebo began to kiss Laura over and over, little soft teasing kisses that kept out of the way of passion, out of the way of Laura's own kisses as they searched for Beebo's lips. Until it was suddenly imperative that they kiss each other right. Laura tried feebly to stop it, but she quickly surrendered. When Beebo relented a little it was Laura who pulled her back, until Beebo was suddenly crazy for her again.

"No, no, no, no," Laura murmured, but she had asked for it. A year and a half of abstinence was too much for her. At that moment she was in bondage to her body. She gave in in spite of herself, rolling over on Beebo, her fine hair falling over Beebo's breasts in a pale glimmering shower, soft and cool and bringing up the fire in Beebo again.

Once again they rested, half sleeping, turning now and then to feel each other, reassure themselves that the other was still there, still responsive. Now and then Beebo pushed Nix off Laura, or out from between them, where he was anxious to make himself a nest.

It was Saturday afternoon before they could drag themselves off the floor. It was Laura who pulled herself to her knees first by the aid of a handy chair, and squinted at the bright daylight. For a few moments she remained there, swaying slightly, trying to think straight and not succeeding. She felt Beebo's hand brush across her stomach and looked down at her. Beebo smiled a little.

An elusive feeling of shame slipped through Laura, disappeared, came back again, faded, came back. It seemed uncertain whether or not to stay. She swallowed experimentally, looking at Beebo. After a minute Beebo said, "Who's Beth?"

"Beth?" Laura was startled.

"Um-hm. She the blonde?"

"No. That's Marcie."

"Well, baby, seems to me like it's Beth you're after, not Marcie."

Laura frowned at her. "I haven't seen Beth for almost a year. She's married now. It's all over."

"For her, maybe."

"I won't discuss it," she said haughtily, getting up and walking away from her, while Beebo lay on the floor admiring her body, her head propped comfortably on her hands. "It happened long ago and I've forgotten it."

"Then how come you called me Beth all night?"

Laura gasped, turning to look at her, and then her face went pink. "I—I'm sorry, Beebo," she said. "I won't do it again."

"Don't count on it."

Laura stamped her foot. "Damn you, Beebo!" she said. "Don't talk to me as if I were an irresponsible child!"

Beebo laughed, rolling over and nearly crushing Nix, who reacted by licking her frantically and wagging his tail. Beebo squashed him in a hug, still laughing. Laura turned on her heel to leave the room, looking back quickly to grab her slip, and went into the bedroom, slamming the door. Within seconds it flew open again and Beebo leaned against the jamb, smiling at her. She sauntered into the room.

"Now, don't tell me you didn't enjoy yourself last night, Little Bo-peep," she said.

Laura ignored her, moving speedily, suddenly embarrassed to be naked. In the heat of passion it was glorious, but in the morning, in the gray light, in the chill and ache of waking up, she hated it. Her own bare flesh seemed out of place. Not so with Beebo, who sprawled on the bed on top of the underwear Laura wanted to put on.

"Did you?" said Beebo. "Enjoy yourself?"

"Get up, Beebo, I want to get dressed."

"After all, it was your idea, baby."

"Don't throw *that* in my face!" she exclaimed angrily, ashamed to remember it.

"Why not? It's true. Besides I'm not throwing it in your face, I'm just saying it."

Laura turned away from her, unbearably conscious of her own slim behind, her dimpled rump, and her long limbs. She yearned to be shrouded in burlap. "Beebo, I—I couldn't help myself last night." She worked to control her voice, to be civilized about it. "I needed—I mean—it had been so long."

"Since Beth?"

Laura fought down a sudden impulse to strangle her. "I was a fool," she said, and her voice trembled. "A fool with my roommate and now with you. It got so I couldn't stand it at home. It got intolerable."

"So you came down here. And I was a nice convenient safety valve."

"I didn't mean that!" she flared.

"Doesn't matter what you mean, baby. It's a fact. Here you were, desperate. And here was I, ready and willing. You knew I wouldn't turn you down."

Laura's face began to burn. She had a wild idea that her back was blushing with her cheeks.

"What would you have done if I *had* turned you down, Laura?" Beebo spoke softly, insinuatingly, teasing Laura, enjoying herself.

But Laura was too humiliated to tease back. "I don't know," she exclaimed miserably. "I don't know what I *could* have done." And she covered her face with her hands.

"I'll tell you, then. You'd have begged me. You'd have gotten down on your knees and begged me. Sometime you will, too. Wait and see."

Laura whirled toward her, insulted. "That's enough!" she said harshly. She pulled her underthings forcibly from under Beebo, but Beebo caught the shoulder strap of her brassiere and hung on to it with both hands, her heels braced against the floor, laughing like a beautiful savage while Laura yanked furiously at it.

"You're going to get about half," she said. "If you're lucky. I'll get the other half. Half isn't going to hold much of you up, baby."

Laura let go suddenly, and Beebo fell back on the bed, grinning at her.

"Laura hates me," she said, "Laura hates me." She said it slowly, singsong, daring Laura to answer her.

Laura glared at her, defiant and fuming. "You're an animal!" she hissed at her.

"Sure."' Beebo chuckled. "Ask Jack. That's his favorite word. We're all animals."

"You're nothing but a dirty animal!"

"What were you last night, Miss Prim? You were panting at me like a sow in rutting season."

Laura's eyes went wide with fury. She grabbed the nearest thing—a hairbrush—and flung it violently at Beebo. Beebo ducked, laughing again at her young victim, and Laura turned and fled into the bathroom. She slammed the door so hard it bounced open and she had to shut it again. With frantic fingers she tried to turn the lock, but Beebo was already pushing on the other side. Laura heaved against it, but Beebo got it open and she fell back against the wall, suddenly frightened.

"Don't touch me!" she spat at her.

Beebo smiled. "Why not? You didn't mind last night. I touched you all over. Did I miss anything?"

Laura shrank from her. "Let me go, Beebo."

"Let you go? I'm not even touching you."

"I want to leave. I want to get out of here." Laura tried to push past her but Beebo caught her, her strong hands pressing painfully into Laura's shoulders, and threw her back against the wall.

"You're not going anywhere, Bo-peep," she said. And began to kiss her. Laura fought her, half sobbing, groaning, furious. Beebo's lips were all over her face, her throat, her breasts, and she took no notice of Laura's blows and her sharp nails. Laura grabbed handfuls of her hair, wanting to tear it out, but Beebo pulled her close, panting against her, her eyes hypnotically close to Laura's. And Laura felt her knees go weak.

"No," she whispered. "Oh, God no. Oh, Beebo." Her hands caressed Beebo's hair, her lips parted beneath Beebo's. All the lonely months of denial burst like firecrackers between her legs. Once it had started her whole body begged for release. It betrayed her. She clung sweating and heaving to Beebo. They were both surprised at the strength and insistence of their feelings. They had felt the attraction from the first, but they had been unprepared for the crescendo of emotion that followed.

It was a long time before either of them heard the phone ringing. Finally Beebo stood up, looking down at Laura, watching her. Laura turned her face away, pulling her knees up and feeling the tears come. Beebo knelt beside her then, the hardness gone from her face.

"Don't cry, baby," she said, and kissed her gently. "Laura, don't cry. I know you don't want to make love to me, I know you *have* to. Damn that phone! It's not your fault. Laura, baby, you make beautiful love. God grant me a passionate girl like you just once in a while and I'll die happy."

"Please don't touch me. Don't talk to me." She was overwhelmed with shame.

"I have to. I can't help myself any more than you can. I had no idea you'd be like this—Jesus, so hot! You look so cool, so damn far above the rest of us. But you're not, poor baby. Better than some of us, maybe, but not above us."

Laura turned her face to the wall. "Answer the phone," she said.

Beebo left her then and went into the living room. Laura could hear her voice when she answered.

"Hello?" she said. "How are you, doll? Fine. Laura's fine. No, I didn't rape her. She raped me." Laura sat straight up at this, her face flaming. Beebo was laughing. "Tell her what? It's all fixed up? You mean I can send her home to Marcie?" Her voice became heavily sarcastic. "Well, isn't that too sweet for words. Okay, Jack, I'll tell her. You what?...With who?...Oh, Terry! Yeah, I've seen him. You got a live one there, boy. Hang on to him, he's a doll...Okay, don't mention it. It's been a pleasure. Most of it. She's lovely...So long."

When Beebo returned to the bathroom, Laura was standing at the washbowl, rinsing her face, trying to compose herself.

"What did he say?" she asked Beebo.

"It was Jack."

"I heard."

Beebo put her arms around Laura from behind, leaning a little against her, front to back, planting kisses in her hair while she talked. "He says you're forgiven. He handed Marcie some psychological hocus pocus about a neurosis. You are neurotic, love. As of now. As far as Marcie's concerned, you have attacks. She should have a few herself."

"Don't be so sarcastic, Beebo. If you knew what I've been through—how scared I was—"

"Okay, no more sarcasm. For a few minutes at least. God, you're pretty, Laura." Like Jack, like Marcie, like many others, she realized it slowly. Laura's singular face fit no pattern. It had to be discovered. Laura herself had never discovered it. She didn't believe in it. She grew up convinced she was as plain as her father seemed to think, and when she looked into the mirror she didn't see her own reflection. She saw what she thought she looked like; a mask, a cliché left over from adolescence. It embarrassed her when people told her she was pretty.

"Don't flatter me," she said sharply to Beebo. "I hate it."

Beebo shut her eyes and laughed in Laura's ear. "You're nuts," she said. "You are *nuts,* Bo-peep."

"I'm sane. And I'm plain. There's a poem for you. Now let me go."

"There's no rush, baby."

"There is. I want to get home." She twisted away from Beebo, turning around to face her.

Beebo let her hands trail up the front of Laura. "Home to Marcie?" she said, and let them drop suddenly. "Okay. Go home. Go home, now that you can stand it for another couple of days. And when the pressure gets too great, come back down again. Come back to Beebo, your faithful safety valve."

"You said you wouldn't be sarcastic."

Beebo wheeled away, walking into the bedroom. "What do you want me to do, sing songs? Write poems? Dance? Shall I congratulate you? Congratulations, Laura, you've finally found a way to beat the problem. Every time Marcie sexes you up, run down to Beebo's and let it off. Beebo'll fix you up. Lovely arrangement."

She turned to Laura, her eyes narrowed. "Laura gets loved up for free, Beebo gets a treat, and Marcie stays pure. Whatever happens, let's not dirty Marcie up. Let's not muss up that gorgeous blonde hair."

"Don't talk about her!" Laura had followed her in the bedroom.

"Oh, don't get me wrong, Bo-peep. I'm not complaining. You're too good to me, you know. You give me your throw-away kisses. I get your cast-off passion. I'm your Salvation Army, doll, I get all the left-overs. Throw me a bone." She was sitting on the edge of her rump on her dresser, legs crossed at the ankles, arms folded on her chest—a favorite stance with her.

Laura was suddenly ashamed of the way she had used Beebo. Beebo was hurt. And it was Laura's fault.

"Everything's my fault, Beebo," she said. "I'm sorry." There was silence for a minute. Laura was acutely aware that "I'm sorry" was no recompense for what she was doing to Beebo.

Beebo smiled wryly. "Thanks," she said.

"I am, Beebo. Really. I didn't come to you last night just because of Marcie." It was suffocatingly hard to talk. She spoke in fits and starts as her nerve came and left her.

"No?" Beebo remained motionless with a "tell-me-another" look on her face.

"No. I came—I came because—" She covered her face with her hands, stuck for words and ashamed.

"You came, baby. That's enough," Beebo finished for her, relenting a little. "You came and I'm not sorry. Neither are you, not really. The situation isn't perfect." She laughed. "But last night was perfect. It isn't like that very often, I can tell you."

Laura looked at her again. Then she moved toward her clothes, afraid to stay naked any longer, afraid the whole thing would start over again.

Beebo came toward her, pulling the slip from her hand and dropping it on the floor. "There's no hurry," she said.

"I'm going, Beebo. Don't try to stop me."

For a moment Beebo didn't answer. Then she scooped up some of Laura's clothes on her foot and flung them at her. "Okay, baby," she said. "But next time, you don't get off so easily. Clear?"

"There won't be a next time." Laura concentrated on dressing, on getting her body covered as quickly as possible. "I'm grateful to you, but I'll never do it again. It isn't fair, not to you."

Beebo laughed disagreeably. "Don't worry about being fair to *me,* baby. It didn't bother you last night."

"I couldn't think last night! You know that."

"Yes. I know that. I'm glad. I hope I drive you out of your mind." Beebo's eyes bored into her and made her rush and stumble. She was afraid to confront her, and when she had her clothes on she caught her jacket up with one hand and headed for the door without looking back.

Nix pranced after her. Before she got the front door open, Beebo caught her and turned her around. "Good-bye, Beebo," she said stiffly.

Beebo smiled, upsetting Laura with her nude closeness. "You'll be back, Little Bo-peep. You know that, don't you." It was a statement, not a question.

I'll never come back, she told herself. *I'll never open this door again.*

And, confident that she meant what she said, she turned and walked away. Within minutes she was riding uptown on the subway. In less than half an hour she was climbing the flight of stairs to the penthouse, her heart pounding.

The door was open. Laura went in, feeling her legs start to shake. There didn't seem to be anyone around. She walked through the apartment: no-one. She slipped her jacket off and went into the kitchen to find something for breakfast. Out on the roof she could hear people laughing, while competing portable radios squeaked from different corners. The population of the apartment building had taken to sunning itself on the roof on fair weekends.

Laura ate some toast and orange juice, sitting quietly on the kitchen table. *She's out there on the porch. I know she's out there,* she told herself. She was afraid to face her, afraid to go looking for her. She wanted to fall into bed and sleep, but she knew she would never rest until the thing was straightened out.

Laura emptied her orange juice glass and put it down resolutely on the table. She set her chin and slipped off the table, heading for the door. She bumped flat into Jack as he came in.

Laura gave a little scream and jumped backwards. "Oh," she said, shutting her eyes for a minute to let her heart come back to normal. "It's you."

"Say it like you're glad to see me, Mother," he said, smiling wistfully.

"I am," she exclaimed, coming toward him then and taking his hands. "Oh, Jack, I am. I don't know what I would have done—"

"Now you're embarrassing me," he said. "They're out on the roof sunbathing, by the way."

"They?"

"Burr's here."

Laura started for the door, but Jack caught her sleeve. "Are you cracked?" he said. "This isn't the time. Wait till Burr leaves." Laura stopped, unsure. "You don't want to go out there and try to explain it to her now, do you?" Jack said.

"I just want to get it over with."

"It'll keep. Don't be pushy."

Laura rubbed her forehead. "You're right," she said. "I can't talk to her in front of Burr." She laughed a little. "I *am* cracked. People have been telling me that all day."

"You don't have to say much anyway," Jack said. "I did a smooth patch job. She thinks you're a little goofy. But harmless."

Laura smiled at him in relief. But as they gazed at each other the ghost of Beebo came up in her mind and she was suddenly blushing without Jack's having said a word. "I—I think I'd better go in and lie down, if you'll excuse me," she said, anxious to get away from him.

"Didn't get much sleep last night?" he said.

"Not much." She looked at the floor, not quite forgiving him for leaving her in the lurch the night before. "You sent me home with her," she reminded him.

"I didn't send you to bed with her. I gave her orders. I told her no monkey business. She promised to behave." He was still smiling, curious to hear her defend herself.

Laura wondered quickly whether she could get away with a lie, ashamed as she was of the truth. But she knew her hot cheeks would betray her. They always did.

"She did behave, Jack." His eyebrows went up skeptically. "She—what I mean is—it was me."

He looked at her sideways. "You mean you just sort of fell into each other's arms?"

"Well, sort of."

"By mistake? In the dark?"

"I—I—"

"You're fibbing. I know Beebo. Who made who?" He opened the icebox and fished out a beer. "Do I have to say it, or are you going to tell me?"

"Well, damn it, who are you?" she exclaimed. "You have no right to know anything."

"Okay. I'll get it from Beebo. She says you raped her."

"She's a liar! I heard her say that. Damn!"

Jack laughed, opening the beer. He sniffed it. "God, what awful stuff," he remarked. "I only drink it before noon. Cheers." He drank, and held the can toward her. "Want some?"

"At this hour?"

"Your stomach doesn't know what time it is."

"Your stomach, maybe."

"Did Beebo jump you, Laura? If she did I'll break her head." He asked it suddenly and quietly, and she saw that he meant to help and comfort her. He had to stick a few pins in her, only to pull them out and offer first aid. It was the way he did things.

"She didn't—no," Laura said, turning away. "Jack, don't make me talk about it."

"You could talk to me before."

"You turned me down last night," she said pettishly.

"I had to. There was someone else last night."

"I...oh damn it, Jack, I'm ashamed of myself. It was my fault, I made it so easy. No, that's a lie. I did it on purpose." A wave of tears welled through her and subsided, leaving her with her hands over her face. Jack started to speak but she silenced him with a wave of her hand. "It's been so long, Jack. It's been hell. I've been so lonely. I didn't know a person could be that lonely and live. And then I moved in with Marcie and it was suddenly torture. All these months I've been here. And most of the time I've been dying for her. And last night—I was so tired, so mixed up and I had a couple of drinks—"

"You sounded nuts on the phone."

"I felt nuts. I felt awful. She took me home, and she was very decent. She really was. She wanted to, I know that. But she didn't. She gave me her bed and she went in the living room and slept on the couch. I thought I'd fall right to sleep. But I couldn't. I just tossed and turned, and every time I heard her turn over I was on fire. It got too strong for me. I finally gave in. *I* did it. It was my fault, Jack."

"Poor Laura." He said it sympathetically. "Come here, honey." He put his arms around her and held her, stroking her back. When he did it, she didn't mind. She'd have resented any other man... except maybe Merrill Landon. But Merrill Landon never showed affection to anyone.

"I know how it is, believe me," Jack said. "You're starving, and somebody puts a feast in front of you. What happens after that is

Instinct. Overwhelming. You eat. Or you die of hunger, right there, with all that food in front of you."

Laura clung to him, letting herself cry softly and gratefully into his shoulder.

"Let me give you just one little word of advice, Mother. Don't starve yourself anymore. Or that hunger is going to kill you."

She looked at him with wet eyes. Her face was strangely different, and Jack could see it. A night of love, a night of luxurious satiation, had changed her. For all her fatigue, her shame at herself, her body was happy and relieved. She couldn't help that. She felt physically good, for the first time in over a year, and she had Beebo to thank for it.

"You're different," Jack said, smiling. "You look good. I don't care how tired you are. It's becoming—love."

"That wasn't love."

"What was it, then?"

"Just purely physical. Animal. Vulgar."

"Love has a body, Laura. Eyes and lips, legs and sex. We humans can't help that."

"Love is bigger and better than that. There hasn't been any of that with Marcie and me, but I love her."

"That's idealistic crap."

Laura gasped, her eyes widening in sudden anger, but he interrupted her sharp retort before she could make it.

"Love is no bigger and better than the people who feel it," he said. "What has your love for Marcie got you? A fat neurosis, a lot of misery, and a night in bed with somebody you hardly know because you couldn't stand it any longer. If that's what makes it bigger and better, the hell with it. Feed it to the crocodiles." And he turned brusquely away.

Laura stared at him, unable to answer him. It struck her harshly that he might be right. "But I love Marcie," she whispered hoarsely.

"Sure. You love her because she looks like Beth, or whatever the hell her name is."

Laura was shocked. "No, no, Jack you don't understand. That has nothing to do with it. I love her." He turned to look at her, cynicism written plain on his face. "I love her because—"

"Because she's under the same roof with you, two feet away when you go to bed at night. Because she's young and pretty. Because you can't have her."

"Because I can't have her!" she exclaimed contemptuously. "That's exactly why I'm so miserable, you idiot! I love her so much—"

"We all do. She's a great girl," he said, so vaguely and quietly, that it calmed her a little.

But when Marcie said, "What are you two talking about?" Laura jumped, visibly startled. "Oh, I didn't mean to scare you," Marcie said. She had made up her mind to treat Laura gently and carefully. Burr came in noisily behind her. "Hi, Laura," he said, and stared at her pale face.

"I didn't hear you coming," Laura said nervously. She wondered what Marcie had told Burr, and suddenly it was too much to stand there and face them. "I'm going to bed," she said suddenly, briefly. "I didn't sleep much last night." It came to her then that she didn't know what she was supposed to have done last night at all. Jack hadn't told her.

Jack, faster than Laura when he was on the spot, said, "Laura spent the night with Beebo Brinker. She's an old friend of mine." He spoke to Burr, who apparently didn't know what to think.

Damn Jack! Laura thought. *He didn't have to say her name. That ridiculous name!*

Chapter Nine

Marcie tried to be understanding with Laura when they were alone later. She said, "Jack told me all about it, Laura. I understand."

What did he tell you? What do you understand? Why didn't he tell me? She didn't know how to act with Marcie. Her discomfort made her awkward and for the first time she found herself wishing to be without her for a little while. She didn't want Marcie to try to comfort her. She just wanted to let it blow over.

But Marcie was a warm-natured girl, and she was curious. She wanted to sit on Laura's bed and talk about it. She kept saying, "Tell me about it, Laur. Tell me what happened. Don't you know I wouldn't be shocked?"

At this point Laura revolted. "No, I *don't* know!" she said, and was immediately sorry. She raised her hand to her mouth. "Marcie, please. Please drop it."

"I'm sorry, Laur. I can't do anything right tonight." She looked so disheartened that Laura had to smile at her a little.

"You do everything right, Marcie," she said soothingly. "I'm the one who's wrong. No, it's true. I'm not like you. I can't confess to people."

"You tell Jack things."

Laura was suddenly alert, alarmed. "How do you know?" she demanded. "What things?"

"Oh, you're always going off and talking. Like this morning. Why don't you have long talks with me?"

Laura sighed, relieved. "I don't know. Jack is so easy to talk to, Marcie."

"Does that mean I'm not? I try to be." She smiled invitingly.

Laura, who had been lying on her bed, raised herself up on her elbows. "I never say these things like I mean them," she apologized. "I only mean, I—" *I can't talk to you because I'm in love with you, that's what I mean. But that's not what I can say.*

She rolled over on her stomach and buried her face in the pillow. Marcie sat motionless for a minute, afraid to say anything and start her off again. Then she leaned over her and touched her shoulders. "You don't have to tell me, Laura, honey," she said. "I guess I shouldn't pester you. Jack says you've been through a lot and that's why you're nervous. I don't want to make you unhappy, Laura. I'm afraid I do sometimes. I don't know why, I just get the feeling now and then, when you look at me, that I make you sad. Do I?"

Laura's nails cut into her smooth white forehead. "Marcie, don't torture me," she said. Her voice was low and strained. It was such an odd thing to say that Marcie withdrew, and climbed into her own bed.

"I'm sorry," she whispered, pulling the covers up and turning out the light. Then she put her hands over face suddenly and sobbed.

"Oh, Marcie!" Laura was out of bed before she had time to think, sitting next to Marcie and holding her. "Don't cry, Marcie. Oh God, why can't I ever say anything right?" She implored the ceiling for an answer. "I didn't mean to hurt you."

Marcie slowed down and stopped almost as suddenly as she began. "I know," she said. "I know what it is. I used to drive Burr nuts this way, asking questions and talking and talking. And when he wouldn't answer, I just kept asking more and more till I drove him crazy. I don't know why. I guess I *wanted* to drive him crazy. But I don't know why I do it to you." She looked away, embarrassed. Laura's arms tightened involuntarily around her. She had no idea how to answer this unexpected outburst. She was afraid to try to comfort Marcie, for the very act of soothing her brought Laura's own emotions to a boil. The safest course was to get back in bed at once and forget it. Or at least, stop talking. But Marcie was clinging to her and she couldn't roughly shake her off.

"I've learned a lot from living with you, Laur," Marcie said quietly. Laura listened, her nostrils full of the scent of flowers. "This may sound silly to you but—don't take this wrong, Laura—but I admire you, I really do. You have a quality of self-control that I could never learn. You keep your thoughts to yourself. If you don't have anything to say, you don't *say* anything. If you don't want to talk, you don't."

She looked up and laughed a little ruefully. "I talk all the time, as if I had to. Just living with you, I'm beginning to see it. I talk all the time and say nothing. You almost never talk, but when you do it's worth listening to."

Laura began to squirm uncomfortably, but Marcie grasped her sleeves and continued. "You know something, Laur? I think I just drove Burr crazy. I talked him to death."

"He still loves you, Marcie." Laura found her hand on Marcie's hair, without quite knowing how she had let it happen. "He wants you back."

"I know. We've hardly quarreled at all this week, Laur. You haven't been around much, you haven't seen us. But we've been getting along unusually well. But the screwy part is, it's not like I thought it would be."

"You mean, you miss the quarrels?"

"I mean I just wish he wouldn't come around so much any more. I want time to change. To think."

"Think about what?"

"About me. No, about anything *but* me. That's all I ever thought about before. You think about other things. You know what's going on. You come home at night and you read all these books that are sitting around. You can't even talk to me about them, because you know how stupid I am."

Laura was astonished. All these critical thoughts had gone through Marcie's head, and Laura hadn't been aware of it. Marcie had been watching her, admiring her, and she hadn't known that either. *I'm plumb blind,* she thought. *And I thought I couldn't know Marcie any better. Because I love her. And she talks like this to me. God!*

"Marcie, you don't need to read books. It's just a bad habit for introverts." Marcie shook her head silently while Laura went on. "Beautiful girls like you don't need to read," she said.

"That's just it," Marcie said. "I'm not going to be just another pretty idiot. I want to know something. I'm sick of knowing absolutely nothing. I want to be different. I want you to help me."

She wants me, Laura thought happily. *She wants me.* It was all she heard.

"When you were gone all night with Jack—" She paused and looked away. "—I started to think. I couldn't sleep, I don't know why. I was thinking about you, Laur. I was wondering why you never talk to me, why we have so little to say to each other. We sit at the breakfast table and read the paper and go off without anything more than 'good morning.' At night we go to bed and sometimes I talk, but it's not a conversation. You listen, I guess you listen."

"I do!"

"And I say the wrong things. And you go to pieces, like last night."

"No."

"Or else you run away. You go sleep with Jack."

"Marcie!"

"I know you were with Jack again last night. He didn't have to lie to me about it."

"But he didn't. I wasn't!"

"Now don't *you* lie to me!"

Laura stared at her, unable to speak.

"Help me, Laura," Marcie said, leaning toward her. "I want to change. I'm sick of myself. I'm sick of Burr."

The strangest craziest feeling started up in Laura; just an echo, faraway in herself. *She wants me to help her, to be with her. She admires me. Dear God, I'm afraid to wonder how much.* A very small smile curved the corners of her mouth.

"I have to start somewhere," Marcie said. "I want to talk to you like an intelligent human being, not an ignoramus."

Laura smiled at her. Almost without her realizing it, her hand had stolen back to Marcie's yellow hair. "Do you, Marcie?" she said. It was a simple question, but it asked a thousand others.

"Yes."

"Why?"

"Oh, I'm fed up with myself. I never realized, till I lived day-in-day-out with you, how much I'd been missing. Give me a book to read, Laur."

"In the morning." Laura smiled at her and got up, edging away from her bed.

"Now."

"It's too late, Marcie. You won't read anything now."

"I want to tell Burr I read a book."

"I'll give you something later," Laura said. It sounded strangely insinuating, the way she said it. She scared herself. She ducked into her bed as into a safe harbor, and hid her body under the blankets.

With a sigh Marcie turned the light out. After a moment's silence she whispered, "Laur? Will you talk to me after this? Really talk to me? Tell me things?"

"I'll try," Laura murmured, frowning in the dark. She lay in bed daydreaming for hours, seeing the first signs in Marcie of an influence she had been unaware of. Where would it lead? What doors would it open? Would it lead them both to bitterness? Or mutual ecstasy?

In the morning Laura was very matter-of-fact. She almost ignored Marcie. She made her work for her attention and it delighted her that Marcie was willing to work for it. Instinctively Laura knew she had to play hard to get, and she liked to play that way for once.

At breakfast, after a few false starts, Marcie blurted, "I'll be late tonight." She put her paper down and faced Laura.

Laura looked up slowly. "Date with Burr?" she said.

"No. Mr. Marquardt is having some out-of-town guests for dinner downtown. He asked some of us to go. I told him I would."

"Have fun," Laura said, and looked back at the front page.

"Ha! Some drunken idiot of a reporter'll probably pester me to death."

"A reporter?" Laura looked up again suddenly.

"Oh, I don't know." Marcie saw Laura's interest and it sparked her own. "A journalist, or something. It's a convention—professional fraternity, I guess."

"What fraternity? What's it called?"

"Ummm." Marcie bit her lip and concentrated. "It's Greek. Let's see. Something the matter?"

"No. Is it Chi Delta—"

"—Sigma. That's it, I remember. How did you know? Now something *is* the matter, Laura!"

Laura had gone very pale. She swallowed convulsively.

"I just remembered, I was supposed to run an errand for Dr. Hollingsworth. I'd better get going." She got up suddenly and went into the bedroom for her jacket.

Marcie stood up and followed her. "You didn't finish your breakfast, Laur," she said, concerned, a line of worry in her forehead.

"I'm not hungry. I'll see you tonight," she said, and turned quickly to almost run out.

Marcie came after her, bewildered. "Laura, you don't make sense," she said. "What's the matter with you?"

But Laura was running down the stairs to the elevator. Marcie turned and went back into the kitchen and drank her coffee standing, gazing perplexed at Laura's plate.

Chapter Ten

Merrill Landon. *Merrill Landon. My father. My father is coming to New York. He never misses these damn things, he goes every year. Oh, God, help me.* Laura rode down to work on the subway, her fists clenched in her lap, her face set like a mask to cover the torment inside.

He doesn't know I'm here, that's one good thing. He'll never find me, either. How long will he be here? It must be in the papers. I missed it at breakfast.

She picked up the *Times* on the corner where she left the subway. She took it up to the office with her, impatient to look at it. Sarah was already there.

"Hi, gorgeous," she said.

Laura looked up, startled. "Hi," she said. "Who's gorgeous?"

"You are. You must be, you've got a man."

Laura stared at her blankly, her mind full of the threat of her father's presence in the city. Finally it came to her. "Oh, you mean Jack," she said.

"Did you talk to him?"

"Oh, yes. Yes." *Now what the hell does she mean? Why would I—Oh! I promised her a date.* Laura felt suddenly sunk. All those reports to do that should have been done before. Lies to tell, at nine in the morning. Merrill Landon somewhere in New York. It was too much. The day stretched away in front of her like an endless obstacle course.

"What'd he say?" Sarah said eagerly.

"He's working on it. Maybe this weekend."

"Gee, that sounds great."

Laura had to look at the paper; she *had* to. It gnawed at her, as she sat at her desk, sneaking through it between reports and unable to find anything. Her father's name ran through her mind like a robot tune from a TV commercial.

It was a rushed day. Sarah didn't take a break on days when they were behind, but nothing could have stopped Laura. She got up and almost ran to the washroom at eleven, the paper in hand. She felt herself trembling, going over the pages again and again, until she suddenly found it at the bottom of page 12. "Chi Delta Sigma, national journalism fraternity, opens its convention today at the McAlton Hotel. The convention will last until next Saturday, at which time..." etc. There was an agenda listed, a few names—the national officers. There it was—Merrill Landon, corresponding secretary. Laura shut her eyes and groaned a little.

The day dragged. She typed until the small round keys seemed to weigh a pound apiece under her fingers, and still the reports piled up.

Laura sat hunched over her machine for a long time after the others had left for the day. She meant to work, but she never did any. She wanted to cry and she couldn't. She wanted to move, to talk to someone, to explode, and she just sat there until the cramps in her back made her groan. She got up stiffly and put her jacket on and stood for a moment, aimless and lost. There was nowhere to go, nothing to do. Marcie wouldn't be home yet.

She rummaged idly in her pockets, pulling out some change and a shopping list. The list was from the week before and she started to drop it in the wastebasket, when she noticed something on the other side. A phone number—Watkins 9-1313. And the initials B. B. Laura crumpled it in her hand, seized with an uncontrollably pleasant shudder. Then she threw it indignantly into the wastebasket, wondering when Beebo had scribbled it out. And then she leaned over slowly and took it out of the wastebasket and shoved it furtively back into her pocket, without looking at it. She sat down abruptly in her chair and put her head down on her arms and wept.

"Father…" she whispered. "Why did we have to hate each other? We're all we have…Father…"

She got up fifteen minutes later, turned out the light, and stole out, quiet as a thief.

She walked over to the McAlton Hotel. She had no idea what she expected to find or to do. But she went into the big softly carpeted lobby and walked, almost as if she were sleepwalking, toward the desk. It was crowded and noisy, with that ineffable air of excitement that big hotels seem to generate.

Laura felt gooseflesh start up all over her. Many of these people must be conventioneers. If Merrill Landon didn't see her one of his Chicago friends might, and the secret would be out. He would run her down if it took the whole New York City police force.

She leaned apprehensively on the marble-topped counter of the desk, waiting until a clerk could serve her. He came up after a couple of minutes, looking enormously efficient and busy. "May I help you, Miss?" he demanded.

"Is a Mr. Merrill Landon staying here?" she asked.

"Just a minute, please." He disappeared briefly and Laura looked around the lobby, her hand partially covering her face.

He might see me. I must be out of my mind to come here. But she waited nonetheless.

"He's in 1402," the clerk said loudly in her ear.

Laura jumped.

"Shall I call him?" asked the clerk.

"Yes, please." She had no idea why she was doing this. She felt as if she were two people, one acting, the other watching; one compelled to act, the other shocked by the action.

"Who wants to see him, please?"

"His daughter." She almost whispered it, and he made her repeat it. Then he buzzed off. She watched him, perhaps ten feet from her but impossible to hear, as he lifted the receiver, gave the number, waited. Then his face lighted into a business-type smile, and she saw his lips form the words, "Mr. Landon?" He went on, and she watched him, feeling almost sick with anticipation.

The clerk came back after a brief conversation. "Well, Miss—" he began, eyeing her closely.

"What did he say?" Laura looked at him with her stark blue eyes. Her chin trembled.

"He says he has no daughter, Miss," the clerk drawled. He grinned. "Tough luck. Want to try someone else?"

Laura's mouth dropped open. Her face twitched. She couldn't answer him. She turned and ran, bumping into people, stumbling, until she found a phone booth empty in a row of booths along a far wall and she took refuge there. She buried her face in her hands and wept. "Merrill Landon, go to hell, go to hell," she said fiercely, under her breath. "I hate you. Oh, God, how I hate you!" And she sobbed until somebody rapped on the door of the booth. She wiped her eyes hastily, knowing they were red and swollen, and turned to glare at the impatient rapper. He glared back.

Defiantly she put a dime in the phone and lifted the receiver. She called Jack.

A voice answered almost at once. A strange masculine voice. "Hello?" it said.

"Jack?" Her voice trembled.

"Just a minute." He called, "Jack, it's for you."

A few seconds later Jack answered.

"Jack, it's Laura."

"Are you all right?"

"I have absolutely nothing to say," she said. "I'm only calling because—because I'm in a phone booth and some fool wants to use the phone. He's rapping on the door."

"Mother," he said slowly, "you have a screw loose. Now listen carefully and do what I tell you. Just go along quietly and don't tell them anything. I'll send my analyst over right away."

"My father's in town." Her breath caught while she spoke. "Oh! No wonder. Did you tell him to go to hell?"

"The desk clerk called his room and said his daughter wanted to see him." She stopped to swallow the fury in her throat.

"And he told you to go to hell?"

"He said he had no daughter." Her voice trembled with the immensity of it

Jack, for once, was momentarily speechless. Finally he said, "He is a bastard, Laura. By God, he is. Don't mess with him. Come on over, I'll buy you a drink."

"Thanks, Jack." She broke into tears again.

"Don't cry, Laura. Just think what satisfaction that would give the old s.o.b."

"You're right!" she said sharply, pulling herself up. "I won't. I'll be right over."

Jack was waiting for her on the front stoop, sitting on one of the cement railings and looking up at what few stars were available between the roofs. Without a word he got up, slipped an arm around her, and turned her away from his apartment. They walked over to a small bar she hadn't seen before called Mac's Alley, without speaking to each other.

The bar was in a basement and you walked down a flight of twisting stairs to reach it. There were booths around the walls, tables and a jukebox in the middle, and a long bar ran across the back. Laura walked halfway toward the bar with Jack before she realized that there were no other women in the place. She turned to Jack with anxiety.

"Do they want me in here?" she asked.

He smiled. "They're not going to give you a rush, Mother. I'll stake my life on it."

"I didn't think they liked women in a place like this."

Jack guided her to a barstool. "Oh, they're friendly enough. They know you wouldn't be here if you weren't gay. They figure, you leave them alone and they'll leave you alone."

Laura looked around her uncomfortably. "I can't help thinking I embarrass them."

"Maybe they embarrass you. Would you rather go over to The Cellar?"

"No...I don't know."

"You don't want to run into Beebo. She's usually out making the rounds about now. That's why I brought you here."

Laura smiled gratefully at him. "Thanks," she said. "I should have seen it myself." But she found herself so shaken by the sudden idea of Beebo loose among scores of desirable girls that she couldn't concentrate for a minute.

Jack ordered them a drink. Then he turned to her, pushing his glasses back into place on his nose. They tended to slide down to the halfway mark. "Well?" he said, and paused. "Let's tear Papa Landon apart."

"I don't want to talk about him," Laura said.

"Then why am I buying you a drink?"

She turned to snap at him and then saw he was kidding her. "Sorry, Jack," she said. Looking at him brought back her faith in him, and she smiled a little. "I always knew he was a hard man," she said softly, "but I never dreamed he'd go as far as this. I always thought, in spite of everything, in spite of all the bitterness and misery we've had together, that he must love me a little. After all, I'm all he has left...of my mother, my brother...his family. I was five when it happened, and I wish to God I could remember what he was like before. But I can't. I like to pretend he was generous and gentle and kind. And I can remember sitting on his shoulders when we went to a Fourth of July parade. It was that same summer, before our vacation. I remember he hoisted me up and bought me a balloon and held me while the parade went by so I could see. Afterwards he walked around and talked to his friends, and he didn't make me get down. I felt like a queen on a throne. It's been my one good memory of him, to this day. But Mother was with us. Maybe he did it for her sake.

"I remember her better than him from those years. Sometimes I miss her terribly. She was very loving."

"Maybe," said Jack, "your father wouldn't hate you so now if he hadn't loved you so much before."

"You give him too much credit," she said. "After what he did to me tonight, I'll never speak to him again. I'd kill him if I could. But I wouldn't go near him, even for that. I wouldn't give him the satisfaction of seeing my face. He has no daughter, has he? All right, God damn him, I have no father! Two can play at that game."

"Don't hate me for saying it," Jack said, "but I think you still love him. I think you'll see him again."

She turned on him. "You're crazy!" she said. "You don't know anything! What makes you think such a thing?"

He shrugged. "Only that it matters so terribly to you."

Laura finished her drink and placed the glass carefully on the bar, trying to sort out her thoughts. "If I do see him again," she said, "it'll be when I can tell him I'm a success. Financially. Socially. Every way. I want to tell him, 'I have a good job, nice friends. I can get along fine in this world without you, and I'll never need you again.' And you know what else I'd like to say to him, Jack?"

"Yeah." He lit a cigarette. "'Father, I'm queer. And it's all your fault. Shove that up your rear and live with it!' Yeah, I know. Shock the hell out of him. I tried that on—on a close relative once."

"What happened?"

"I don't really know. When his face went blue I took off. I haven't been home since. I can't go home to find out, as a matter of fact. I'm—shall we say—not welcome." He said this with slow sarcasm.

"Jack, I'm sorry," she said gently, and looked at him sympathetically. It occurred to her now, when she found his own troubles paralleled her own, that he was very human and not a slick witty party boy without real feelings. He was lonely. *Everybody's lonely,* she thought. *Marcie for a perfect mate. Beebo for a perfect girl. Jack for an affectionate boy. Me...Poor Sarah...*

That recalled Sarah to her mind. "Jack, I have a friend," she said.

"Congratulations."

"—named Sarah."

"Does Beebo know?"

"And she wants a date."

"With a girl?"

"—With a boy. She's straight."

"What a shame."

"Can you help me out?"

"I can help *you,* Mother, but can I help Sarah?"

"You must know somebody. How about that boy who answered your phone tonight? Could he take her out?"

"If he does I'll break his head for him," he said and laughed softly, knocking his cigarette ashes into a scorched aluminum tray in front of him.

"Who is he, Jack?' she asked.

"A friend. No, a lover. For the moment, anyway."

Laura put her hand on his arm. "Don't be so cynical," she said.

"These things never last." He shook his head. "Better to face it at the beginning."

"He must see something worthy in you or he never would have come to you in the first place." She spoke awkwardly, but with sympathy.

"He sees dollar bills." Jack smiled.

"Jack! Don't be so hard on yourself. It hurts me." She didn't like to see him stick the pins in himself. It was all right when he did it to her, because it was fun. She didn't mind, she understood his need. But when he hurt himself he hurt in dead earnest.

"Besides, you aren't rich," Laura said. "If that's all he wanted, he'd find somebody else."

"I have a little put away," he said. "I save it up in between affairs. When somebody irresistible comes along, I spend it like a fool. Makes a wonderful impression the first couple of weeks. Then I'm flat broke and all alone again. My chronic condition."

It was a pathetic revelation. Laura was taken aback by it. "You shouldn't do it, Jack," she said.

"I can't help it. I'll hang on to him with anything. Anything I've got. Even dollar bills."

"If all he wants is your money he's not *worth* your money! Or your time, or your friendship."

"Laura, this isn't friendship. This is another subject entirely. Honest to God." Laura blushed. "A man can't buy a friend. But there's always a little love for sale."

"Not real love."

He shrugged. "I don't ask for the moon."

Laura finished her drink. "What's his name?" she said.

"Terry."

"Terry what?"

"Just Terry."

"You don't trust me." She said it quietly, but she was hurt.

"Terry Fleming." He spoke the name gently and Laura saw a look on his face that changed him entirely. She studied him, surprised.

"Jack, I think you're in love." Once said, it sounded gauche and unfair.

But he only said, "I think so, too."

Laura was lost. What do you do on the spot like this? "I don't know whether to give you my congratulations or my sympathy," she said seriously.

Jack laughed. "Both, Mother. That's a beautiful sentiment, whatever it is. Thanks."

He seemed unable to talk about it and Laura finally returned to Sarah. "Is there somebody in the office you could get for Sarah?" she asked. She described her to him. "She's not pretty, but she's just a swell girl."

"I know, there are a million of 'em," he sighed. "I wish to God I were straight. I'd marry her, poor kid." Laura stared at him, then smiled. "I guess I can arrange something," he said. "Do we have to double with them?"

"She expects it. I hate to ask."

"Okay, okay. It won't kill me. But dinner only. And I'll be in a hurry."

"Thanks, Jack."

"I'd better find a tame one for her," he mused and then laughed a little. "Whatever that means. Jesus, the poor girl has probably dreamed all her life of a good thorough raping. But I can't assume the responsibility. Maybe Jensen can go. I'll call you in the morning on it."

"Thanks. She'd be so happy." Laura finished a second drink. Jack was two up on her. She looked at him out of the corner of her eye, wanting to tell him about the change that had come over Marcie but afraid of his sarcasm. Finally she said, in the characteristic blunt way that disguised her uncertainty, "Jack, Marcie is different. Something's happening to her. I—I'm scared." She could go no further. She looked away from him.

Jack chuckled. "Well, what's she doing, filching undies from Macy's basement?"

"She doesn't want to see Burr anymore."

Jack frowned slightly. "She's finally coming to her senses? That was a screwy match to begin with. Burr wants to worship one gal. Marcie wants to raise a little hell with every other man she sees."

"She wants to be like me. That's what she said. She wants to read books. Spend more time at home. She wants me to help her."

"Help her what?'

Laura frowned. "I don't know what. She says she's sick of herself and she wants to be a better person."

Jack bit his underlip reflectively. "I know what you're thinking. And you're wrong. She's not turning gay."

"I didn't say that." Laura turned to him indignantly.

"You don't have to. You're thinking it so hard I can hear the wheels going around in your head." He looked at her. "Once and for all, Laura, she's *not* gay. Maybe she's got room in her somewhere for a little curiosity. Maybe living with you really has made her dissatisfied with herself. If so, so much the better. But she's not mooning for you every night."

"She acted so funny, Jack. Like—like she enjoyed having me near her. Like she wanted me to touch her. I mean, comfort her. You know."

"The more you want her to enjoy it, the more it'll seem like she does."

"I'm not making up stories," Laura said with some heat.

"No, Mother, I know. I believe you. I'm just telling you a fact. I've known Marcie for a couple of years. From the time she and Burr started dating right through their divorce. She's capable of—let's say—wondering. Like the night she wanted to touch tongues." Laura shivered involuntarily. "Once in a while she gets a kick out of a fling in the Village. Maybe she just wants to see how far you'll go. Maybe she's egging you on, Laura. Did you ever think of that? Just to see what the hell you'll do?"

"She wouldn't do that," Laura said positively, somewhat shocked. "Never."

Jack gave a little snort. "Okay, maybe not. But she's not about to fall for you. Not now or ever."

"She meant it when she talked to me last night. She was sincere."

"Sure she meant it. She's on a book kick. She's obviously very impressed with you. It shows when she talks about you. Temporarily, you're somebody to imitate, somebody to admire."

"Temporarily?"

"Don't fall into a trap." He put a hand on her knee.

"It's no trap! She's too innocent to set me a trap."

"Innocent?" He laughed. "Don't count on it. Besides, you're too innocent to avoid one. Right now you have a lot to learn."

Laura glared at him. "I'm not stupid."

"No, you're not. You're very bright, honey. You're just uninformed. If you want to learn, go scout up Beebo and take the Grand Tour of the Village."

"I could no more fall for her than I could fall for—for—"

"For me?" He laughed.

She smiled suddenly and laughed with him. "Oh," she said with a wave of her hand, "You're taken."

"Mother, that's a beautiful one-line definition of my dilemma. My analyst could use you."

"Are you being analyzed?" she asked.

"Aren't we all?"

"Answer me!"

"I did. Let's go. I hate to keep people waiting."

"Who's waiting?"

"My friend, Mr. Fleming."

She slipped off the barstool, pulling her jacket on. "I'd like to meet him."

"If it lasts another couple of weeks, I guess it'd be safe." He took her arm and steered her through the crowd. They stared at her but it didn't disconcert her so much now that she had had a drink or two.

"Where's your adoring roommate tonight?" Jack said as they went up the stairs.

"Having dinner downtown."

"Why don't you go over to The Cellar? Let Beebo tell you some fairy stories. She's got a million of 'em."

"I couldn't take Beebo tonight."

"Suit yourself. I'll walk you to the subway."

"No, don't bother. I know you want to get home. Thanks a lot, Jack. I don't know why you're so good to me."

"My interest is purely academic. Your innocence amazes me."

"You make me feel like a hayseed," she said.

He laughed. "Okay, Hayseed. I'll call you in the morning on what's-her-name."

"Sarah."

"Sarah. See you." And he turned and walked off.

Laura walked toward the subway but she knew she wasn't going home. She knew she would walk right past it and she did. She walked for four blocks, seething with a renewed fury at Merrill Landon. Her hot hand was cramped around the slip of paper with Beebo's number on it, in the pocket of her jacket...

I'll pay her back. I'll just give her the money I owe her, have one drink, and go home. She looked at her watch—a little past nine. For a moment she stood at the head of the stairs looking down at the double doors that opened into The Cellar, feeling her heart pound nervously. She never seemed able to walk into this place confidently. There was always a moment of fear and reluctance. But the need to be with her own kind quickly overpowered it.

She walked in, heading for the bar, ignoring the curious stares that greeted her. She stood at the end of the bar and when the bartender came up he recognized her.

"Hi," he said. "What'll it be?"

"Whisky and water, please," she said. She looked around the place, up and down the bar, around the tables, but she didn't see Beebo. She drank half her drink, and then walked back to the ladies' room, looking into the rear of The Cellar, but Beebo wasn't there. In extreme irritation she walked back to the bar, wondering whether to crush her pride and ask the bartender where Beebo was, or let it go. She finished her drink and decided if she had come this far she might as well go the whole way.

"Where's Beebo tonight?" she asked the bartender the next time he got near. "I owe her some money," she explained compulsively. He smiled.

"Oh, she's been and gone already," he said. "She's probably over at The Colophon. She likes it over there. No boys." He grinned.

"Thanks," said Laura, slipping off her seat at the bar and heading for the door. She was embarrassed enough without asking him where The Colophon was. She didn't want to advertise her "innocence."

Near the door a slim pretty girl, who had kept an eye on her at the bar, approached her. The girl wore her hair in a short soft curly cut. She was blonde and feminine. Laura let herself be approached simply by returning the girl's gaze as she came near her. She stopped when the girl spoke.

"Excuse me," the girl said. "We noticed you were all alone. My friends and me. Like to have a drink with us?" She nodded toward a table where three other girls were sitting watching them. One of them, sitting alone on one side of the table, stared coldly at Laura.

Laura was flattered. But the feelings in her were too personal, too rough, to dissipate with strangers. "Thanks," she said. "I'd like to, but I'm looking for somebody. I'm in a hurry."

"Who're you looking for? Maybe we can help you out," said the girl, stopping Laura as she started to move away.

Laura realized the girl was interested in her, and it made her turn back once more. "Oh," she said with a little shrug, "you wouldn't know her."

"Somebody might. We're over here a lot. What's her name?"

Laura was dead certain they'd know Beebo, who came over here all the time. The last thing she wanted was to have everybody run up and tell Beebo that Laura had been looking for her. The bartender would no doubt tell her. That was bad enough.

"What's her name?" the girl prompted, and then smiled. "Don't want to tell?"

Laura blushed and backed away from her. "I just owe her some money. I thought she'd be down here tonight."

"Who?" the girl goaded her, with a pretty smile.

"Beebo Brinker." Laura didn't mean to say it. Yet saying it was better than trying to hide it and getting laughed at. They could always ask the bartender who she was looking for after she left, and she would look even worse. They would take her stammering reluctance for infatuation. She said the name as casually as she could.

"Oh, Beebo!" The girl laughed. "She left half an hour ago. She's over at The Colophon. She said this place was dead tonight. I guess if she'd known you were coming she would have waited— hm?" She smiled.

"I guess," said Laura briefly. She stared at the girl. It occurred to her that she saw a slight resemblance to Beth in her face. Then she turned and walked out.

The slim girl walked back to her table. Her partner said peevishly, "Maybe that'll teach you you're not irresistible."

"Oh, shut up," the slim girl said quietly. "She's Beebo Brinker's girl."

"Beebo's girl, hell. Beebo's got a dozen girls. She can really pick 'em, though, I'll say that much. I should get one like that." And she made a face at the slim one by her side.

Chapter Eleven

Laura went home. She arrived before ten, but Marcie wasn't back yet. Laura put a book she had been reading on Marcie's bed and climbed into her own bed. She tried to read herself, but she couldn't. An hour went by, and no Marcie. Nervously, Laura shut her book and dropped it to the floor. She got up and went into the bathroom to brush her teeth, and remembered she had already done it.

Then she went to the phone. She didn't know what was coming over her. She only felt a deep will-defying unhappiness. She pulled out the phone book and looked up the number of the McAlton Hotel. She sat for a moment with the book open in her lap, unable to move. Then she reached slowly for the phone.

Suddenly it rang. Laura screamed, a small quick cry of extreme surprise. Her heart had taken a tremendous leap at the piercing bell sound in that still apartment. She let it ring twice more while she caught her breath. *It must be Marcie,* she thought. *Maybe she's in trouble.* She lifted the receiver. "Hello?"

"Hello, Bo-peep."

Laura's heart gave another bound. She felt the sweat break out. "Beebo?" she said faintly.

"How are you, sweetheart? I hear you were looking for me tonight."

"You didn't waste any time." Her voice was sharp.

"I hate to keep a lady waiting. What's on your mind?"

"I just dropped in for a drink. I was down there in the Village to see Jack and I just wanted to pay you back." She spoke in fits and starts.

"You don't owe me a thing, Bo-peep. Not a thing."

"A drink." Laura hated to owe anybody anything. She was meticulous about her debts, however small the sum.

"You're right." Laura could feel her smile. "I nearly forgot. Okay lover, you owe me one drink."

"Beebo, I can't talk now, really."

"You're doing fine. What's the matter, Marcie breathing down your neck?"

"It's not that."

"You don't have to say you love me, you know. Just say you'll meet me tomorrow night. About eight."

"No."

"Don't be late, doll. I'll call Marcie and ask her where the hell you are."

"You wouldn't! You won't! Damn you, Beebo!"

"I would and I will." She laughed. "Eight on the dot."

"I won't be there."

"Want to bet?"

Laura hung up on her. She was trembling. Angrily she slammed the heavy phone back into place, switched out the bedroom light, and got into bed.

The black night settled around her but it brought more restless tossing than repose. The hours slipped by. No Marcie. No sleep. Only an endless bitter reviewing of what her father had done to her; the look on the clerk's face when he gave her the message; the impotent fury and shame that besieged her. At last she turned the light back on and began to pace the room. The electric clock on Marcie's dresser said two-thirty. Laura wondered whether to call Burr. Or Jack. She was getting afraid for Marcie. But nobody knew how to reach her. There was nothing to do but wait.

It was a few minutes past three when Marcie came in. Laura had left the living room light on for her and she heard her come in laughing and heard a male voice answer her. Not Burr's voice. Somebody else. A deep mature voice. Laura peeked out through the crack in the kitchen door but couldn't see him. Marcie was gig-gling, as if she were tight, and pushing him away. Laura could see her now and then.

Marcie said, "I'll call my roommate. She'll make you go home."

"I can't go home tonight. I live in Chicago."

"That's where she's from!"

"Who?"

"My roommate."

"To hell with her. Come here, Baby."

"No!" High as she was, she nevertheless sounded a little scared. She had stopped laughing.

Laura threw a coat hastily over her pajamas and went into the living room. A large man, partly bald and handsome in a heavy fea-tured way, had Marcie wrapped in a bear hug and was trying to drag her to the couch.

"All right," said Laura sharply. "Get out."

She startled them both so much that they froze where they were. The man stared at her. He was drunk, and his balance wasn't the best. Laura, pale and silver blonde, her long hair falling down her shoulders, her face strange and sensitive and imperious, looked like an apparition to him. Without taking his eyes off her he asked Marcie, "Who the hell is *that?*"

"My roommate." Marcie took advantage of his interest to slip free. Laura took her arm firmly and sent her through the kitchen door. Then she turned back to the man.

"All right, you," she said as if he were a servant. "Out."

The impudence of it amused him and angered him at the same time. "You can't talk to me like that," he said.

She advanced on him briskly, pulling the door open sharply and facing him. "It's my home and I'll speak as I please," she said. She looked as cold and unapproachable as she was hot and angry. He stared at her, not sure how to take her, and then came toward her to put a hand on her shoulder.

"Marcie's no good," he said confidentially "Let's you and me—"

Laura swept his hand off her shoulder. "Get out of here or I'll call the police," she said.

He got mad. "Jesus, what a chilly little bitch you are!" he growled.

"Get out," Laura said, so cold, so controlled, that she froze him into submission. She shut the door after him, resisting the urge to slam it. *Dear God,* she thought intensely. *If I could do that to my father. Just once.*

"Laura? It was just a party, Laur," Marcie said. "We went out after dinner. Just for kicks. He got sort of out of hand. Thanks, Laur, I don't know what I'd have done."

"Come on to bed." Laura turned and walked toward her and Marcie preceded her into the bedroom. It occurred to her then that she was behaving with Marcie much as Beth used to behave with her. She was asserting herself, taking the lead. She liked it; with Marcie, anyway. She felt her influence and reveled in it. A feeling of tremendous strength swept through her when the man turned and left, like the other poor demented little fellow who pestered her on the subway. Only he was such a weakling he hardly counted. She had a mental image of herself treating Merrill Landon that way, and it worked a strange exaltation in her. She smiled.

Marcie grinned at her crookedly. "I thought you'd be sore," she said.

"No. No, of course not. Why should I be?"

"I don't know. Maybe because I felt kind of guilty going out with somebody besides Burr. But I had fun. Up to the end, anyway. I wouldn't have minded that if he hadn't slobbered so much." She giggled and Laura ignored what she said. They were standing less than a foot from each other and suddenly Laura reached for her and gave her a little hug. "I'm not mad. I'm just glad you're all right," she said.

Marcie submitted, but she seemed embarrassed, and Laura quickly released her. With the release came a letdown, a loss of strength and confidence. She slipped quietly into bed and spent the hours till dawn wrestling with the bedclothes.

Laura didn't feel much brighter than Marcie in the morning. She got to work on time, but all she wanted to do was sleep. *I've got to catch up. I've got to catch up,* she kept telling herself. *Less than three weeks and Jean'll be back. And I haven't done a really good day's work since she left. Even if they like me, they can't keep me on as a charity case.*

The episode at the McAlton flamed up in her mind and gave her an angry energy through most of the morning. Sarah said nothing to her, but she kept looking at her over her typewriter, apparently afraid to bring up the date subject again. It wasn't till Jack called that Laura even remembered it.

"All set," he said. "Carl Jensen can go. Friday night. Dinner and a show. What's Sarah's number?"

Laura got it from her and made her face light up with expectation. Jack put Carl on the phone, and Laura gave her end to Sarah. It gave her a momentary lift to see somebody else stammering with pleasure and anticipation. But the day she lived through was endless, bleak with undone work, dragging will, impotent anger.

"You're late," Marcie said when Laura walked in. "I wanted you to tell me about that book Burr brought over last week."

"Nothing to tell." Laura felt too low to talk, to joke, even to eat. She picked listlessly at her food. After a while Marcie fell silent, too.

When the dishes were done Marcie said, "I called Burr. Broke our date tonight." She looked expectantly at Laura, as if this were a significant revelation, and she wanted a proper reaction.

But Laura only said, "Oh?" and walked into the bedroom.

Marcie followed her. "What's the matter, Laur?" she said. And when Laura didn't answer, she asked, "Bad day?"

"Um-hm. Bad day." Laura lay down on her bed, face downward, one leg hanging over the edge, her mind wholly occupied with her father: her hatred, her stifled love for him, her fear of him.

"Talk to me, Laura," Marcie said, coming over to sit next to her.

"Not tonight."

"Please. You said you would."

"I can't, Marcie. I can't talk. I'm too tired." She rolled over and looked at her. "Don't look like that," she said. "I'm—I'm worried about my job, that's all. I'll be all right."

"What's wrong with your job?"

"Nothing."

"Oh, Laura! God! Make sense!" Marcie exclaimed. But when she evoked no response she dropped it with a sigh. "Let's go out on the roof," she said, "and get some fresh air. It's a beautiful night."

"Looks like rain."

"How would you know? You're staring at the ceiling."

"It did, earlier."

"That's what's beautiful about it. Maybe there'll be thunder. I love to stand naked in the rain." She glanced down slowly at Laura.

But Laura turned back on her stomach without a word. A terrible apathy nailed her to the bed. Not even the nearness of Marcie could arouse her. They sat quietly for a few minutes, Laura lost in herself, and Marcie searching for a way to cheer her up. The phone rang.

"I'll get it," Marcie said, and got up. She walked across the room and picked up the receiver when Laura suddenly remembered Beebo. She sat up in a rush.

"No," Marcie was saying, "I can't. I'm sorry. I don't want to argue, not any more. I've had enough, that's all. I won't talk to you, Burr. No, it's not her fault, it's nobody's fault." She looked at Laura stretched out again on her bed. "That has nothing to do with it. No. Good night, Burr."

She hung up and stood for a moment motionless, watching Laura, who lay with her face turned away, apparently relaxed. Burr was getting jealous, impatient. He was ready to accuse anybody of anything to get Marcie's favor back. Their phone conversations were little more than arguments which Marcie terminated by hanging up on him. But he wouldn't be put off for long.

Marcie sat down on her own bed with a book, the one she meant to ask Laura about. She stared at the pages without reading, and wondered about her moody roommate.

Laura was watching her wristwatch. It was two minutes fast. She lay still, but she was alert, poised to jump. At two minutes past eight, by her watch, the phone rang again. "It's for me," she told Marcie, who had no intention of going for it. Laura came across the room and sat on Marcie's bed.

"Hello?" she said into the receiver.

"Hi, lover. Where are you?"

"At home," Laura said sarcastically. "Where else?"

"You want me to come over?"

"I'll be down in a few minutes. I was delayed."

"Okay, but make it fast. I'll call again at eight-thirty. And every ten minutes after that."

Laura hung up without a further word and turned to look at Marcie. "I met him at work," she said, her face flushing. "He's been pestering me. I don't want to see him." She didn't know what she was going to do.

"Oh," said Marcie. *Then why all the fuss?* She looked curiously at Laura's pink face. Laura turned away and began to walk up and down the room, feeling as if there were a bomb sealed in her breast, ticking, about to go off. She knew her nails were cutting her underarms, yet she hardly felt them. It was an expression of terrible tension in her. Suddenly she whipped the closet door open and pulled out her coat.

Marcie, watching her, said quickly, "Where're you going?"

"I'll be back early," Laura said, heading for the door, propelled by the tight violence that was boiling inside her.

"Laura!" Marcie jumped up and followed her. "Damn it, Laur, please tell me, I'm worried about you."

Laura turned abruptly at the door. "I'm just going out for a little while," she said. "I won't be late." She tried to leave, but Marcie grabbed her arms.

"You're not fit to go anywhere, Laura. I never saw you so upset," Marcie said. "Except once. And you—you spent the night with Jack that time. It was my fault. Is this my fault? Am I driving you out again?"

"No, no, nothing's your fault." Laura covered her face with her hand for a minute and when Marcie's arms went around her to comfort her, she wept. "Please don't let me go," she whispered. "I mean—God!—I mean, let me go. Let me go, Marcie." She began to resist.

But the curiosity in Marcie had taken over. "You're trembling all over. Come to bed, Laur. Come on, honey, you're in no shape to go anywhere. Come tell me about it," she coaxed, trying to guide Laura away from the door. But Laura knew what was in store for her if she obeyed. She uncovered her face to gaze for a moment at Marcie, so close to her, so tantalizing. And that terrible storm brewing inside her made her feel as if she might do any wild thing that her body demanded of her. She was afraid.

"Please," Marcie said softly. "I'll give you a rubdown, I'm a great masseuse. My father taught me how." She smiled. "Please, Laur."

"Your father?"

"Yes."

"Do you love him very much?"

"Yes." Marcie frowned at her.

"And he loves you?"

"Of course."

"You're lucky, Marcie."

"That's the way it's supposed to be, Laur. I'm not lucky. I'm just normal. Ordinary, I mean."

Laura stared at her. The emotion in her simmered dangerously near the top. With a sudden swift movement, Laura kissed Marcie's cheek lightly, leaving the wet of her tears on Marcie's face, and then whispered, "So lucky...so lucky..." Then she turned and ran down the stairs to the elevator.

Marcie sat down on a living room chair and put her head in her hands and tried to think. Laura's strange behavior made her tickle inside. She felt close to the storm that had barely brushed past her, and yet she remained untouched. There was only the wet on her cheek as a token, and she brushed it off, inexplicably embarrassed.

Laura made the taxi driver take her past the McAlton. She counted to the fourteenth floor, as nearly as she could figure it, and stared at the golden blocks of windows, and wondered which ones opened into 1402. And if Merrill Landon was in his room.

She walked in quickly when she reached The Cellar, with no hesitation, and made for the bar. It was a little past eight-thirty by her watch. She hoped anxiously that Beebo hadn't called Marcie again. She saw her at the far end of the bar talking to two very pretty young girls. They looked like teenagers. Laura was dismayed at the flash of jealousy that went through her. She walked right up to Beebo, without being seen, until she stood next to her. She took a seat beside her, watching Beebo while she talked, until one of the teens nudged her and nodded curiously at Laura. Beebo turned and broke into a smile.

"Well, Bo-peep," she said. "Didn't hear you come in. How are you?"

"Am I interrupting something?" Laura looked away.

Beebo laughed. "Not a thing. This is Josie. And this is Bella. Laura." She leaned back on her stool so they could all see each other.

The younger girls made effusive greetings, the better to exhibit luscious smiles, but Laura only said, "Hello," to them briefly. Beebo laughed again, and leaned closer to her.

"Jealous, baby?" she said.

"I owe you one drink," Laura snapped. "What do you want?"

"Whisky and water."

Laura nodded at the bartender.

"Is that all you came for, Bo-peep?"

"Don't talk like that, Beebo, you make me sick." Laura still wouldn't look at her.

"I didn't last time."

"Yes you did. I hope you've bought your friends there one of Dutton's cartoons. It's the quickest way to get rid of them I know."

"Why didn't it work with you?" Beebo laughed softly in Laura's ear. "You came home with me that night, if you recall."

Laura turned angrily away from her. "What happened was in spite of the God damn juvenile cartoon, not because of it. I nearly walked out when he gave it to me."

"But you didn't."

"I should have."

The bartender came up and Laura started to order. She wanted to buy Beebo the drink and have one quick one herself, and then get out. Go home. Forget she had come. But before she could give an order, Beebo said, "Come home with me, Laura."

"No."

"Come on." Beebo spun her slowly around on the barstool with one arm. Laura looked reluctantly at her for the first time since she had been noticed. Beebo smiled down at her, her short black hair and wide brow making her face more boyish even than Laura remembered. She was remarkably handsome. Laura was deeply ashamed of what she was feeling, sitting there on the barstool, letting herself be influenced by this girl she tried so hard to despise.

"Why don't you invite Bella?" she said.

"She's busy."

Laura's cheeks went hot with fury, and she shook Beebo's arm off and started to get up, to walk past her, to get out. But Beebo caught her, laughing deep in her throat, thoroughly amused. "By Jesus, you *are* jealous!" she said. "Sorry, baby, I had to know. Come on, let's go."

Laura, who was pulling against her, suddenly found herself going in the same direction as Beebo, heading for the door, all her resistance dissipated.

"Beebo, I didn't come here for that! I came to keep you from calling Marcie. To pay you back that drink."

"I want you to owe me that drink all the rest of your life, Bo-peep."

Laura gasped. Then she walked hurriedly ahead of Beebo, trying to get far enough ahead to escape. In the faces around the tables she spotted the slim little blonde who had approached her before about Beebo. She was laughing and the sudden humiliation that filled Laura sent her running up the steps to the street. But Beebo was close behind her, and Laura felt her arms come around her from behind, and Beebo's lips on her neck, and her own knees going shaky.

"No, no, oh Beebo, please! Not here, not here *please.*"

"Laura, darling." Beebo kissed her again. "Not here is right. Come on." She put an arm around her and led her away as she had before, and suddenly, strangely, Laura felt like running. She felt like running with all her strength until they reached Beebo's apartment. For there was no doubt about it any longer, that was where they were going.

She wanted her arms around Beebo, their hot bare bodies pressed together as before. Almost without realizing it she began to speed up and then to run. Instantly Beebo was after her, then beside her, laughing that pagan laugh of hers. She caught a handful of Laura's streaming hair, silver in the street light, and pulled her to a stop, whirling her around. In almost the same gesture she swept her into a dark doorway and kissed her, still laughing.

"You're wonderful," she said in a rough whisper. "You're nuts. I love you."

"No, no no no no," Laura moaned, but she returned Beebo's kisses passionately. It was Beebo who had to quit suddenly.

"Oh, God, Laura, stop. Stop!" she said. "We can't come in the streets. Come on, baby." She dragged her on for another two blocks. Laura walked if she were drunk. She had no liquor in her, but she was not sober. Not at all. She felt punchy. She half ran, half skipped, to keep up with Beebo's stride. For the last two blocks they ran as fast as they could go. Beebo led her into Cordelia Street, and through the green door into the court.

Inside the door, standing in the little court, the urgency left Laura. She stood gasping for breath, leaning against the brick wall by the door. She was where she wanted to be, next to a fascinating woman whom she wanted to make love to. It was a huge physical need, an emotional hypnotism, that drew her to Beebo. After the wild race she had just come through Laura wanted suddenly to slow down. To tease, to tantalize. She felt like somebody entirely different. Not the tightly controlled Laura who lived anxiously with Marcie, with an uncertain job, with the spectre of a hated father. Not the nerve-tortured cautious girl her roommate knew, but a warm excited woman on the verge of the ultimate intimacy. She wanted it, she asked for it, she accepted it. She stood watching Beebo, her eyes enormous with it, her nostrils flared, her lips parted. Beebo came toward her, smiling, but Laura slipped away.

She moved, almost glided, to a circle of benches in the center of the court. Beebo followed her. And again when she reached for her, Laura slipped around the benches. Beebo reached again, and Laura faded out of her grasp. And suddenly Beebo was on fire.

"Come here, come here, baby. Pretty baby. Pretty Laura," she chanted like a spell. But Laura eluded her, moving just a little faster each time, until they were running again, and Laura felt the laughter coming out of her, soft and light at first, but growing wilder, uncontrollable. She fled, inches from Beebo's hands, into the dark hallway, and scrambled up the stairs, losing her footing, and nearly losing her freedom, twice. Beebo was so close behind her near the top that she could hear her breath. With a little shriek of unbearable excitement she fell against Beebo's door, and felt within a second Beebo's weight come hard against her. The laughter burst out of her again until Beebo got the door open and they almost fell into the living room.

Nix was all over them instantly, but Beebo, dragging Laura by the neck and Nix by his collar, locked him in the bathroom. Then she turned on Laura. Laura, seeing her, suddenly stopped laughing. Beebo looked unearthly. Her black hair was tumbled, her cheeks were crimson, her chest heaved. But it was her eyes that almost frightened Laura.

Laura let her jacket drop from her shoulders slowly, provocatively, and Beebo approached her. They stood motionless, so close that just the tips of Laura's breasts touched Beebo, and they stood that way, without moving, until Laura shut her eyes, letting her head rock back on her shoulders, and groaned.

"Do it, Beebo," she said. "Do it. I can't stand it, do it to me."

"Beg me. Beg me, baby."

Laura's eyes opened. She didn't know how hard her breath was coming, how strange and wonderful she looked with all her inhibitions burning up in her own flame of desire. "Beebo, Beebo, take me," she groaned.

Still Beebo didn't move. Her breath was hot and pure on Laura's face when she spoke. "When I start, Laura," she said slowly, "I'm never going to stop." She put her hands against the wall over Laura's head and leaned on them, her eyes boring into Laura's, her body closing gently in on Laura's, pressing. "Never," she whispered.

"Do it, Beebo. God! Do it!"

"I'll never stop. Never." Her lips grazed Laura's brow. Laura shook all over. She couldn't talk, except to repeat Beebo's name over and over and over, as if she were in a trance. Beebo's hands came slowly over her hair, her face, her breasts, her waist, her hips. And then one strong arm went around her and Laura groaned. They sank to the floor, wracked with passion, kissing each other ravenously, tearing at each other's clothes.

They never heard Nix's indignant barking from the bathroom, or the phone when it rang a half hour later. They never felt the chill of the rainy night nor the hard discomfort of the floor where they lay. Or the phone when it rang again. And later, yet again. It was not until late morning and brilliant sunshine invaded the room that they were aware of anything but themselves.

Once again it was Laura who woke up first. She was too bewildered to think straight at first, and the sight of Beebo, turning over slowly and opening her eyes, did nothing to straighten her out. Physically she felt wonderful. For a few moments she luxuriated in her body, letting her mind go blank.

She rubbed her hands gently over herself and discovered a bruise on her thigh. The little ache gave her a sudden hard thrill and she remembered how Beebo made the bruise with her mouth. She had to fight hard against the need to roll over on Beebo and start loving her all over again. She touched the small bruise once more and felt the same shameless pleasure. She stretched, more for Beebo's benefit than her own.

Beebo caught her and pulled her down and rubbed her black hair against Laura's breasts. Laura laughed and struggled with her.

"Beebo, I've got to get up. I have to get to work."

"To hell with work. This is love."

"Don't keep me, Beebo. This job means the world to me. I don't want to be late." She spoke the truth, yet she had no idea of how she was going to get up and get out.

"What time do you think it is, baby?"

"I don't know."

Beebo peered over her head at the dresser clock. "Eleven-thirty," she said.

Laura gasped and tried to get off the floor, the surprise giving her impetus, but Beebo held her. "You're going nowhere, Bo-peep," she said. Her tone, her self-assurance, brought out the fight in Laura.

"I've got to get there. You don't know how far behind we are. I could lose my job. And if my father ever—" She stopped, still squirming to get up. She got as far as her knees but Beebo grasped her wrists and held her there.

"I said, you're not going anywhere, baby," she said, and she wasn't kidding.

"Beebo, be reasonable. Please. You can't know how important it is to me." It was suddenly important in a new way, too; it meant distance between her and Beebo. She was vaguely afraid that Beebo was strong enough to overwhelm her, to dominate her life. She needed something else to keep her perspective, her independence.

"You don't know how important *you* are to *me,*" Beebo returned. "What the hell, you're half a day late already. Call 'em and tell 'em you're sick."

"I can't."

"Why not?"

"I can't lie worth a damn, Beebo."

"You can say 'I'm sick' can't you? It's a cinch, I do it all the time. Come on, let me hear you say it."

"I can't. I turn bright red when I lie."

Beebo released her and turned over on her stomach, laughing. "Jesus, Laur, you could turn bright green. Who's going to see you over the phone? Do your damn radiologists have X-ray eyes?"

Laura was on her feet and heading for the phone in Beebo's kitchen. She dialed the office, while Beebo got up and followed her to listen.

"Sarah?" Laura said.

"Laura! Are you all right?"

"Yes. I'm all right. I'll be down as fast as I can get there. I'm terribly sorry. Is Dr. Hollingsworth mad?"

"No. You know him. He's awfully nice about these things. He did ask if you called in, though. He asked twice. Are you sick?"

She looked at Beebo, who grinned at her. "Yes, I'm sick," she said, setting her chin.

"Well, gee, maybe you'd better not come in, then."

"No, I'll be all right." She glared at Beebo, who was laughing at her red cheeks. "I'll be in right away." She hung up and brushed past Beebo haughtily without looking at her.

"Laura," said Beebo, coming after her, her arms crossed over her chest. "You're not going to work."

Laura picked up her wrinkled clothes and said, "Do you have an iron?"

"You won't need it."

"I can't go out like this." Laura held up her rumpled dress, trying to shake it out.

"Then you just can't go out." Beebo stretched out on the bed and made a clucking noise at her. "Poor baby," she said.

"Why is it you're such an angel in bed and a bitch out of bed?" Laura snapped.

For answer, Beebo only lay on her back and laughed at her. Laura looked at her lithe body and after a moment she had to turn away to keep from lying down beside her. "I don't even like you, Beebo," she said harshly, hoping it would hurt. "I don't know why I can't keep away from you."

"It's because I'm such an angel in bed, Bo-peep," Beebo said. "That's all you care about. That's all you want from me."

Laura whirled and threw one of her shoes at her. "Bitch!" She exploded. The hurt had backfired. Beebo spoke the truth. And then Laura turned away to hide the surprise she always felt when the passion in her burst to the surface. In silent embarrassment she slipped into her panty girdle, burningly aware of Beebo's amused stare while she pulled it over her hips.

"I wouldn't bother, baby," Beebo said lazily.

"Why not?" Laura wouldn't look at her.

"Number one, I hate the damn things. Number two, you don't need one. Number three, you can't go to work in a girdle. Period. And that's all the clothes you're going to get."

"What?" Laura turned around.

Beebo had gotten off the bed and with two or three sweeping gestures she grabbed Laura's clothes and headed for the bathroom.

"Beebo, what are you doing? What's the matter with you? Give me those things! Beebo!" Laura tugged at her but Beebo, laughing, was too much for her. Nix burst out of the bathroom as Beebo shouldered in. She turned on the shower full force and threw the clothes over Laura's head into the drink. And while Laura was still spluttering at her she threw Laura in, too, gently, dumping her on the clothes. Everything, everybody, was soaked.

"Beebo, you animal! You're impossible!" Laura said furiously. She turned off the water angrily and snatched up her clothes, wringing them out into the tub. She was trembling with anger. She faced Beebo with a crimson face and threw the clothes at her.

"Take the girdle off, Bo-peep," said Beebo with unconcern. She threw the clothes over a wooden drying rack. "It doesn't do a thing for you."

Outraged, Laura tried to scratch her, but Beebo pinned her back against the bathroom door and kissed her. Laura bit her and only made her laugh. With a feeling of excitement so strong it almost made her sick, Laura knew what was coming.

"No!" she exclaimed, suddenly sobbing. "No, I won't! No!" But it was submissive, helpless. Beebo forced her to her knees. Standing spreadlegged beside her, she put her strong hands behind Laura's neck and pressed Laura's face into her belly. "I said I'd never stop, Bo-peep. I said never, remember?"

"Please, Beebo…" Frustration and desire were both so strong in Laura now that she was nearly out of her mind. Her weakness had got her again, and Beebo would make the most of it.

It was late afternoon before she called Marcie. She had left under such peculiar circumstances that she was afraid of what Marcie must be thinking. She didn't want to call. Marcie was angry with her, to Laura's surprise.

"You told me you were coming right back," she said.

Laura was bewildered. "I meant to," she said. "I swear, Marcie."

"You lied to me."

"No, I didn't, I just didn't know—I mean—"

"Don't lie to me anymore, Laura. It makes me sick. I thought we were finally getting close to each other. I thought we were finally going to be friends." She sounded upset.

"But Marcie, we are."

"I know where you went, Laura."

Laura went white, and Beebo, who was lounging around the kitchen making dinner, turned to watch her with a frown. "What do you mean, Marcie?" Laura said.

"I nearly lost my mind," she said. "I would have called the police and made a fool of myself. But I called Jack first, thank God. Laura, why won't you tell me the truth? Why won't you just admit that I make you nervous? This isn't the first time I've driven you over to Jack's. If you don't tell me what I'm doing wrong how can I ever do anything right?" Her voice broke. "I feel as if I'm making your life intolerable. As if you'd rather move in with Jack and live in sin than put up with me. You might as well, you spend so much time in his bed."

"Marcie! Marcie, I don't!" Laura was thunderstruck.

"I've already talked to him, so don't deny it, Laura."

"Marcie, honey, listen to me. I—" She looked up at Beebo and the look on Beebo's face silenced her. "Marcie, we'll have a long talk tonight. I'll try to explain it to you. We can't talk over the phone."

There was a brief pause on Marcie's end. Then she said, "Are you at Jack's now?"

"I—no—I'm at the office."

"You must have just gotten there. I've been trying to get you all afternoon."

Laura got more bewildered, more tongue-tied, the more she lied. "Marcie, I can't talk now," she said urgently. "Please. I'll come right home. I'll explain."

"All right, Laura. But I'll tell you right now, I'm ready to move out if you want me to. I'm sick and tired of getting on your nerves and not knowing why."

Laura shut her eyes and tried to control her voice.

"Laura? Are you still there?"

"Yes." She cleared her throat. "I'll see you tonight, Marcie." She hung up and turned a pale face to Beebo.

Beebo snorted and opened the refrigerator door. "She still straight?" she asked sarcastically.

Laura was stung. "No," she flung at her. "She's falling in love with me."

"Don't kid yourself, Bo-peep."

"I'm not kidding. And I'm not blind. She's jealous of Jack. She thinks I spent the night with him and it's her fault. She wants me home."

"How sweet," said Beebo and chucked her under the chin. Laura pushed her hand away impatiently.

"My clothes should be dry by now," she said, getting up.

"Call Jack," said Beebo. "Ask him what he told your roommate."

Laura hated to do anything Beebo suggested, just because Beebo suggested it. But Beebo was right. Laura called him at the office. She got him five minutes before closing.

"I found out from Mortin—the bartender at The Cellar," he said. "And if you pull another fast one on me, Mother, by Jesus, I'm going to let you stew in your own juice. I called you a dozen times last night. You must have been out on Cloud Nine. Marcie's mad as hell. She thinks I'm corrupting you."

"I know. I'm sorry," Laura said earnestly. "Jack, what would I do without you?"

"I don't know. But I wish to hell *you* did. Marcie'd like to see me behind bars."

"Jack, isn't that a good sign? I mean she seems almost jealous."

"Oh, Christ," he said, and then he laughed. "You're really goofy for her, aren't you?"

Laura looked up at Beebo. "Yes," she said. "I am."

"Well, watch it. I don't know what to tell you. Nothing seems to register. If I say 'she's not gay' to you once more I'll sound like a broken record. But she's not. I don't want to see you get stabbed, that's all. Better you should blow off steam with Beebo until you get over Marcie."

"I've blown off about as much steam as I can stand," Laura said, and Beebo laughed. "I'm through."

"Don't be so dogmatic, Mother mine. You'll only have to swallow your words and you'll look like an ass doing it."

Laura wouldn't believe him when he told her Marcie was straight. She wouldn't because she didn't want to. She had told him, she had even told Beebo now, that Marcie was falling for her. She didn't dare believe it herself, but if somebody else did, maybe somehow that would help. Her desire, her pride, trapped her. "Thanks again, Jack," she said. "One of these days I'm going to do the same for you. I swear."

"One of these days you may have to. And Laura—"

"Yes?"

"Watch out for Burr. You're on his black list."

"What'd I do?"

"He thinks you're turning his pretty little sex-pot into a neurotic. He's jealous."

Laura smiled, surprised.

"Well?" said Beebo, when she hung up. "Going home to your little wife?" She grinned.

"Beebo, sometimes you make me sick."

"I know. I'm enough to make you go straight. Go sleep with Jack tonight, it'll do him a world of good."

"Oh, shut up!"

"At least it'll give him a whopper to tell his analyst."

Laura turned on her heel and left the room. She felt her clothes, hanging in the bathroom. They were still damp, but dry enough to iron. She brought them into the kitchen. "Where's the ironing board?" she said.

"Pretty determined, aren't you?"

"I certainly am."

"I've got dinner ready. You can eat before you go." There was a faint tone of pleading in her voice, as if she knew the time had come when sheer force was useless. Laura had made her mind up.

"I don't want another thing from you, not even dinner."

"No, not for another day or two," Beebo said and her voice became rougher as she talked. "You just want to run down for kicks once or twice a week. I'm pretty damn convenient, aren't I?"

She pulled the board out from the wall and plugged the iron in, her movements sharp and angry. Laura felt a little afraid of her. Her blue eyes snapped and there was no trace of her usual humor in her face.

"You're the bitch, Laura, not me. You're using me," she said. "Go on, iron the damn thing." She waved a hand at Laura's dress and Laura spread it out on the board.

"I'm sorry, Beebo," Laura said, taken aback.

"Sure you are."

"All right, Beebo," she said softly. "I won't bother you anymore. Ever."

Beebo snorted at her. "You try it and I'll beat you, I swear I will," she said. "I've had enough from you, Laura. I'm not made of stone. Am I nothing to you? Am I supposed to *believe* I'm nothing to you? Do you think I like to stand and listen to you slobber over that simpering little roommate of yours? Can she give you what I can give you? Well damn it, *can* she?"

Laura couldn't face her, much less answer her. She only worked the iron over her dress and glanced at Beebo's shoes.

Beebo's voice softened a little. "Jesus, what a mess," she said, leaning on the refrigerator. "Here I am falling for you. I ought to have my head examined. I ought to know better." She came over to Laura and took the iron out of her hands and Laura had to look at her. "Laura," Beebo said, leaning toward her, "I'm nuts for you. I wasn't kidding." They gazed at each other, Laura surprised and scared and flattered all at once. "I need you, baby," Beebo whispered. "Please stay."

"I can't, Beebo," Laura said.

"You don't really think you're in love with that little blonde, do you?"

"Yes."

Beebo shook her head and shut her eyes for a minute. "Jack says she's straight. Jack is a shrewd boy. Don't you believe him?"

"No."

"You want to get the Miseries, baby? That's the quickest way."

"You don't know her, Beebo. Even Jack doesn't know her as I do. She's changing. She seems interested in me. She's sort of approachable. She doesn't even want to see her ex-husband anymore. She wants to stay home at night with me. She breaks dates with him to do it."

"All right." Beebo turned away. "Suppose she's gay. Suppose she is. What then?" She turned to look sharply at Laura.

Laura was stumped. She had never looked beyond the present into that possibility. What would it be like, just the two of them, both gay, living together, in love? "Well, then everything will be wonderful," she said.

Beebo gave a short unpleasant laugh. "Yeah," she said. "Wonderful. You walk hand in hand into the sunset."

"I didn't mean to hurt you, Beebo. I never made a secret of my feelings for Marcie."

"I never made a secret of mine for you, baby."

"We'd never do anything but fight, Beebo."

"Fight and make love. I could live forever on such a diet." She smiled a little.

"It would drive me crazy. I couldn't take it."

"Do you think there won't be fights with your little Marcie if she turns out gay?"

"I suppose there will."

"You know damn well there will. And if she's straight, what happens? She reads you the Riot Act. Calls the cops. Sics her husband on you."

"She wouldn't do any of those things, Beebo. She's a sweet girl. She wouldn't get wild like you."

"Not according to Jack. You've known her four months. Jack's known her for years." Beebo lighted a cigarette and blew the smoke through her nose. "Want to know something, Bo-peep? Want to know what it's like? I've had it happen to me—more than once. If you're gay, it just happens now and then, that's all. You get

150

the bug for some lovely kid and you can't keep it to yourself. You get closer and closer. And if she plays along it's worse and worse. And finally you give in and you grab for her. And she turns to ice in your arms."

She looked at Laura and there was a deep regret in her eyes. "And she gets up with the God-damnedest sort of dignity and walks across the room and says 'I'm sorry. I'm so sorry for you. Now go away. Don't talk, don't try to explain, I don't want to hear. It makes me sick. Just go away, and I won't tell our friends. You don't need to worry. Just so I never see you again.' It makes you heartsick, baby. You get so sick inside. You give yourself the heaves. All you want in God's world is to get the hell out of your own skin and be normal. Fade into the crowd like a normal nobody." She crushed her cigarette out, grinding it into the ash-tray with her thumb till the paper burst and the brown tobacco spilled out.

Laura felt closer to her. All the insults of the day faded in her mind. She walked over to her, her pressed dress over one shoulder. "Beebo," she said softly.

But Beebo wasn't ready to let herself be touched. "Just remember one thing," she said. "Too many Marcies in your life, and you commit suicide. That's what it is to be gay, Laura. Gay." Laura stepped back a little shocked. "Sometimes all it takes is one," Beebo said.

"No," Laura whispered. "Oh, no."

"Okay, baby, go find out for yourself. I can't stop you, Jack can't stop you." Beebo's eyes were brilliant with bitterness, with the hard knowledge of her own experience. "Go play with your little blonde. You'll find out soon enough she has claws. And teeth. And when you get to playing the wrong games with her, she'll use them."

"Never!" Laura said. "Even if she's straight she won't hurt me. She's not that kind."

"She doesn't *have* to hurt you, idiot. Can't I get that through your head? All she has to do is say 'no thanks.' Kindly. Sympathetically. Hell! If you want her bad enough, you'll die of it. I know, Laura, I know!" And she took Laura's shoulders and shook her head until Laura felt like sobbing. Beebo released her suddenly and they stood in silence, unable to talk, heavy with feeling, trembling.

Finally Beebo said quietly, "Go on, baby. Go home and get it over with. You've been warned." All the fight seemed gone out of her.

When Laura left, Beebo came to the door with Nix at her heels. She was unsmiling. "Come back, baby," she said. "To stay. Or don't come back at all." And when Laura turned away without answering she called after her, "I mean it!"

Chapter Twelve

Laura entered the penthouse and walked slowly back to the bedroom. It was hard to imagine Marcie's mood. Marcie looked up from her bed, her hair in pincurls. She was a relief to Laura's eyes after the stormy, ranting handsomeness of Beebo. Marcie looked beautiful, even with tin clips in her hair. But she looked cool, too; ready for a fight.

Laura slipped her jacket off without a word, thinking of the loud quarrels she and Beth used to have. And how they resolved them with love. A little curl of excitement twisted around her innards.

"Well?" Marcie said sharply. "Did he throw you down in the street?"

Laura was startled, offended. Marcie had no right to say such a thing. "What do you mean?" she said.

"Your dress," Marcie said, nodding at it.

Laura looked down at it. Beebo had dragged it over the bathroom floor and the dirt, together with a hasty pressing job, made her look like she'd been through a scuffle. "Marcie," she said, trying to control her voice, and not sure when she started talking what she was going to say, "Marcie, I didn't sleep with Jack."

Marcie turned her eyes down to the book she was holding and her expression said, Tell me another one. "With who, then?" she said.

Laura pressed her lips together and sat down on Marcie's bed. *I won't yell at her,* she told herself. *I can't take the chance. I'd say the truth, I'd blurt it out by mistake.*

"Marcie, I just ended up down in the Village."

"Did you wander around all night?"

"No. No." She looked down at the floor. "Well, I—"

"You what?" Marcie looked at her.

"Marcie, I *didn't* spend the night with Jack." Her voice begged for understanding.

"Jack has friends."

Even in her mounting irritation Laura sensed jealousy and it thrilled her. "Yes, Jack has friends. And they aren't all men."

"Don't tell me you spent the night with a girl. Ha! That's even better. You just hang around with anybody who's handy, don't you."

"You aren't very choosy yourself, Marcie."

"Only with Burr!" Marcie flashed angrily. "I only sleep with Burr. And I was *married* to him. Besides, I haven't let him touch me for weeks. You've never been married, not to Jack or anybody else."

"And I've never slept with Jack or anybody else."

"I don't believe you!"

Laura stood up and looked down at her. "You don't have to, Marcie," she said. "What the hell do you care who I sleep with? Or why? Are you guardian of my morals? Yours aren't perfect, you know. I haven't slept with Jack, for your information. Not once. But if I had, what would it matter? You thought it was all a good joke at first."

Marcie's face began to color. She put her book down and looked diffidently at Laura, who was standing by her dresser taking off her clothes. Marcie ran her fingers over her lips, as if warning herself to shut up, and Laura thought to herself, *Just like me. Just like me when Beth used to taunt me. I wanted her so. And I was so afraid.*

"I didn't know it would get so serious, at first. With Jack," Marcie said, her attitude softening. "I feel like it's my fault, what you're doing, and I—I feel real bad about it. I'm scared. Maybe you'll get into trouble, maybe you'll blame me then. You get so *odd* sometimes. I guess I'm just being selfish, Laur. But—" She gave an audible sigh that made Laura turn to glance at her. "Laur, will you tell me—will you *please* tell me—why you keep running out of here at all hours of the night? What am I doing wrong? If you don't tell me, I'm going to move out of here tomorrow, I swear. I can't stand it!"

Laura had to tell her something. She had to lie and she couldn't lie and as she walked toward Marcie's bed, she felt something like panic at the thought of losing her. But when she sat down beside her something popped into her head and saved her. She didn't have to stammer and blush, and she didn't have to confess her homosexuality. She told Marcie about her father.

She was almost ashamed to recount what had happened. It was humiliating, and it looked like a bald bid for sympathy. And yet she wanted terribly to touch Marcie's heart, to win her compassion. "He told the clerk he had no daughter." She finished. Her shame made her drop her gaze and cover her face with her hands. But Marcie, suddenly moved, put her arms around Laura and cried.

"Forgive me, Laura," she whispered. "I've been a stupid idiot about this. I don't know what got into me. Honey, forgive me, I should never have tortured you about it. Whatever your father did to you, he must be a beast. He doesn't deserve to live."

But that was going too far, even for Laura. There had been violent moments of shame and rejection, when she wanted to kill him. But there were others when she wanted only to be allowed to love him. "Don't say that, Marcie."

Marcie looked up at her, her face so close that she gave Laura a start. "Don't tell me you still feel anything for him?" she said. "After what he did to you?"

"I don't know what I feel. I hate him sometimes, Marcie, I hate him so much sometimes that I'm terrified of myself. I think 'If he were with me right now—if he suddenly appeared—I'd kill him. I'd *kill* him!'" And she said it with such force that Marcie shuddered.

"And then, other times, all I want to do is cry. Just cry till there aren't any tears left. Get down on my knees and beg him to love me."

"It seems so crazy, Laur. My Dad is so nice and ordinary. I couldn't take it if he ever hurt me like yours. God, you must feel so alone. Laura, let me be close to you. Let me be friends with you. You haven't up to now, you know."

Laura began to feel dizzy. *This is too much, this is too easy,* she thought, and pangs of conscience came up in her. *All I have to do is pull her close, caress her, kiss her, all I have to do—oh, my God! But I can't! It'd be like corrupting her, like leading her astray. Damn! Why have I got a conscience? Beth didn't have one. Neither does Beebo. Why me? Why can't I just take her?* But she was too afraid.

"Laura, talk to me. You're off in another world again."

Laura looked down at her, balanced between desire and fear, between desire and conscience, between desire and…desire, desire…

"Marcie," she whispered. "Remember the night you wanted to touch tongues?"

Marcie laughed a little, embarrassed. "Yes," she said. "I told Burr about it. He says I'm cracked."

Laura was shocked. "You told Burr?" she said, hurt by the betrayal.

"Well, don't look so horrified." Marcie giggled. "Don't tell me you didn't tell Jack?"

And Laura, by her sudden confusion, admitted that she had. With the admission, and the shock, came a clear head. She stood up. Marcie watched her. "I'm going to bed," Laura said. "I'm too beat to talk. I'm just worn out."

Marcie let her go without a word. Her eyes followed Laura around the room. Laura ignored her studiously. She was asleep within minutes after she lay down, too tired even to worry.

Laura knew she would have to lie to Sarah in the morning about where she spent the day before. She made up her mind to do it fast and simply. She organized a little story about a sick headache and she delivered it quickly, even before Sarah had a chance to ask. Sarah took it at face value.

At the end of the day, she called Marcie and told her she'd be late. "I've got to stay here and catch up," she explained. "I've done nothing but get behind the whole time Jean's been away. I just can't seem to get the work done. I'm not going to lose this job."

"You're wearing yourself out, Laur. I think you're crazy. You can get a much softer job and earn a lot more money. In fact I talked to Mr. Marquardt about you."

"You *what?*"

"Yes." She laughed. "Today. I thought it would be fun if we could be in the same office. Besides, I never saw anybody work like you do. It's insane, when all you have to do is sit around."

"Marcie, I don't *want* to sit around! I don't need help! I can do this myself. I know you did it out of friendship but damn it, I *want* to work. I don't want to sit around on my behind all day, counting the minutes till the next coffee break."

Marcie was taken aback by the forcefulness of it. "Laura, I didn't mean—" she began, and her voice was hurt.

"I know, I know. I'm grateful, Marcie, forgive me. But I have something to prove, staying here. It's only hard at first, when you're learning. It'll get easier. And in another two weeks there'll be three of us at the office."

She knew she had hurt Marcie's feelings and when she hung up she wondered if it was worth it. *Why don't I quit? Why don't I take a soft job, like Marcie?* But she knew what scorn her father would pour on a job like that. It was only the tough ones, the ones that took it out of you, that demanded your best, that he had any respect for.

Laura stayed on until nearly eight by herself. The building was crypt-quiet and she was deep in the last round of reports she intended to do, when the door opened and a voice said, "Laura!"

Laura gave a gasp of shock, throwing her hands over her face. She was so startled that she found herself trembling all over. For a moment she was unable to move. "Laura?" he said again.

Laura turned slowly around in her swivel chair, taking her hands away from her face. She looked up, her face cold and white and resentful. It was Burr. She didn't say a word. She only stared at him in surprise. She felt overflowing with hatred for him, as if Merrill Landon were standing there.

Burr was somewhat taken aback. "Marcie said you were down here," he said, a little awkwardly. "I wanted to talk to you." He shrugged, and pulled Sarah's chair out from her desk, sitting down about five feet from Laura. She said nothing.

"Laura," he said, embarrassed. "We started out to be pretty good friends, you and I." He turned his hat around and around in his hands, studying it while he talked. "Then—I don't know why—we seemed to—well, we just didn't have anything to say to each other. I guess maybe because we always talked about books. And Marcie. You don't seem to be reading any books anymore. And Marcie— well…" He seemed at a loss for words here. He twirled his hat assiduously, as if that might give him some answers. But it was no help. "Of course, I haven't been around much lately, either," he said.

Laura was suddenly a little scared. But she was determined not to be any more helpful than his hat. She only glared at him. She still hadn't said a word to him.

After all, she thought, *I haven't done anything. He still hasn't said what he wants.*

"Well, frankly Laura, Marcie's changed. I don't know what the hell's come over her. I thought maybe you could help me out." He eyed her closely. "I guess it sounds pretty silly. But I love her, and all of a sudden I can't even see her anymore. I can't get near her. She's just not interested." When Laura still said nothing he went on, "I mean, I know it's not your problem, but I thought, being her room-mate, you know, you might help me out." He looked up at her, smiling a little, but his smile faded when he saw the look on her face.

Laura was thinking, *Why the hell should I help you?* But she said, "Why don't you stop fighting with her, Burr? Maybe that would help." Her voice was faintly sarcastic.

"When we fought," he said, "at least we could always make up. That was fun. We both enjoyed it. Then all of a sudden, a couple of weeks ago, Marcie wouldn't fight anymore. I don't know what the hell got into her. She just got quiet and thoughtful. She wouldn't fight and she wouldn't make love. I'm beginning to think she needed to fight before she could make love. Maybe that's the only thing that excited her." He looked quizzically at Laura.

"How would I know? Maybe *you* needed it," Laura said and shrugged.

By her reticence she had made Burr uncomfortable. "Well, I know it isn't exactly the sort of thing to bother you with," he said, making a visible effort to control his temper. "But damn it, Laura, I love her. She's my wife. I still think of her that way, I can't help it. I was a fool ever to let her have that divorce."

"Do you think getting married again would change any of that?" Laura said. "Don't you think it would just be the same old fights all over again?"

"I don't know." He shook his head. "Maybe. But I'd rather live with Marcie and fight than live without her and be this miserable."

"Does fighting make you happy?"

"I don't mind it. Not enough to make me give her up again."

"You talk like a kid, Burr," she said, wondering what authority gave her the right to pronounce judgments. And then she reasoned that Burr himself gave her the right. He asked for it. Okay, he'd get it. "If you want to win Marcie back, find out what's the trouble and change it. If you want my opinion—and I guess that's why you're here—I don't think you should go back together. I think Jack's right; you were never meant for each other. It's purely physical."

These were hard words, but even so Laura wasn't prepared for the effect they produced. Burr went pale and his mouth dropped open. Suddenly he stood up. "Jack said that?" he said incredulously. *"Jack?"*

And Laura went a little sick. She had violated a confidence, without even meaning to. The one person she couldn't bear to hurt, to alienate right now, was Jack. "Maybe I'm mistaken," she said quickly. But who else could it be? "It was me, Burr, I don't know why I said that. It wasn't Jack."

"Oh, it was *you!*" He had been surprised into a fury. He had been nursing his grievance, trying to talk calmly to Laura. Now his feelings got out of control. "Well, I'll tell you something, Laura. I don't believe you. It was Jack or you wouldn't have said so. You're a lousy liar. Now suppose you explain something to me." He leaned with his fists on her desk.

Laura leaned away from him, frightened now. "Calm down, Burr," she said, but he ignored her.

"You and Jack can both go to hell!" he said. "You've been psycho-analyzing the situation over a couple of beers in your spare time. A couple of cocktail hour psychologists. Oh, don't think I can't see it. Well, I don't give a damn what you think. I love Marcie!" He was shouting. "I love her! And I'd like to know why the hell she doesn't love *me* anymore. *Why,* Laura? *You* tell me. Why would she rather stay home with you at night than go out with me? Why does she talk about Laura, Laura, Laura all the time? Laura reads this, Laura does that, Laura says! God, I'm sick of it!" His ugly suspicions exploded in her face.

"She doesn't, Burr, you're mistaken."

"Mistaken!" he roared, his face turning scarlet "Mistaken! Oh, you're a bitch, Laura! Mistaken! And she won't make love to me anymore. She won't see me. You're the only one she gives a damn about. She can't get enough of you at home, she's got to get you a job in her own office. Yes, she told me about it," he interrupted himself, when Laura gave a little gasp.

"Burr, you fool, you're making things up," Laura said. She looked cold and controlled, but there was a terror inside her that he couldn't see. She rose in her seat and faced him, their faces not a foot apart. "Now get out of here." It had worked before with other men. It had to work now with Burr. She would give him no satisfaction.

"Don't tell me you're not up to some God-damn funny business," he growled.

"I'm not up to any God-damn funny business," she replied quietly.

"Then what's all this crap about touching tongues? In the dark? In bed? Why does Marcie follow you around like you were Svengali?"

"She doesn't."

"Don't tell me she doesn't!" he shouted in a fury, bringing his fist down with a huge thump on her desk. "I know she does. I know!"

"Burr, you're insane with jealousy."

"What's going on between you two?"

"Nothing. Absolutely nothing. I'm a bad liar, you said it yourself. If I had ever touched Marcie I couldn't lie about it." She glared at him, her face a mask, almost white; her eyes brilliant and her body tense.

"You want her. Admit it." He was quiet now, but it was the quiet of hatred.

"I won't admit anything. Who the hell are you? I don't owe you any explanations."

"She's my wife."

"So she's your wife. She's *my* roommate. She prefers to live with me." Laura was dangerously near throwing her advantage in his face.

"You *are* queer! By God, I knew it!"

"How dare you!" And the hot blood came to Laura's face. "Get out of here! You bastard!"

"All right, deny it, then."

"I'm not accountable to you, Burr. I won't admit or deny anything. I don't have to. I'll call the police if you don't get out of here. I'll sue you for libel if you make that accusation in public. I never laid a hand on Marcie."

"That's not what Marcie said."

For a shocked second Laura was unable to move or respond. Then she gasped and staggered a little. There was a terrible silence, heavy with the awful meaning of his words.

Laura sat down shaking. She began to cry.

Burr watched her in silent fury for a moment. Then he said, "I thought that'd get you, you bitch." His voice was low and dry. "I came here to talk to you like a human being, to give you a chance. But you act like a God-damn queen. You act like I was in the wrong, not you! Like I was an animal. Well, you're no better. You're a pervert, Laura. And I'm going to get Marcie away from you if have to call out the cops to do it. You're not going to touch her again." He turned sharply and started out.

"Burr! Burr! My God, wait! What did she say? What did she tell you?"

"Can't you guess?"

"She made it up, Burr, believe me. Please believe me." She was begging him now. "You know how she is."

"Yeah, I know how she is. She didn't make this up."

"She did! She's lying."

"She's telling the truth. You're perverting her. It's obvious, even I can see it. Perverting her! My Marcie!" He almost wept when he said it, and Laura instinctively put a hand to her throat as if to protect herself.

"Burr," she said, and her voice was deeply intense and quiet, "I swear to you by God and Heaven and everything I hold sacred, I never—"

"You hold nothing sacred! You're a walking profanity! You're a mockery of womanhood. You're queer. *Queer!* And you're infecting Marcie. I'm going to get her away from you. Now, tonight!" And he turned on his heel and walked out.

Laura called after him until he walked into the last operating elevator and disappeared. She sobbed wildly for a minute, collapsed in her chair. Then, as if electrified, she picked up the phone and dialed the penthouse, as fast as her trembling fingers would let her. She almost died of impatience before Marcie answered. "Hello?" Marcie said.

"Marcie! Marcie, what have you done to me? Answer me!"

"Laur?" Marcie's voice sounded small and frightened. "What's the matter, honey?"

"Burr just left me. I thought he was going to kill me. Marcie, what did you tell him?"

"Oh, Laura." Marcie's voice was only the faintest whisper. "I had no idea he'd—I didn't think he'd bother you. I didn't think he'd even mention it."

"What did you tell him, Marcie?" Laura's voice sounded almost hysterical.

"I—we quarreled." Marcie was crying quietly while she talked. "We quarreled, for the first time in weeks. It was terrible. As if to make up for all those weeks when we didn't fight at all. He accused me of—forgive me, Laura, I'm ashamed to say these words—of falling in love with you."

Laura groaned despairingly.

"Laur, I'm so sorry. I guess I talked about you all the time. I get interested in somebody, or something, and I just don't talk about anything else for a while. I talked about you because I admire you so much. I—well, you know. He got the wrong idea, that's all. But I didn't realize it, I swear I didn't, Laur. I would have stopped him if I had. And then we had this quarrel tonight and I said some things I shouldn't have."

"What things? *What things,* Marcie?"

Marcie sobbed. "He accused me of trying to tempt you, of egging you on. Oh, Laura, this is too horrible, I can't go on."

"Tell me!"

"And I got so furious. It was so unfair. You know we haven't done anything! He was just determined to believe it. He can't believe I just don't want to see him anymore, that's too hard on his damned pride. So he was just waiting for somebody to blame, and there you were. And I was so damn mad at him. It was hopeless, there was no talking to him. He was losing me because somebody else winning me, that's the only way he could see it was. So I finally just shouted at him, 'All right, have it your way, you big fool.

Believe what you want to believe, I can't stop you!'" She was interrupted by her own sobs.

"Marcie," Laura said, making a huge effort to control herself. "Did you tell him that I..." She could hardly get the words out.

"... made love to you?"

"No! No, Laura!" Marcie cried.

"Did you tell him anything specific?"

"Absolutely not, I swear!"

Laura gave a sigh of relief. She began to cry again herself. After a moment she said softly, "Marcie, he's on his way to the penthouse. He says he's not going to let you spend another night in the same apartment with me. I'm infecting you."

"Oh, Laura, honey. God!"

"So you'd better lock the door."

"We don't have a key!"

"Get one from the janitor."

"I'm afraid of him. He's down in the basement. It's so dark down there and he always tries to make a pass at me."

"I shouldn't think that would bother you." Laura couldn't help the dig; it made her feel better.

"Laura, he's nuts. He's a meatball."

"Well, damn it, do *something!*" Laura cried, exasperated. Then she forced herself to speak quietly. "All right, call the police," she said. "Say your former husband is threatening you. Say you're afraid of him, you think he wants to kill you. Say anything! Tell them he's on his way over right now and you want protection."

"Laura, I've never done such a thing in my life! Poor Burr! I've known him since I was a kid, I worshipped him."

"You stopped worshipping him in a hurry when you had to live with him. Listen to me, there's not much time. If you don't want him to do something violent you'd better get some protection. I can't fight him off for you. Unless you want to go with him tonight."

"Go with him! That bastard! After what he did tonight? He can go to hell. Without me."

"That's where he'd like to see *me,*" Laura said. "I'd better not show up. I'll stay down here for another hour or so. I'll call you before I come home, to be sure the coast is clear."

"Laura? I hate to call the police, Laur. It makes me sick." She sounded miserable.

"Marcie, for God's sake, you're a taxpayer. You're entitled to protection. Burr was in a fit when he left here."

Marcie began to weep again. "Laura, I'm so sorry. I'm so sorry," she said softly over the phone.

Laura's heart softened too. "Oh Marcie," she moaned. "I guess it really isn't anybody's fault. Burr's still in love with you. None of us realized how much. He had to be jealous of somebody, and he knew you weren't dating anybody else. We've all been pretty stupid about the whole thing. I just hope to God it blows over." All of a sudden she felt powerfully tired.

"It's all my fault," Marcie said. "Everything's my fault. I'll make it up to you, Laura, I promise."

"Never mind, honey. Just keep out of trouble tonight. I'll be home about ten. I'll call you first."

"Okay." Marcie was still crying when she hung up.

For a long time Laura sat at her desk, staring into space. The windows were black, gold-spangled with the city night, and everything was still.

She got up, feeling weak and tired, and yet not desperate or frightened any more. Burr had no proof of anything. Marcie would deny everything. And if things went as it seemed they must, Burr would act like a crazy man and convince the police he was bent on violence. Marcie would be genuinely frightened and it would show. There ought not to be any difficulty about it. She got her things together and turned out the office light.

The hall to the elevator was bare and echoing as she walked down it. The elevator boy was silent, as if he too had been touched by the vast quiet of the night.

Laura walked out on the street. People hustled by, lights shone, cars honked. But it all seemed far away, not very real. Her senses registered only half of what they perceived.

Where shall I go? I'd better not try to go home for a while. Not till Burr leaves. Another hour, at least.

She looked at her watch: eight-thirty. She walked slowly, gazing ahead of her like a sleepwalker. *I'll go somewhere where I can sit down and read,* she thought. She bought a magazine from a corner stand and sauntered on another couple of blocks until she saw the McAlton on the next corner.

She almost exclaimed aloud, as if the hotel had been sneaking up on her while she marked time on the sidewalk. She stopped in her tracks to stare at it and then looked self-consciously into a shop window. After a few minutes she moved on to the hotel.

If I just sit in a corner, as if I'm waiting for somebody, they can't do anything. I'll just read this thing till nine-thirty or so.

A tiny unworded excitement knotted itself around her heart and stuck there, prepared to stay for as long as Laura stayed in the lobby. She didn't go over to the desk. She just sat down in an alcove on a leather-covered sofa next to a fat middle-aged woman. She read until nine-thirty.

Then she got up and walked halfway across the lobby to the phone booths, entered one, and dialed the penthouse. Marcie answered.

"Is everything all right, Marcie? It's Laura."

"Yes." She sounded tired, reticent.

"What happened?"

"Nothing. The policeman got here right after Burr did. Burr was yelling like a crazy man. The policeman took him out and told him to stop bothering me or they'd take him down and book him. He was furious. He cried. But he went. Damn it, he deserved it, after what he did to you."

"Are you alone now?"

"Yes."

Laura suddenly felt enormously relieved. "Thank God," she said. "Will you be right home?"

"Yes. Right away." She hung up and left the booth, putting some change in her purse. She felt much better. Burr was mad as hell, that was certain. But for the moment he would have to watch himself; he would have to be careful. Marcie was disgusted with him. Obviously force was the wrong way to get her back. And suddenly Laura saw her father.

Merrill Landon was about twenty feet from her, his face turned profile to her, talking to some men.

Laura gave a low cry, almost inaudible, and her heart stopped. The knot around it gave a tremendous squeeze, like a big angry fist, and stopped it altogether for a moment. It started again with a tremendous thump. She darted toward the little alcove, her face averted, but found all the seats taken. She stood facing away from him for a minute, her heart kicking wildly, wondering frantically what to do.

I've got to be calm, I've got to be calm, she said under her breath, but each time she said it it seemed more hysterical. She gulped convulsively and barely heard someone say in her ear, "Excuse me, dear. Are you all right?"

"Yes. Yes, thanks," she said, her voice staccato, afraid to identify her questioner.

She shut her eyes tight for a minute. *If I just walk out quickly, he'll never see me. The lobby is full, there are dozens of people in here. He's not looking for me, he's talking to some men, he won't see me. I'll just walk out.*

She took a very careful glance behind her. He was facing her now, but not seeing her, gesturing, talking, engrossed in his words. He would never see her. For a second she permitted herself the luxury of looking hard at him; his big maleness, his strong face that could never be called handsome and yet compelled interest. That face that almost never smiled at Laura since she was five years old. That face she was condemned to love.

Laura turned away then and began to walk toward the door, keeping her face averted, hurrying, her heart pounding as if she were running up a steep hill. Near the door she slowed down a little. *I'll never see him again,* she told herself fiercely. *Just one more glance. It will have to last me my life.* She turned around slowly, carefully, just five feet from the door and safety.

He was looking at her. Looking straight at her, as if he had been following her through the crowd with his eyes, not quite sure but wondering. For a split second Laura didn't believe it; thought he didn't really see her and was just looking that way. But then he cried, "Laura!" in his big rough voice, and her eyes went huge with fear and she gasped and turned and ran as if the devil were after her. She ran headlong, panicky, her heart huge and desperate, struggling to get out of her throat. She ran with all her strength and with an unreasoning terror whipping her heels, all the way to the subway. She never once looked back. People turned to stare, they jumped out of the way and she collided with a dozen of them. She almost fell down the subway steps and ran and dodged and shoved her way into the ladies' rest room.

There, she fell on the floor, whimpering, crying despairingly, unable to lift herself off the filth of the black floor and completely unaware of anything but the hysterical fear that gripped her. After a while she felt hands on her shoulders and she gave a wild scream and sat up. A terrified Negress was bending over her, saying, "There now, there now." Her eyes were all whites.

Laura panted, speechless, gasping for breath. She leaned exhausted against the door of a booth until her wind came back to her and then she tried to get up. The Negro woman helped her, handling her like heirloom china, watching her every second for fear she would take off on another fit.

Laura half staggered to the wash basin and turned the water on. She looked at her haggard face in the mirror and an attack of real crying, soothing relief with real tears, overwhelmed her. "Father, Father, Father," she cried softly, her face in her hands.

"Can I help you, Miss?" the colored woman asked. She was scared by Laura's behavior, but fascinated.

Laura shook her head.

After a moment's pause the woman said, "You came in here like a bat out of hell. You was out of your mind, honey, that's for sure. Was some sonofabitch chasin' you?"

Laura put her hands down to look at the woman in the cracked mirror over the basin. She nodded.

"Well, I never seen a girl so scared in my life. Never." She shook her head positively. "You better get yourself some help, honey. Is he still out there?"

At this Laura went so white that she frightened the woman again, who said, "There now, there now. Didn't mean to start nothin'. Don't go off like that again."

Laura turned around to look at her. And in her awful unhappiness she went to her and put her arms around her, to the bottomless astonishment of the woman, and wept on her shoulder. "I never had a mother," Laura sobbed. "I never had a mother." And her heart was broken.

The woman held her like a child and said, "There now, there now. Everybody's got a mother, even you."

"Nobody knows me. I don't even know myself. I don't know what I'm doing here," she said brokenly. "I'm a stranger in this world."

"Well, now," said the woman, "Everybody's a stranger when you look at it that way. But everybody got a chance to find a little love. That's the most important thing. When you got a little love, the rest don't seem so strange or sad no more. There now, honey, there now."

Laura suddenly shied away from her. "Don't call me honey!" she said, her face twisted with misery.

The Negro woman let her go, shaking her head. "You pretty sick, girl," she said. "You need a doctor, and that's the truth."

Laura turned and walked out of the rest room on shaking legs. Outside she looked warily up and down the waiting platform. Only a handful of people were there. A train had gone through just after she entered the rest room and had taken most of the crowd with it. She waited in silence for the next train.

The woman came out of the rest room after Laura. She stood some distance from her, staring at her with a mixture of distrust and pity, until the train arrived and the crowd separated them.

Laura came home too exhausted to talk about it, to be embarrassed with Marcie about the fight with Burr. She was so full of her experience, so absorbed in her father, that nobody else seemed real. She almost fell into her bed, with hardly a word to Marcie, and lay there wrapped up in herself, crying quietly for a long time.

Things were no better in the morning. Somehow the enormity of Burr's accusation hung between them like a curtain. They could look at each other only furtively; they couldn't speak. They were embarrassed, a little afraid of each other, and it made them overly polite. All they said was, "Excuse me," "Pass the cream, please," "I'm sorry." Laura had the additional burden of her terrible flight from her father to keep her both silent and preoccupied.

She was unable to figure it out. She knew she didn't want to talk to him, to show him any forgiveness at all, to satisfy his curiosity about her—if he had any. She only wanted a glimpse of him; she wanted to reassure herself that he was still in New York, even though she knew he was. And she knew he might see her if she hung around his hotel. And she was ashamed that he should see her and know how important he was to her, even after his cruel denial of her. All these things were plain to Laura and yet when she looked back on the night before it seemed incredible. Especially her own terror.

They parted for work without more than a perfunctory good-bye. Laura knew it was going to be a rough day. She had had almost no sleep. And for the first time since she took the job she didn't even give a damn what happened. She was too engrossed in herself and the urgent unnamable feelings that plagued her. Not even the head start she had given herself the night before encouraged her. It only reminded her of Burr and the ugly quarrel they had had. The thought of her father, which usually spurred her on, even on the darkest days, now filled her with a shaky apprehension and so engaged her mind that it was hard for her to think about anything else.

Bombshells fell around her all day. Marcie called in tears at ten to say she couldn't stand it any longer and wouldn't Laura forgive her. And Laura was forced to take time out, while Dr. Hagstrom was in the room, to reassure her. Marcie wouldn't be put off; there was no help for it.

Sarah reminded her that they were all going out for dinner that night. They had arranged to meet Jack and Carl Jensen at a small bar a couple of blocks away for cocktails and to go on from there. It wasn't until Sarah mentioned it that Laura even remembered it, and then she was dismayed.

Just before lunch, Jack called.

"Laura," he said firmly, "what the hell are you trying to do to me?"

"Nothing. What's the matter, Jack, can't you make it tonight?"

"Tonight be damned. I'm liable to get skinned alive. Right *now.*"

"Did something go wrong with Terry?" Laura was startled into attention.

He paused a minute before answering, taken aback to hear his lover mentioned right out on the phone. "No," he said. "I spoil him rotten, but that's nothing new. Guess again."

"Well, Jack, I don't have time for guessing games, we're—"

"I know, you're behind. Burr told me you stayed late last night to catch up."

"Burr told you? Oh!" Suddenly she remembered. "What's the matter with me?"

"You tell me. I'd like to know. Burr was real sweet. He told me I was a lousy bastard and no friend of his, and I could take my psychoanalysis and cram it. Oh, he told me some very interesting things. He told me you're queer and you're perverting Marcie, and you two are lovers, and Marcie sicked the cops on him last night, and God knows what else. Would you care to explain to me what the hell is going on? Just so I won't put my foot in my mouth? You know how it is." There was no forgiveness in his bitter humor and it made her miserable.

"Jack, I'm so terribly sorry," she said. "I blurted out something about the way you felt about Burr and Marcie. I was trying to calm him down. I should have known better. He was out of his mind."

"Since when are you and Marcie lovers?"

"We're not! I would have told you, you *know* that." She glanced surreptitiously across the office at Sarah, but Sarah had her eyes on her work. "Burr got it into his head we were because Marcie talked about me so much. Because she stayed home and wouldn't go out with him. When he accused her, it made her so mad she just told him, 'Okay, believe it.' And he did. I thought he was going to kill me last night."

At this Sarah did look up, but Laura didn't notice.

"Well, that's a hell of a story," Jack said.

"It's the truth, Jack! I swear."

"Never mind the truth. You've got me in a lovely mess. Burr thinks I promoted the whole affair."

"My God! Jack, what'll we do?"

"What *can* we do? Have you done anything with Marcie you wouldn't want to write home about?"

"Nothing! I wish to God now I had. As long as he's going to believe it anyway."

"Oh, no! Christ! Whatever you do, Laura, don't touch Marcie. Not till Burr straightens out. Never, if you have any sense."

Laura wouldn't answer him. She felt closer to winning Marcie, in spite of their awkwardness with each other this morning, than she ever had. She wouldn't make any promises to Jack.

"You hear me, Mother?"

"Yes."

He apparently took that for a promise. "And one more thing."

"I can't take any more right now."

"This won't hurt. What have you done to Beebo?"

Done to her? Nothing. Ask her what she's done to me," she said, and her voice was hard. Sarah watched her with considerable interest now.

"Keep your voice down, Mother," Jack said. "Beebo's goofy for you. And when she gets a girl on her mind, that girl had better watch out. She's a stubborn bitch."

"So am I," Laura snapped.

"She's in love with you, Laura. Don't cross her."

"I'd walk all over her if I could. She treats me like a slave."

"Christ, keep your voice down," Jack said, and Laura was surprised at her own lack of caution. Usually she was meticulously careful. Today, nothing seemed to matter. "She's in love with you," Jack said. "That explains a lot of things."

"It doesn't excuse them. Besides, she isn't. How do you know she is?"

"She said so."

"When?"

"Last night."

Laura couldn't help being flattered. The pleasure in her was warm and sudden and overwhelmed her bad conscience briefly. "I'm not going to see her again," she told Jack. This time she almost whispered, which intrigued Sarah still more.

Jack laughed. "Have it your way," he said. "Only don't drag me into your messes anymore, Mother. I've got enough of my own."

"Is everything all right between—I mean—" She looked over at Sarah for the first time and surprised Sarah staring at her. Sarah went quickly back to work and Laura felt suddenly nervous. "Jack, I'd better hang up. We'll talk tonight."

"Okay. See you at five-thirty."

Laura spent the rest of the day reassuring herself, *I'll never go back to that hotel. He'll be gone tomorrow. Or Sunday at the latest.* The thought gave her considerable relief.

Chapter Thirteen

Carl Jensen was a clean cut young man, very fair with freckled skin. He engaged Sarah in conversation right away; it was a part of what he considered good technique to get a girl talking, and he wasted no time.

Jack and Laura had dinner with them, but Jack was obviously chafing to get away. They hadn't even finished their after-dinner coffee before he was whispering in Laura's ear, "Let's get the hell out of here." Laura, who was almost wordless through dinner, agreed.

Jack did the dirty work. He told them a joke, he made them laugh, and then he said he had a meeting the next day up in Albany. Very unexpected. Would they mind, etc.

They were a little startled, Jensen especially, for he had expected Jack and Laura to stick with him and lend moral support through the evening—but they replied, almost together, "No, go ahead. We don't mind."

As soon as they were in the street Jack sighed, "God. I couldn't have stood another minute of it. Straight people are so depressing."

Laura smiled at him and noticed for the first time that evening how tired and worried he looked. She was so wound up in Laura Landon that nobody's troubles counted for her but her own. But now she saw Jack's anxiety and she was afraid she had caused it. She started to apologize. "Jack, I want you to know..." she began.

"Skip it."

"Please."

"I said skip it." And his voice was harsh enough to hurt her.

They walked along in silence for a minute and finally Laura said, "Jack, I have to talk. I feel awful about it. I saw my father last night. He saw me, too. I don't know what came over me. I've never been so terrified in my life, as if he were the devil and I had to get away from him. I ran all the way to the subway. I think I was hysterical."

He looked at her and then he sighed. "Everybody's hysterical. Even me."

"There was an old colored lady there. In the rest room. She said something I didn't understand then, but I've been thinking about it. She said everybody is a stranger in this world until he finds a little love. That's the most important thing."

"Wise lady," Jack said.

They walked without talking for half a block. "How's Terry?" Laura asked.

"He needs a spanking. I act like a lovesick cow with him. I can't help it. I know I'm doing it, and I can't help it. He laughs at me." Jack looked at the pavement as he walked, his hands shoved into his pockets. "Mother," he said slowly. "Do you want to get back in my good graces?"

"I do," she said gently. "Yes. I do."

"Well," he said, and stopped walking. She stopped beside him and saw that he was embarrassed. "This is a rotten thing to do. But I'd do it for you, bear that firmly in mind." He poked her chest between her breasts, as if he were making a point with a fellow businessman. It was intended to lighten the atmosphere a little, but the atmosphere was too heavy already.

"I'll help you, Jack, you know I will. Any way I can. You've been so wonderful to me. I don't know what I would have done."

"Okay, okay." He stopped her abruptly and then seemed unable to speak himself for a minute. Finally he said, quickly, "I'm losing him, Laura."

"Oh, Jack!" She was suddenly full of sympathy, but he cut her off again.

"What the hell," he said cynically. "I expected it. I *predicted* it. And I know why."

"Why?"

"Mother, you have a short memory." He smiled wryly. "My little friend likes nice things. Nice things cost money. And besides," he looked at his shoes, scraping one toe along a crack in the pavement, "I can't handle him. I should shove his teeth down his throat. I should make him behave. And I can't. I feel more like falling on my knees and worshipping him. He has no respect for me." He spoke so softly that Laura had to strain to hear him.

She put her hands on his arms. "Jack, he's not worth your time," she said. "Anybody who would take advantage—"

"No, no, no, it's normal. In this abnormal world we live in, you and I. If I were young and beautiful, he'd settle for that. But I'm not. I'm middle-aged and ugly. And a sap. So it takes something else...money. I wish had the knack of being a millionaire."

"Damn it, Jack, you need somebody who can appreciate you." He laughed bitterly, but she went on. "You make me hate Terry already without ever having seen him."

"No, Laura," he said seriously. "Don't hate him. He's very young. He'll learn. It's my fault. I can't give him what he needs."

"Dollar bills?"

Jack sighed. "That's my last chance. I know it takes something else, but I haven't got it. And now I haven't got the dollar bills, either."

"If I were a boy I'd fall madly in love with you," Laura said.

This was such a startling remark that Jack had to drop his cynicism and take it in the spirit in which it was given. "Thanks, Mother," he said softly. He looked at her, his ugly intelligent face prey to a number of strong emotions that he made no attempt to hide. It was a measure of his regard for Laura that he could let her see him stripped of wit and laughter like this. "How much do you have in the bank, Laura?"

Laura stared a little at him. But then she said quickly, "All I have is yours, Jack. It's not much, but if it'll help...

He smiled a little and then he leaned over and kissed her cheek. "You're a doll," he said. "We both know this is a losing investment. But it'll give me a few more days with him. After that…" He shrugged. "Well, I always seem to live through these things. I don't know why."

They stood uncertainly on the corner for a minute and suddenly he asked, "Where are you going now?"

"Home."

"To Marcie?"

"Yes. I hope Burr hasn't tried to bother her."

"He's pretty sick about the whole thing. I think he'll drink it off for a day or two. You should, too. The whole thing looks screwy to me." He looked at her. "Come have a nightcap with me."

"Where?"

"The Cellar. Where else?"

"I'm afraid I'll run into Beebo."

He shrugged. "I've gotten to know her better." He gazed away from her thoughtfully.

"You have?"

"She calls me all the time. 'Where does Laura work, what does Laura like, tell me all about her.'"

"She asked you that?" Laura was slightly incredulous, but once again, she liked it. She was sorry she liked it, but she did.

"Yeah. I'm beginning to think I like her."

"You liked her before."

"I know." He laughed. "I'm not making sense. I guess I mean I feel sympathetic toward her. We're both unlucky in love. At the moment." He looked hard at her then and said, "Please come with me, Laura. I don't want to go home."

"Why not?"

Again he laughed, not so pleasantly this time. "I'm afraid of what I'll find."

"Like what?"

"Like somebody else in my bed with Terry."

After a moment of shocked silence, Laura put her arm in his. "Okay," she said. "Let's go somewhere and flatter the hell out of each other."

He chuckled at her. "Mother, damn it, sometimes I suspect you of having a sense of humor."

They went down to The Cellar, in spite of Laura's misgivings. Jack seemed so unhappy that she wanted to indulge him. It was crowded as always on Friday nights, but Beebo wasn't in sight.

"She'll be in," Jack observed. "She's late on Fridays."

They stood at the bar until a couple of stools were vacated and then sat down.

"What does she do?" Laura asked rather shyly.

"Who? Beebo?"

"She must get money somewhere. She has to pay the rent like everybody else."

"She runs an elevator. In the Grubb Building. They think she's a boy."

"My God—an *elevator.*" It seemed wrong, even ludicrous. Beebo had too much between her ears to fritter her youth away running an elevator. "What does she do *that* for?"

"She doesn't have to wear a skirt."

Laura was stunned. It was pathetic, even shameful. For the first time she saw Beebo not as an overwhelming, handsome, self-assured individual, but as a very human being with a little more pride and fear and weakness than she ever permitted to show.

Laura didn't know how long they had been there when Beebo walked in. She only knew she had had plenty to drink and it was time to go home. Beebo walked up to her, and Laura saw her face first in the mirror. She turned around with a start and stared at her. Beebo was wearing a dress.

A dress. And high heeled shoes. She was over six feet in the high heels. Strangely enough she wasn't awkward in them, either. She wasn't comfortable, but she could walk a straight line and keep her balance.

"Hello, Bo-peep," she said quietly in Laura's ear.

Laura felt a grateful response flow down to her toes from the ear. "Hello," she said to the mirror image and then turned to face her. "Hello, Betty Jean." She looked at her skirt.

Beebo gave her a wry smile. "You remembered?" she said. "Do you remember the good things, too?"

"Yes," said Laura, smiling back. And surprised herself. For a moment she felt curiously receptive. She had no idea why.

Beebo gazed at her and then she put a hand on Jack's shoulder. "Hello, fellow sufferer," she said.

"Hi, doll." He turned around. "We're drowning our sorrows." He gestured at Laura with his glass.

"So I see. Mind if I drown a few with you?"

"We'd be delighted."

Beebo nodded at the bartender, who nodded back and fixed her a whisky and water. Beebo was on good terms with the bartenders in all the gay bars. They knew what she drank and they served her without being told. Beebo leaned on the counter between Jack and Laura.

"Where've you been, doll?" Jack asked, waving a hand at her dress. "Masquerade ball?"

"Party," she said laconically, hoisting her newly arrived glass.

"Gay?"

"Straight."

"How dull. What's the matter with you, Beebo? You're no fun anymore. You wear skirts and go to straight parties. Jesus."

Beebo grinned at him. "I have one dress, lover. I get it out once a year and wear it. In honor of my father. He likes dames."

"Yeah, but he's not around to appreciate it."

"Well, you are, Jackson. Give me a kiss." And she took his chin in her hand and extracted one from his reluctant mouth.

"God!" he said, and made a face. Beebo laughed. And Laura sat and watched them and wondered what they were all doing there and why they laughed at themselves when they were all aching inside from unspeakable hurts. She felt vaguely jealous to think of Beebo at a party with people she didn't know and had never seen. Beebo surrounded by women. Laura looked at her until Beebo returned the stare without talking, only looking at Laura until Laura had to lower her eyes. "What's eating you, Bo-peep?" Beebo said, running a finger around the edge of her glass.

"Are pants really that important?" Laura said. She said it sarcastically because she was afraid of her tears.

Beebo laughed a little. "I don't know. How important is *that* important?"

"Why don't you get a decent job?"

"Oh," said Beebo as she understood. She finished a second drink. "I've got one, baby. I'm a lift jockey. Very elevating work."

"Not funny," Laura said. "You work all day at a lousy job like that, and then you drink all night."

"Does that bother you?"

"Yes. Not very much, of course. You're not worth it. But it seems awful. All for a pair of pants."

Beebo laughed. "Reform me, baby."

"I don't have time."

"What do you have time for?"

"Work."

"And Marcie?"

"And Marcie." Laura didn't know why she said it. She knew how badly it would hurt. But she was high, the go-to-hell feeling was still with her from the morning. It was either hurt or be hurt; sarcasm or tears. She looked up slowly at Beebo. At her blue eyes and her lips turned down, with an unaccustomed trace of lipstick on them. Laura wanted to hurt her. She couldn't stop herself. She turned on her stool to face her. "You're ridiculous," she said. "You're a little girl trying to be a little boy. And you run an elevator for the privilege. Grow up, Beebo. You'll never be a little boy. Or a big boy. You just haven't got what it takes. Not all the elevators in the world can make a boy of you. You can wear pants till you're blue in the face and it won't change what's underneath."

Beebo just stared at her, her face suddenly pale and frowning, in silence. Then she turned, leaving her cigarette still lighted in a tray on the bar, and left them without saying a word to either.

Laura and Jack sat in silence for a while after she had gone,watching her cigarette burn itself out. Finally Jack said, "If Terry had done that to me, Laura, I'd have strangled him."

Laura put her head down on the bar and cried.

The weekend was a stalemate for Laura and Marcie. Laura was so deeply involved in her conflicts that it was impossible to talk about them. In two weeks Jean would be back. In a day her father would be gone. Burr would start hounding Marcie, and Laura still didn't know why Marcie had let him think they were lovers. And Beebo...Beebo...that hurt the worst, somehow. It was so needless, so brutal. The kind of thing Merrill Landon had done to her when he was in a temper. Just to blow off steam, to dissipate the mood. Only he went even farther. He would shout and call her names, slap her, call down the wrath of his dead wife and son on her head.

Marcie couldn't get through to Laura, hard as she tried. She, too, began to get moody. She launched into long self-reproaching speeches which tortured Laura until she begged her to stop.

On Monday Laura went to the bank before she went to the office and withdrew one hundred and ninety-two dollars. She was going to leave herself twenty, just in case, but she left herself five instead. She had a little at home. She could get along until the end of the week. The rent wasn't due and there was food in the house.

Jack came by at five and picked it up. "Come out for dinner with me," he said. "I seem to have come into a little money."

"No, thanks."

"My treat," he said, directing his sarcasm at himself and waggling her dollars at her.

Laura smiled faintly. "Take it," she said. "I can't talk to anybody tonight."

"How's Marcie?"

"Brooding. I get on her nerves, I guess."

"That's only fair. She's made a mess of yours. How's Burr?"

"He called her. They talked for a few minutes. He asked her to see him."

"Will she?"

"No."

"Not yet, hm?"

"Never," Laura said sharply. "She's fed up with him."

"Well, if not Burr, somebody else." Laura covered her face with her hands suddenly and Jack looked at her sympathetically. "Just won't believe me, will you, Mother? You love Marcie so sooner or later Marcie will have to give in and love you."

"No!" she said, looking up. "I know it's not that simple. It's just that I'm convinced I have a chance. I live with her, I know her, and she was willing to have Burr believe we were lovers."

"She was willing to get him the hell out of her hair after a bad quarrel," he said. "That's all. She just let him believe it to get rid of him."

"Please Jack," she said with forced patience. "How's Terry?" *If he's going to torment me, I'll give him the same treatment,* she thought.

Jack lifted his eyebrows slightly and shrugged. "Healthy," he said. "And hungry. Jesus, how that kid eats. And he likes smoked oysters."

Laura had to smile, though she didn't feel like it. "Get him a bale of smoked oysters," she said, "and leave me alone for a while. Please."

Jack gave her shoulder a squeeze. "Okay." He started out and then turned to ask, "How did Sarah like Jensen?"

"She said she liked him. She has a crush on Dr. Hagstrom, but she liked Carl anyway."

"He's smitten. Says he's going to call her again."

"Good." They smiled a little at each other. "Somebody's doing it right," Laura said wistfully.

Jack laughed. "Never mind," he said. "Someday we'll die and go to heaven. All the angels are queer, you know." And he left.

Laura followed soon after. She knew just where she was going—the McAlton Hotel. She would walk right in and ask for Merrill Landon and the clerk would say he had left, the convention was over, and Laura could quit suffering over him. He would be hundreds of miles away and she could start to forget him.

She walked over to the hotel in a matter of minutes and went into the lobby with a confidence she had not felt during the week her father had been there. She was out to kill her ghost. She looked forward to great relief.

At the desk she waited for a moment or two until a clerk could take care of her. She recognized him from one of her previous visits but fortunately he didn't seem to remember her. "Yes?" he said.

"Is the Chi Delta Sigma convention over?" she asked.

"Yes, ma'am it is."

"Oh. Then I guess Merrill Landon isn't staying here anymore."

"Oh, yes he is."

Laura was startled. "He said a young lady might be asking for him," the clerk said. "He left a message." He looked at her dubiously, unnerved by the strange expression on her face. "Would you be his daughter, by any chance?"

Laura shook her head numbly. The clerk brought her an envelope and Laura opened it and read, in her father's hand: "Laura, I will be here till the end of the month. Come up to my room any evening after eight." It was not even signed. *Nice and sentimental,* she thought. *Just like him.*

"Thank you," she told the clerk.

"Will there be any answer?" he asked.

"Yes," Laura said. She took the pad of paper he pushed toward her and wrote on it, "Go to hell." Then she folded it, put it in the envelope, sealed it, and wrote "Merrill Landon" on the front.

She shook all the way home. He was still there, still haunting her, waiting to pounce on her and punish her. When Marcie asked her what was the matter, Laura couldn't tell her. It was Laura's problem, it was intimate and awful, and she had no wish to share it. She hardly noticed how little she had looked at Marcie the past few days, how little she had responded to her. And yet in the back of her mind the question rankled: Why did Marcie let Burr believe that lie? Even for a short while? Why hadn't she fought it harder?

But the fact of her father's physical presence in New York obliterated other considerations. He was waiting for her around every corner, in every doorway. She was even afraid to answer the phone, and afraid to return to his hotel for fear he would have the police there waiting for her. She didn't know on what grounds he could arrest her, but she believed her father could do anything violent and forceful. Her work suffered still more at the office. And she hadn't the interest to stay late and make it up.

Sarah talked to her one afternoon at the end of the week. "Guess what?" she said, to start out in a friendly vein.

"What?"

"Carl Jensen called me again. We're going out tomorrow night."

"How nice, Sarah. I'm glad for you." But she spoke without enthusiasm.

"Are you?" Sarah's voice was pointed enough to catch Laura's attention and warn her that something was wrong. She looked up. "Yes, of course I am, Sarah. I'm sorry, I'm not myself lately. I—"

"You've been in a fog all week. Another one of those headaches?"

"No. I mean yes. I don't know. I just don't feel alive." She laughed listlessly.

Sarah sat down beside her. "Laura," she said firmly, "you could do real well in this job. If you wanted to. Everybody here likes you. Everybody's pulling for you. You're a good typist and you're a smart girl. Jeanie liked you a lot, and she'll be back here in another week. There'll be three of us, and things could go a lot better...but Laura..."

"But I haven't worked out too well," Laura said for her. "Is that it?"

"You haven't worked at all sometimes. Other times you work your tail off. That's the trouble, Laura, you're so erratic," Sarah said. "You stay late and knock yourself out one night, and then a week goes by and you can't do a damn thing. You drag along all day, you just don't seem to care.

"I hate to pull a philosophical on you, but gee, Laura, we're dealing with sick people. Sometimes these X-ray reports spell life and death for somebody. We can't dawdle over them. Doctors are waiting all over the city for these things. Dr. Hollingsworth is swamped. We can't let him down."

"I know." Laura felt the way she had in third grade when she feigned sick to get out of playing a role in the annual spring pageant. The teacher had talked to her in much the same tone of voice, and used much the same arguments. "Everybody's pulling for you, we all like you, don't let us down, Laura, don't let us down." But the thought of going out on that stage had appalled her. The whole audience melted down to one man—Merrill Landon. She had done it, finally, to prove she could. But his amused criticisms afterward had nearly killed her.

"I haven't been feeling well," she murmured to Sarah.

"Well, you'd better start feeling better, honey. Because Dr. Hollingsworth and I had a little talk today. He asked me what was wrong with you. He thought maybe if you and I talked it over you might tell me what was the matter." She spoke carefully, in a discreet voice.

But Laura stood up, offended and frightened. "Nothing's the matter," she snapped. "If he doesn't like my work let him come to me and tell me about it himself."

Sarah stood up, herself slightly offended at this display of ingratitude. "He came to me because he wanted to spare you any embarrassment, Laura. I should think that would be obvious."

Laura relented a little. "I'm sorry, Sarah. I can't explain it. I just can't, it's impossible. If he wants to let me go, I have no choice. I'll leave." But she was not as resigned to it, as stoical, as she sounded.

"Can't you *try* to do a little better, Laura?" Sarah said kindly. "If I could tell him we had a little talk and you promised to try to do better. Or you'd been sick, or had a problem at home, or something. *Anything.*"

Laura gave an unpleasant little laugh. Then her face dropped and she said, "I have no excuses, Sarah. I'm not a good enough liar to cook one up. I just—" And here she burst unexpectedly into tears and Sarah had to try to comfort her.

"Look, honey," she said, after Laura had recovered a little. "Do you want the job? Do you?"

"Yes," Laura said. "I want it."

"Will you try to be more consistent, then? And I'll tell Dr. Hollingsworth you've been having trouble at home you don't want to talk about."

"That's such an obvious fib, Sarah."

"No, it's no fib. I heard you talk to Jack on the phone last week," Sarah said. "I know there's something going on."

Laura went shaky and pale, and the blue shadows that had been growing in the past weeks under her eyes deepened. "What do you know?" she demanded.

Sarah became alarmed at her appearance. "Well, nothing really, only you sounded so upset, I thought maybe—"

"What did I say?"

"Oh, I don't remember." She tried to push it off casually, but she had thoroughly scared Laura, who recalled with biting clarity now Jack's voice saying, *For God's sake, Mother, keep your voice down.* "What did I say, Sarah?"

"Nothing so very bad, Laura." Sarah stared at her. "I just got the impression you had a quarrel."

"You had no right to listen!" Laura exclaimed harshly.

"You had no right to make personal calls during working hours, for that matter," Sarah said defensively.

Laura picked up her purse and ran out of the office without another word. She went into a phone booth and called Jack. "Can I come over?" she said.

"No. I'm in a mess."

"Please, Jack."

"Mother, for Christ's sake! Be empathic for once, will you?"

"All right, I'll call Beebo."

"No don't. She's p.o.'d at you. She may never speak to you again after what you said to her."

Laura felt frantic. "Well, what am I supposed to do?" she said, half crying into the receiver. "I've practically lost my job."

Go home to Marcie, Mother. Do *something*. I can't help you out tonight. I'm sorry, honey." And he was.

"Oh, Jack, say something to me. Say something kind. Anything."

After a pause he said, "I love you, Mother. Only I'm not *in* love with you. I wish to hell I was, it couldn't be worse than Terry. Now be a doll and let me go. I'll call you tomorrow."

She felt the urgency to get away in his voice and let him go. For a moment she sat in the booth and dried her tears. She felt sick about Beebo but she was afraid to call her.

It was another torturous weekend for Marcie, who was beginning to feel as if she had ruined Laura's life. It was Sunday night before they actually made any sort of communication with each other.

Burr had been calling Marcie every night, trying to talk her into leaving the apartment. Their talks were short but the animosity had faded from them. Laura listened to them listlessly; she could not avoid hearing them in the small apartment. Marcie said things like, "Yes, she's here." "No, you *know* I don't want to see you." "No, we aren't, and don't bring that up again." "I know I did. I know what I did, Burr, don't throw it in my face." She refused to see him.

Laura winced at all this, and finally she took to going out on the roof when he called. The windows were wide open, the weather being soft and pleasant now, and Marcie's voice carried even out there. But it wasn't so pervading, so persistent. On Sunday night, Laura went out and looked at the city while Marcie talked. The time passed almost without Laura's being aware of it. She gazed across New York in the direction of the McAlton, wondering if her father was sitting in his room waiting for her. And then she looked down toward the Village and her heart gave a sick squeeze at the thought of Beebo. Beebo, who told her how terribly a love affair could hurt. Beebo, who told her to beware and then got caught in her own trap. Laura wondered if Beebo really loved her. If she could ever forgive her. Laura had attacked the very basis of her being: her body, her pride, her deepest needs. In that one quick wicked speech, Laura had ridiculed her. She felt the tears come. And she could hear Jack saying, "If Terry said that to me, I'd strangle him." It was shameful.

She grew very depressed, thinking of the necessity of going back to work in the office the next morning, with Sarah trying to put on cheerfulness and Dr. Hollingsworth—so kindly, so tolerant—watching for signs of steadiness and application in her. And herself, so heavily aware of their good will toward her, their frustration, and her own overwhelming complexities that sapped her strength and effort.

She was startled when Marcie said at her elbow, "Burr wants to see me." When Laura didn't answer, Marcie said, "He feels Godawful about the whole thing. He wants to apologize to me." Another silence. "I want to apologize to *you,* Laura. But you won't let me."

Laura shut her eyes in pain for a moment, as if to avoid the sight of Marcie's face. And then she opened them and without looking at her, said, "We've been all through this before, Marcie. I don't want your apologies. You have nothing to apologize for."

"I do."

"You don't!"

Marcie gave a long sigh of exasperation. "All right, then why won't you speak to me?"

"I *will,* Marcie. When I can."

"When will that be?"

"I don't know."

"Why not now?"

"I guess I'm sick. Maybe Jack was right, I need to see his analyst." She tried to smile a little.

"Because of your father? What he did to you?"

Laura looked down at her arms, folded on the cement railing. "I guess so," she almost whispered.

"Laura, say something to me. This is unbearable." Marcie was pleading with her, as Laura had pleaded herself with Jack on the phone. She turned and looked at Marcie, standing close beside her, two delicate lines between her eyes betraying the tension inside her. For a moment Laura just looked at her. It had been over a week since she looked at Marcie that way. In the soft spring night, in the golden light fading up from the streets below, with the myriad muffled noises that are the music of a great city around them, they gazed at each other. And Marcie was very beautiful with her hair lifted gently in the breeze and her eyes big with anxiety. She was wrapped in a blue silk negligee and the lines of her slim young body showed through it.

Finally, prompted by the necessity to speak, Laura said, "It's so hard to talk, Marcie. Words are so inadequate sometimes."

"Any words will do, Laura. Except 'Excuse me.' That's all you've said to me for days on end."

They smiled a little at each other, and Laura took her hands. She pulled just a little on them, and Marcie responded softly, coming toward her. "Laura, tell me I'm forgiven. Don't say there's nothing to forgive me for. I just want to hear you say it."

"No."

"Please." Her voice broke.

"No, no, no," Laura said, gazing curiously at Marcie. Did she really feel so guilty? She hadn't done anything that bad. Laura had a strange feeling of finality, of the end of things, of everything ending at once so that nothing really mattered anymore. As if Marcie would turn and walk out of her life, and her job would end, and Beebo would never see her, and Jack and Terry would break up. It made her pensive and sad. She wondered at all the new feelings in her: the inability to care about her job, her meanness with Beebo, her unreasoning fear of Merrill Landon in the hotel lobby. Nothing seemed very real, up there on the roof. It didn't seem to make much difference what she did. She gave another little pull and Marcie came still closer, touching her up and down the length of her body.

Laura touched her hair. "You look so much like a friend of mine," she said. Marcie reminded her of Beth again at this moment; the Beth she had lost so long ago, a million years ago, it seemed.

"I do? You never told me that."

"I forgot."

"What's she like?"

"Oh, she was tall, short dark hair, purple eyes. Rather boyish."

"You talk about her as if she were dead."

"She is. As far as I'm concerned."

Marcie frowned at her. "She doesn't sound at all like me."

"No, I guess she doesn't," Laura said. "There's something about your face; I don't know how to define it. I thought I saw a resemblance." She had seen it in Beebo, too. And even in the curly-headed little blonde who had approached her in The Cellar the night she was looking for Beebo. They couldn't all look like Beth. It was very strange.

"Were you good friends?" Marcie asked.

Laura smiled a little and put her arms around Marcie. In the still night she answered simply, "We were lovers." It was very quiet, dreamlike, as if she spoke in a trance.

Marcie stared at her, motionless, as if to determine whether she were joking. She stood in Laura's arms, unable to move one way or the other; uncertain and a little scared.

Laura saw her consternation, but it didn't worry her. She spoke again, still feeling as if it weren't real, any more than the glittering city below was real, or her father's wrath, or Jack, or Beebo, or the doctors and Sarah... "That was the 'great love' I told you about, in college," she said. "It was Beth."

After a long pause, Marcie said in a whisper, "What happened?"

"She got married," Laura said.

Marcie was dumbfounded. "I'm sorry," she said awkwardly and then retreated into herself, embarrassed. She had no idea what to say, what to do.

Laura could see that, but at first she didn't try to interpret it. It didn't frighten her yet. "That's why I was so shocked when Burr said you told him we were lovers," Laura said. "I wish we were, Marcie. But I never touched you." Marcie was studying her now, her eyes brimming. "When he accused me of it, and believed it and said you told him so, I was so hurt I didn't know what to do or say. I thought of a million crazy explanations. The only one that seemed to make sense was that you felt the way I do." She looked hard at Marcie. Their faces were very close together, and Laura was holding her tightly, her arms locked around Marcie's small waist. "Do you, Marcie?" Laura whispered. "Do you?"

They stayed that way for a while, not moving, looking at each other. Laura felt her breath speed up and she felt a powerful longing to kiss Marcie. It grew stronger by the second. She began to press Marcie against her rhythmically and suddenly all the months of repression exploded inside her and came out as kisses on her lips. She began to kiss Marcie intensely—her face, her neck and arms, her ears, her throat. "Marcie," she said hoarsely, suddenly holding her tight with the strength of desire. "I've wanted you for so long. I thought I'd die of it. Living with you, so close to you, seeing you all the time...undressing, bathing...It drove me

191

crazy. Marcie, you're so beautiful, so sweet. Oh, God, it feels so good to say it. You're impossible. I want you so terribly, so terribly. You want me too, don't you? I know it, I always knew it. Oh, Marcie, let me, let me. Don't stop me! Please!" A note of anguish crept into her voice when Marcie began to resist her. "Please, Marcie!" she implored her.

But Marcie put her arms up and pushed hard against Laura. "Let me go!" she said. "Let me go!" And she began to cry. Laura, shocked, released her so suddenly that Marcie staggered backwards a little. She gave a cry, recovered her balance, and stared at Laura with her eyes wide for a moment. Then she turned and ran inside.

Laura stood where she was for a long time, afraid to think or feel. She had no idea how much time had passed before she dared to go inside. Had she frightened Marcie? Revolted her? Would Marcie greet her with love or hatred? As a witch or a lover? She was in a state of nervous agony when she finally gathered the strength to walk around to the penthouse door.

She opened it and walked slowly through the living room and kitchen. She pushed the bedroom door open slowly. Marcie was sitting on her bed, her back toward Laura. She had apparently sat like that without moving for some time. She turned very slowly when she heard Laura come in, and looked up at her. Laura felt her heart turn over. Marcie was so lovely, so miserable. It showed plainly in her face. Laura went to her and dropped to her knees in front of her and put her head in Marcie's lap. And when she felt Marcie's hand stroking her head, she wept.

"Forgive me," she begged. "It's your turn now, Marcie. I frightened you. I didn't mean to, I didn't!"

And she caught Marcie's hand and kissed it.

"Laura," Marcie said quietly. "I've been trying to talk to you for weeks and you wouldn't let me. Now it's eating me up. I'm going to tell you something. And you're going to listen." Her voice trembled so that Laura looked up at her.

"Laura, I'm so ashamed, so ashamed."

"Tell me, Marcie. Tell me. I'm listening now." She searched her face anxiously.

Marcie swallowed her tears and with a tremendous effort, said, "I did an awful thing, Laur. I've known for a while about you." She looked away, struggling with herself; her shame, her pity, her shaking voice.

"You—you knew?" Laura whispered, going white.

"Yes. I couldn't help knowing. You couldn't hide it, Laura. You couldn't come near me without it showing—in your eyes, your face. The way you touched me, the things you said, all the crazy moods you had. You seemed afraid of me. You let things slip. You even kissed me once. I've been around enough to know. I knew about you." She wiped the tears from her cheeks embarrassedly and went on, unable to look at Laura, "I should have told you. Or else I should have let it drop. But I guess it interested me. It seemed like a game. I got sort of intrigued, you might say. I even told Burr what I suspected…months ago…" She stifled a sob.

Laura's face was colorless, tortured. Her hands were over her mouth.

"It kills me to say these things," Marcie whispered. I did everything to earn your contempt. I can't lie to you anymore, Laura. I even *bet* Burr I could make you make a pass at me."

"No," Laura gasped. "Oh, no—"

"He thought it was all a joke. He wouldn't even listen to me. Until I got fed up with him and started hanging around here so much. Then he got it into his head that we were having a hot and heavy affair. I couldn't talk him out of it. I'd gone too far for that."

Laura turned away from her and rested her head against her own bed, too stunned, too wounded, to answer or understand half of it.

"Laura." Marcie bent toward her. "I don't know what crazy imp gets hold of me sometimes. I swear I don't. I never even wondered what I'd do if it ever came to this, if you ever tried to make love to me. I guess I thought it would be a game, like everything else. I guess I thought it would be a lot of kicks. Or just a stupid silly thing that wouldn't really matter. To either of us. I guess I didn't think at all.

"And just now—on the roof—when you told me how you felt, and how you wanted me—Laura, I had no idea you could love like that. I didn't know it could be beautiful, or touching, or tragic. I thought it was mostly play-acting. I thought the only real love was between men and women. But you made it beautiful, Laura. I don't know what else to call it. I'm ashamed. Clear through my soul. I played you for a fool, and all the while you were an angel."

Laura began to sob.

"I'd do anything for you, Laur," Marcie whispered. "Anything to make it up. If I could love you the way you want me to, I'd do that. I'll even try, if you want it."

Laura slumped to the floor, her arms over her head, and sobbed helplessly.

Marcie knelt beside her, profoundly afraid and ashamed. "Laura," she said, "Do whatever you want with me. I've hurt you so terribly. Hurt me back if it'll help. Do something. Do anything. I can't stand to see you like this. Oh, Laura, Laura. Please don't cry like that. Please."

Chapter Fourteen

In the morning—the bleak morning that came in spite of every-thing and had to be faced—she could hardly look at Marcie. And Marcie, brimming with shame and pity, avoided her, breaking softly into tears from time to time.

At breakfast Marcie said, "Laur, if you think you can bear to live with me I don't want you to move out. Nothing was your fault, nothing."

"I couldn't stand it, Marcie," Laura said hoarsely without look-ing at her. "Neither could you." She got up abruptly and left the table without having eaten a thing.

Marcie got up and followed her. "I wish we could still be friends, Laur."

"We never were."

"Oh, but we were. I like you so much, Laura."

"Marcie, this is unbearable. Don't talk to me. Please don't."

"But I can't just leave things like this, it's too awful."

"I can't help it."

"Laura, I'll never get over this. I'll never forgive myself. I hurt you so."

"Marcie, stop it!" She almost screamed at her. "I was a fool, a blind fool. I wouldn't listen." She was thinking of all the warnings from Jack and Beebo that she willfully ignored. But she caught herself and spared Jack another betrayal. That, at least, was some-thing Marcie didn't know and never would. "Never mind," she finished. "Just drop it." She turned away and busied herself, but Marcie wouldn't let her go.

"You will come back tonight, won't you, Laura? You'll stay here until you find another place? I'll be sick if you don't. This is your apartment as much as it is mine. I'll move out if you'd rather. You know that, don't you, Laur?" She was so anxious, so eager for conciliation, so disgusted with what she had done, that Laura felt a momentary relenting and looked shyly at her. "Please come back tonight," Marcie whispered. "I'll worry myself sick if you don't. Please. Promise?"

Laura shut her eyes for a moment and tried to control her voice. She hadn't the courage to argue. She just said, "Yes," and grabbed her purse and rushed out.

Laura knew, even before she reached the subway, that she wasn't going to work that day. She knew it would be impossible for her to read, to type, to look up words, to answer the doctors, to joke with Sarah. It would be a nightmare of hypocrisy, utterly beyond her strength.

She felt shattered, ready to scream if anyone touched her, like someone with an open wound. But she held herself tightly in check. She rode aimlessly on the subway for an hour or two. She stood in bookshops with a volume in her hands and stared at the pages until the clerks, in turn, stared at her. She sat on benches in Central Park. She stopped now and then to get a cup of coffee, and late in the day, a sandwich. It enabled her to keep walking. She walked, looking at nothing but the pavement ahead of her, for a couple of hours. She paid no attention to where she was going or why. She walked to exhaust herself, to reach that country of fatigue where even the mind cannot operate and the emotions are dead.

Abruptly she found herself standing outside the McAlton in the last hour of daylight. She was not strong enough to feel surprise. On the contrary, it was as if she had been working toward it, all through that empty endless day, knowing she would end up here. And knowing, she had not needed to think of it, to make a decision. It was unavoidable.

She stood outside the main door to the lobby, looking at the people hurrying past and hoping somebody would come up to her, talk to her, even make advances to her. Anything to postpone what she knew was coming. She looked at the door and away again, and then back to it, as if it were a great sinister magnet. Sooner or later she knew she would walk through it.

She stood leaning against the gray stone of the McAlton, her fine face pale and vacant, her body apparently relaxed. She looked like a tired young career girl, waiting at the appointed place for a date. She knew it and took advantage of it. The hotel doorman strolled to her and said, "Lovely evening, isn't it?" And later, "Looks like he's a bit late, Miss." With a little smile.

Laura returned the smile faintly. She tried to engage him in conversation, but he was called away frequently, and finally, with the evening crowd converging on him, got too busy to talk to her at all. The night was violet now, turning fast to black. It was eight o'clock.

Laura turned to the door and walked through it almost automatically. Once inside she was suddenly profoundly afraid. Flashes of fear went through her; long sweeps of tremors and gooseflesh. She didn't bother with the desk this time. She knew what floor he was on. She got the elevator and said, "Fourteenth floor, please." She wondered if her voice sounded as shaky as it felt in her throat. She thought of simply getting off the elevator on the fourteenth floor and taking another elevator right back down. And when she was let off, she stood there in the deep carpeted hall with her heart crying "No-no, no-no, no-no," at every beat.

"He's my father," she told herself. "He won't kill me, after all. He might beat me, but he's done that before and I've lived through it. I'll be twenty-one in three weeks, so he can't say I'm a minor. All he can do is make a speech about my ungratefulness. He's a human being, not the devil." She said the last aloud, in a whisper, and her own voice startled her.

Cautiously, Laura investigated room numbers, half expecting him to burst from his room and discover her unprepared. After a few false starts she found 1402 and standing there, looking at that door, she felt an enormous need to cry. She shut her eyes hard and said softly, "I won't, I won't." Then she opened them, and, with her heart in her mouth, she rapped on the door.

The noise sounded huge. For a moment she wanted to run. But she didn't. *He mustn't see me looking panicky*, she thought. She listened. There was no sound audible. *Maybe he's not in. Oh, dear God, maybe he left.* She didn't know whether to exult or despair. *If I don't face him now, I'll never be able to face myself*, she thought. *I'll never stand alone. I've got to tell him everything.* She felt desperate at the thought of having to go and search him out, to win her freedom from him. The hope that she had missed him, that he had already left for Chicago, was too sweet to banish.

She was ready to flee when the door swung open, without any preliminary sounds to warn her. She blanched uncontrollably and found herself looking at her father's feet. Very slowly, she looked up the rest of him to his face. There was a slight frown on his heavy features but he wasn't at all surprised. He let her stand there until she was miserably uncomfortable, and then—only then—he spoke.

"Come in," he said. Not "Hello, Laura." He spoke as if she might have been the maid come to clean his room. He stepped aside slightly to permit her to walk past him. She clutched herself in her arms, fearful of touching him as she brushed past, and walked quickly across the room to a half open window on the opposite side. She looked resolutely out at the city, afraid to let him see her face.

The minute I look at him, I'll cry. I'll do some damn silly weak thing, and he'll lord it over me, and I'll wind up promising to go home to Chicago with him. I can't look at him. Not yet.

She listened to him moving around the room behind her and felt his eyes on her. But he said nothing. After a few moments, Laura could stand it no longer. She knew he was laughing at her. Not with his voice or his lips, but silently, inside. She turned and looked for him. He was standing across the room, his enormous back planted against the wall, his arms folded over his chest, studying her. She flinched a little, seeing his face.

"I never knew before," he said slowly, savoring it, "how fast you could run." He gave her a slight sardonic smile.

Laura felt her insides turn to water. Her face was white and set as plaster. She forced herself to return his gaze.

"I never knew you could swear, either," he said. "Especially at me. As a matter of fact, I doubt whether you can, now that we're face to face."

It was a dare. Laura, stung, felt a flush of resistance come up in her. "If I do," she said, "you'll beat me. That's your answer to everything."

"It always worked before," he said, mocking her.

"It worked so well that it drove me out of your house forever. It made me hate you, Father."

"You don't need to spell it for me, Laura. I get the idea."

She hated his sarcasm! Her hatred flowed in her now and revived her spirit. "Is that what you wanted? To make me hate you?" she asked. "Because you've done a fine job. A masterful job."

"Thanks. I'm glad we agree on one thing anyway." He stood immovable, still smiling slightly.

He wants to drive me frantic. He wants me to end up on my knees, incoherent. Kissing his feet. God damn him! He doesn't care what he says as long as it'll drive me wild.

"I must say, you took a prosaic way out, Laura. Running away is no way to solve a problem. Running away to New York is the classic cliché. There are a lot of you here in New York, you know. Silly little girls who left one set of problems at home for another set in the big city."

Laura turned her back on him. *I won't even answer him. If I could just hurt him somehow. Hurt him like he hurts me. What would hurt him the worst? Mother. My Mother.*

"Did you slap my mother around the way you do me?" she asked him abruptly.

At this his smile faded and his face grew very hard. "Your mother never deserved it," he said.

"Neither did I," she retorted. "As far as I can see."

"You are notoriously shortsighted, my darling daughter."

"And you, Father, are blind." Her face flushed.

Again he smiled, but his smile frightened her. "What have you been doing, Laura, that gives you such intestinal fortitude in the face of such obvious physical risk?"

She wanted to scream at him, "I hate you! I hate your God-damn sophisticated sarcasm!" But she only said tersely, "I have a job. I have some nice friends. I have money in the bank. I have a life of my own without you. I have a little confidence I never had before." They were all lies, that started out so beautifully true. Almost all lies, anyway. But she had flung them in his face, and now he was not sure. He studied her. "Those are the problems I came to face in New York, Father. Nothing could ever persuade me to trade them for the ones at home." *If I didn't hate him so much I couldn't do it. He started out wrong, trying to drive me in a corner. He gave me a chance without realizing it.*

He moved away from the wall then, his face registering contemptuous amusement. He lighted a cigarette, and, to her astonishment, offered her one. She shook her head. "Well," he observed. "You apparently haven't taken up all the vices yet." He turned away from her and walked about the room, firing questions at her. "What kind of job do you have?"

"Medical secretary."

"Where?"

"With Dr. Edgar Hollingsworth."

"Who's he?"

"The top radiologist in the city."

"Where's his office?"

"Fifth and fifty-third."

"Who are the friends?"

This abrupt switch threw her for a moment. "The friends?"

"You said you had some."

"Oh," she said quickly. "Do you want their names?" The little sarcasms she mustered added to her bravery.

He curled his mouth disgustedly. "Anything that will help," he said. "Names mean nothing. Who are they?"

"Well," she said, "some are men and some are women." For a triumphant moment she felt like laughing in his face. But his face had grown dark, and a flash of fear prevented her. "My roommate," she went on, more timidly. "For one. She's a very nice girl. I've met a lot of wonderful people through her. The doctors have been wonderful to me."

"Everybody's 'wonderful,'" he mimicked.

"I was surprised to find that people can be nice, Father."

"God! If a man accused me of being 'nice' I'd spit in his face."

"And decent and human!" she said hotly.

His face grew dangerous now and his body tense. "Are you implying that I'm not human?"

Her fear grew suddenly quite strong and for a moment she wavered. Then she said softly, "If you're going to beat me, Father, do it now and let's get it over with."

He laughed; an awful laugh she remembered very well. It was usually the prelude to violence. "Well, isn't that noble," he said. "Why don't you pull down your pants and bend over? Make it easy for me?"

"You've beaten me all my life, whenever I displeased you. And I seem to displease you just by existing. I've never seen you beat anyone your own size, Father, but you're awfully damn good at beating *me*."

"My, aren't we grown up!" he said. "We not only talk back to our Father now, we swear at him. That's real sophistication."

"You don't know how much I hate you, Father! You can't know! I've begun to think that's what you want. You've worked hard enough all my life to make me hate you."

His face changed again, became grave and heavy. Her eyes watched him intently, like eyes that have witnessed floods scan the skies for sun. He turned away from her, dragging on his cigarette, knocking ashes into a heavy glass tray on the dresser. "Why do you hate me, Laura?" he asked dispassionately. "Because I discipline you now and then? Isn't that a father's prerogative?"

"Not when it ruins his child's life."

"Is your life ruined?" he said sharply. "You have a 'wonderful' job, 'wonderful' friends. Wonderful money in the bank, wonderful everything. Hell, I seem to have done you a favor."

"A favor! You call it a favor!" She stared at him, his hardness still astonishing her after all these years. And then she felt her resistance begin to wilt. Sooner or later all her arguments were doomed. She never won with him. The sheer physical fact of him, massive and dominant, exhausted her after a while. "I—I never wanted to hate you, Father. You were all I had. I wanted to love you. But you wouldn't let me," she almost whispered. *I mustn't go on like this. I'll cry,* she thought desperately. "I hate you because you hate me!" she flung at him.

He looked at her for some time before he answered quietly, "What makes you think I hate you, Laura?"

She was so taken aback by this that she could only stammer at him. "I don't know, but you know you do."

"Oh, come now. I haven't been *that* harsh with you."

It's a trap! A trap! He wants to soften me up. He wants to see me whimpering. Oh, God, if only I could stop him, freeze him up, like other men. "You've been brutal," she said harshly and the sobs were crowding close in her throat. "You've treated me like a slave. Worse! You've beaten me sometimes for nothing. Just for the exercise."

"I never once beat you without a reason," he said.

"You lie!" And her voice was a furious hiss.

He glared at her. "I'm not in the habit of lying to you, Laura. Your life has been more than beatings. I sent you to the best schools. I let you go to the college of your choice. I let you join a sorority and paid all your bills. And when you came home and quit like a damn coward—without so much as an explanation, I didn't force you to go back. I found you a good job with excellent training and a big future. I've given you a good comfortable home, a lot of clothes, travel." His voice was low, controlled, but it was the calm before the storm and he was tense.

"I would have traded them all for love." Her voice broke and she turned suddenly away, afraid to shame herself with tears in front of him.

"Let's not get maudlin," he said sardonically, and once again smothered the spark of tenderness that had waited so many years in Laura for expression.

"All right," she said sharply. "Let's not be maudlin. I have a good job here and I'm not going to leave New York. That's what I came to tell you. Now maybe I'd better go." She turned and walked resolutely toward the door, but she should have known it wouldn't be that easy. He merely placed himself between the door and Laura and she stopped, afraid to go near him. He smiled slightly at this evidence of his power over her.

"Before you leave," he said, "suppose you explain the filial affection that made you write me to go to hell, in your little billet-doux last week?"

"Why did you say you had no daughter?" she flared.

"To teach you a lesson."

"Are there any lessons left for you to teach me?" she said.

"Quite a few, my dear. You don't know it all yet, even if you are almost twenty-one."

"It almost killed me, Father," she said, the anguish showing. "You don't know how terribly I—" But she stopped herself, ashamed. He didn't know, and she didn't want him to know. She was the one who cared about their relationship, who wanted love and trust and gentleness between them. Not her father. He didn't give a damn, as long as she minded him. "You said you had no daughter," she repeated bitterly.

"You wanted it that way, Laura."

She turned to stare at him, incredulous. "I?" She said. "*I* wanted it that way?"

"You denied my existence before I ever denied yours," he said. "You ran away from me."

"You *forced* me to."

"I did no such thing."

"You made life intolerable for me."

"I didn't mean to." It was an extraordinary admission, completely unexpected, and she looked at him speechless for a moment.

"Then why didn't you show me some kindness?" she said. "Just a very little would have gone a long way, Father."

He crushed out his cigarette in the heavy ashtray with an expression of contempt on his face. "You women are all alike, I swear to God," he said. "Give you a little and you demand a lot."

"What's wrong with a lot?" she said, trembling. "You're my father."

"Yes, exactly!" he said, so roughly that she ducked. "I'm your father!"

"Did you treat my mother this way?" she whispered. "Her life must have been hell."

He looked for a minute as if he would strangle her. She stood her ground, pale and frightened, until he relented suddenly and turned his profile to her, looking out the window. "Your mother," he said painfully, "was my wife. I adored her."

Laura was absolutely unable to answer him. She sat down weakly in the stuffed chair by the dresser and put her face in her hands. Her father—her enormous gruff harsh father—had never spoken such a tender word in her presence in her life.

"I could never marry again, when she died," he said. Laura felt frightened as she always did when her mother's death was mentioned. She expected him to turn on her unreasonably as he had so often before. "I never struck her."

"Then why me?" she implored out of a dry throat.

He turned and looked at her, his mouth twisted a little, running a distraught hand through his hair. "You needed it," was all he would say.

"What for?"

"You *needed* it, that's what for!" And she was afraid to push him further. After some minutes he said, "Laura, you're coming back to Chicago with me."

"No Father, I can't. I won't."

"That's why I waited for you," he went on, as if she had said nothing.

"I won't go to Chicago or anywhere else with you. I'm through with you."

"You could look for work with a radiologist, if you like it so well. I won't insist on journalism. You have a flair for it, it's a waste to leave the field, but I won't insist. You see, Laura, I can be human enough."

She stared at him. She had never heard him talk like this. He glanced at her, annoyed by the look on her face. "I've made reservations," he said, "for June first. That's Saturday. I could probably get earlier ones."

"Father." She stood up. "I can't come with you."

"Don't say that!" he commanded her, so sharply that she started.

"I can't," she whispered.

"You can, and you will. That's all I want to hear on the subject." As she started once again to protest he held his hands up for silence. "No more discipline, Laura. I promise you that. I was a fool. You were too, but never mind that now. I was too hard on you, it's true. I see that. Well, you're more or less grown up by this time. I guess we can dispense with spanking."

"Spanking! It was more than that and you know it!"

"Don't argue with me, Laura." He turned on her, his voice low and fierce. Then, making a visible effort to calm himself, he said, "Get your things together and I'll see about the reservations."

"No."

"Don't fight me, Laura."

"Father, there's something you don't know about me." *I have to tell him. I'll never be free from him till I tell him. Till he knows what he's made of his only child.* "There's something you don't know about me," she whispered.

"I don't doubt it. Now hurry up, we've wasted enough time."

"Father...listen to me." It was almost too hard to say. Her legs were trembling and her heart was wild.

"Well, out with it, for God's sake! Jesus, Laura, you go through more agony...Well? What is it?" He frowned at her tense face.

"I—I'm a—homosexual."

His mouth dropped open and his whole body went rigid. Laura shut her eyes and prayed. She held her lower lip in her teeth, ready for the blow, and felt the humiliating tears begin to squeeze through her shut lids. She moaned a little.

He made up his mind fast and his voice cracked out like a lash. "Nonsense!" he snarled.

"It's true!" Her eyes flew open and she cried again, passionately, "It's true!" It was her bid for freedom; she had to show this courage, this awful truth to him, or she would never walk away from him. She would spend all her life in a panic of fear lest he find her out. "I'm in love with my roommate. I've made love—"

"All right, all right, all right!" he shouted. His voice was rough and his face contorted. He turned away from her and put his hands over his face. She watched him, every muscle tight and aching.

At last he let his hands drop and said quietly, "Did I do that to you, Laura?"

Without hesitating, without even certain knowledge, but only the huge need to hurt him, she said, "Yes."

He turned slowly around and faced her and she had never seen his face like that before. It was pained and full of gentleness. Perhaps it looked that way to her mother now and then. "I did that to you," he said again, to himself. "Oh, Laura. Oh, Laura." His heavy brow creased deeply over his eyes. He walked to her and put his hands on her shoulders and felt her jerk with fear. "Laura," he said, "have you ever loved a man?"

She shook her head, unable to speak.

"Have you ever wanted a man?"

Again she shook her head.

"Do you know what it's like to want a man?"

"No," she whispered.

"Do you want to know?" His eyes were wide and intense, his grip on her shoulders was very hard.

"I'm so afraid of them, Father. I don't want to know."

He seemed to be in another world. Laura was utterly mystified by his strange behavior, blindly grateful for his sudden warmth, and she let herself weep softly.

"Laura," he said, as if he derived some private pleasure from saying her name over and over. "Your mother—you look so much like your mother. You never looked like me at all. Every time I look at you I see her face. Her fragile delicate face. Her eyes, her hair." He put his arms around her. "Come back to Chicago with me," he said gently. "You don't have to love a man, Laura. I don't want you to. I don't want you to be like other girls, I don't want you to go off with some young ass and give him your youth and your beauty. I don't mind if you're different from the rest. I can take that if you are able to."

Laura clung to him, astonished, fearful, grateful, anxious, a whirlwind of confused feelings churning inside her.

"I want you to stay with me," he said. "I always did. I won't let you go."

"You made me go, Father. You punished me so."

"No, no Laura! Don't you see, it was myself." He was holding her so hard now, as if to make up for years of avoiding her, that she ached with it. She began to cry on his shoulder.

"Oh, Father, Father," she wept. "You never told me you wanted me to stay with you. You made me believe you hated me."

"No," he said. "I never hated you." He spoke in a rush, as if he couldn't help himself, as if it were suddenly forcing its way out of him after years of suppression. "Never, Laura, it was just that I was so lonely, so terribly lonely; I wanted her so much and she was gone. And there was only you, and you tormented me."

"I?" She tried to see his face, but he held her too close.

"You were so much like her, even when you were a child. Every time I looked at you, I—oh, Laura, it's myself I should have punished all this time. I *was* punished. I've suffered. Believe me. Laura, please believe me."

Laura was suddenly shocked rigid to feel his lips on her neck. He put his hand in her hair and jerked her head back and kissed her full on the mouth with such agonized intensity that he electrified her. He released her just as suddenly and turned away with a kind of sob. "Ellie! Ellie!" he cried, his hands over his face.

Laura was shaking almost convulsively. At the sound of her mother's name she grabbed the thick and heavy glass ashtray from the dresser, picking it up with both hands. She rushed at him, unable to think or reason, and brought the ashtray down on the crown of his head with all the revolted force in her body. He slumped to the floor without a sound.

Laura gaped at him for a sick second and then she turned and fled. She left the door wide open and ran in a terrible panic to the elevators. She sobbed frantically for a few moments, and then she pushed the down button. She jabbed it over and over again hysterically, unable to stop until an elevator arrived and the doors opened. She stumbled in and pressed into a back corner, helpless in the grip of the sickness in her. The operator and his two other passengers stared at her, but she paid them no heed, even when one asked if he could help her. At the ground floor the operator had to tell her, "Everybody out."

She turned a wild flushed face to him and he said, "Are you all right, Miss?" And she glared at him, violently offended by his manner, his uniform, his question.

"Don't you know those pants won't make a man of you?" she exclaimed acidly. And rushed out, leaving him gaping open-mouthed after her.

Chapter Fifteen

Marcie called Jack late that night. "I haven't heard from her. I wouldn't bother you, but I don't know where she is, and I'm worried," she said. "Is she with you?"

"No. What's the matter, Marcie? It's only ten-fifteen."

"She said she'd be home tonight. She promised."

"Did you call the office?"

"Yes. She wasn't there today."

"Was she sick?"

"No." Marcie was almost physically sick with shame and the fear that Laura would do herself violence. She knew well how passionately Laura could respond, how intensely she could feel. She had been truly alarmed when she called the office in the afternoon and Sarah told her they hadn't seen Laura all day. And they'd damn well like to know where she was themselves.

"She left the house this morning to catch the subway to work. She said she'd be back tonight, but she didn't go to work. And she isn't back," Marcie told Jack.

Jack's first thought was Merrill Landon. "Out with it, Marcie. Tell Uncle Jack everything."

"Jack, I can't—" Jack of all people! Jack, who had a crush on Laura. Marcie would have slit her throat before she would have betrayed Laura to him. She was in no madcap mood any longer. She had wounded Laura with a callousness that shocked even herself when she thought back on it. She had no yen to hurt anymore.

"Come on, doll, we've known each other for years," Jack said. "Spill the beans."

"Jack, I won't hurt her. Not even—"

"Not even if she drops dead because you won't tell me the truth."

"Oh! But she won't!"

"Oh, but she might! Now let's have it."

"Jack, I don't want you to think—"

"I think all the time. It's a congenital defect."

"Yes, but this—"

"Oh, for Chrissake, Marcie. *Say* it. Did you quarrel?"

"I—yes. We quarreled."

"What about?"

"I can't say."

"Now you listen to me, God damn it, I'm getting worried."

"About love." She whispered it.

And Jack knew at once what was the matter. But why hadn't Laura come to him? Why hadn't she told him? She couldn't be that ashamed. She knew he wouldn't hurt her with the knowledge. He would be kind, with the kindness of deep sympathy. Something was wrong—more wrong than Marcie admitted, or more wrong than she knew. Or both.

"I can't explain, Jack," Marcie moaned.

"You don't have to, Marcie. I get the message."

"Should I call the police?"

"No," he said quickly. Jack had an inborn aversion to cops. "I think I have an idea. I'll call you back later. And call me the minute you hear anything."

"I will, I promise!"

Jack called Beebo. "Marcie's straight," he said.

"So what, Jackson?"

"So Laura just found out—the hard way, apparently—and now she's disappeared."

"I couldn't care less."

"I don't believe you."

"Look, Jack, I don't even want to talk about the kid. I don't want to hear her name mentioned. She can go to hell as far as I'm concerned."

"I've got to find her, Beebo, and you've got to help me."

"The hell I do."

"I want you to check the Lessie joints. They won't let me in. I busted the mirror in The Colophon last month and they all hate me."

"That's your problem."

"Beebo, for God's sake. I know how bitchy she was. I'm not asking you to forget it. I'm asking you to help me find her. I think she went to see her father. From what she's told me of him, she might be dead before we find her."

There was a shocked silence and finally Beebo said, "Don't play around with me, Jack. Tell me the truth."

"That *is* the truth. He's a real bastard. God knows what he might have done to her. He has the Devil's own temper and he's been beating hell out of her since she was five years old."

There was a reluctant pause at Beebo's end and finally she said, "All right, damn it. All right. I'll go look for her. If she's with her father I don't know what good it'll do to check the bars down here."

"You never know. Besides, there's not much time."

"Okay, Jack. I'll get going."

"Call me as soon as you get back. Whether you find her or not."

"Right. Where are you going?"

"The McAlton. To check with her old man."

"What about Terry? Can you trust him alone?" she asked with slight sarcasm.

"No," he said matter-of-factly, looking at Terry as he spoke, in a voice that betrayed none of his passion for the boy. "I'm counting on the smoked oysters to keep him out of trouble."

Terry grinned a little but his eyes didn't leave the television set.

Beebo laughed "Okay, doll, I'll help you out, but don't expect me to welcome Laura back and send her flowers. I'm through with that little bitch. If I find her I'll drag her home by the scruff of the neck and dump her."

"That's good enough, Beebo. Thanks."

Beebo scoured the Village. She knew it inside and out and backwards: all the gay bars, the favorite coffee shops, the side streets; the markets, the boutiques, the stalls and the brownstones, the parks, the alleys, the bookshops. Some were closed, some stayed open half the night. Wherever people collected down there, sooner or later Beebo investigated the spot.

The hours stretched out. Every hour or so she called Jack's apartment and talked to Terry. He simply said, "Jack's not back yet. He hasn't called in. Okay, I'll tell him." And as Beebo walked she began to feel a real fear for Laura's safety, a tender concern that welled up in her and aroused her own contempt. At three in the morning she muttered, "Oh, the hell with it. Nobody can cover the whole damn Village in one night." She called the penthouse.

Marcie, wide awake and alarmed, answered, hoping it would be Laura. She wasn't sure if she had a boy or a girl on the phone; she only knew it wasn't Laura.

"Marcie?" Beebo said.

"Yes. Who's this?"

"A friend of Laura's. Is she there?"

"No. Do you know where she is?"

"I wish I did.

"Who *is* this?"

"I'll call you back."

Marcie sat holding the receiver and staring perplexed at the phone some minutes after Beebo hung up.

Jack got back in the first light of dawn to find Terry asleep. He sat down without taking his jacket off, and called Beebo. No answer. Terry rolled over and looked at him. He was a medium-sized well-built boy, bright and handsome and easily bored, affectionate by nature, but spoiled, quick with his temper and quick with his generosity. He was not quite sure, being young and desirable, if he was in love with Jack. He liked being admired by a lot of people. But he was not the money grubber Jack had painted for Laura. He liked to be dominated and he was waiting for Jack to make a move in that direction.

"Where the hell have you been?" he asked Jack.

"Where's Beebo?"

"How should I know? You're the one who knows it all."

"Just this once, don't get smart with me, lover. I gotta find her." Jack was too worried to coddle him.

"She'll call back on the hour. She's been calling in every God damn hour since you went out. I can't get any sleep around here. Who's this Laura, anyway? She must be a living doll."

"I've told you a dozen times. She's a friend."

"You act like she was a lover."

Jack stared at his handsome arrogant young face. "So what?" he said. "You have your affairs. I have mine." And he turned around and walked into the bathroom and left Terry staring after him. Jack never talked that way to him, not even when he caught him *in flagrante delicto.* He never showed an erotic interest in girls, either.

The phone rang fifteen minutes later. It was Beebo.

Terry answered and handed Jack the phone, listening to the conversation with his eyes half open.

"Absolutely no soap," Beebo said. "I've been all over the damn Village. Nobody's seen her."

"She saw Landon earlier this evening," Jack said.

"She did? Does he know where she is?'

"He doesn't know from nothing, doll. She gave him a first class concussion. Walloped him with a glass ashtray. On the back of his head. Must have snuck up on him when he had his back turned."

"God!" Beebo exclaimed.

"And then took off, hysterical, according to the elevator boy. She screamed all kinds of stuff at him. He says. Half of it's crap, of course. But he did tell me one thing—"

"What's that?"

"She told him those pants he was wearing would never make a man of him."

After a surprised silence Beebo gave a wry tired little laugh. "Jesus," she said. "She must have been screwy."

"The elevator boy thought so. It sounds kind of bad. I'd better call Marcie."

"I called her at three."

"God, Beebo, don't make it any worse than it is!"

"Relax. I didn't leave my name. Just asked for Laura and Marcie said she wasn't there. Well, Jackson? Now what? We call the cops?"

"You want us all to get thrown in the jug? They'd love to run in a bunch of queers. No, let's wait a day. She's a sensible girl underneath it all. She'll come to her senses and I'm the first one she'll call." Terry, on the bed beside him, gave a contemptuous snort.

"I wish I felt so confident," Beebo said.

"Yeah," Jack said. "I do too," he admitted.

"Okay, boy, keep in touch."

Jack hung up and sat drooping on the bed, the fatigue showing in his face.

"God, you look old," Terry said with a characteristic lack of tact. "How old are you? You never told me."

"Eighty-two," Jack said.

Terry grinned. "I don't believe you."

"You're not supposed to."

"How old? Tell me."

Jack stood up and turned to face him, in no mood for jokes. "Terry, don't bug me. I've had enough of you today." Terry gaped at him. Jack had never talked harshly to him and now he was doing it every time he opened his mouth. "I love this girl," Jack told him. "I don't know why, but I do know that for once I've found a decent sweet kid who isn't out for every damn thing she can get from me. She can give a little, she doesn't have to take all the time."

"Oh, you love her!" Terry said sarcastically, propping himself up on his elbows. "That's swell. Just swell! Thanks for letting me in on it."

"And I'll probably love her long after you've climbed out of this bed for the last time, you little bastard. You and a dozen other guys. It's a kind of love you don't know much about, Terry." He was too tired, too worried, to take much heed of what he said or how. His resentment spilled out and it felt good to let go with it and he did.

Terry wasn't used to being disciplined. He had managed, in eighteen crafty years, to avoid it. So he was surprised at himself when he reacted to Jack's tongue lashing with a renewal of interest in him. He lay back on the bed and watched Jack strip to his underwear. Jack was not a beautiful man physically; tough and wiry, but not beautiful. Yet Terry watched him with enjoyment, wondering what to expect from him next.

Jack stretched out on the bed next to Terry. There was an hour or so when he could sleep before he had to get to the office. He turned his head a little and saw Terry watching him. "You still here?" he said. "I thought I told you to go."

"I think I'll stay," Terry said, smiling. "I'm a glutton for punishment." He was intrigued by this new side of Jack.

Jack turned over and looked at him, surprised. "You're a brat," he said finally. "A beautiful, unbearable, stuck-up, silly, irresistible brat."

Terry laughed. "That's why you love me, Superman," he said, poking Jack in the ribs.

"Who says I love you?" Jack said wearily and turned away from him.

"Jack, be nice to me."

"I'm worried sick and he wants me to be nice to him. Ha!" Jack told the walls.

"Damn it, I think you *do* love this girl."

"She bought your oysters, lover. You can spare her a little good will yourself."

Terry dropped back on his pillow in silent surprise. It was the first hint he had had of the state of Jack's finances.

Jack went to work. There was nothing to be accomplished sitting around the apartment quarreling with Terry. It wouldn't bring Laura back any sooner, and there was not much he could do to find her now. Except call in the police, and he gagged on that idea. He would wait at least until the next morning.

But at the end of the day things were getting black. Laura was still gone; Marcie was panicky and agitating for a call to the police; Beebo was glowering, furious at herself for caring what happened to Laura and yet calling anyway in spite of herself; and a thunderstorm was brewing.

They waited alone, Jack and Marcie and Beebo, in the gathering dark: each with his own peculiar fears and hopes. Jack drank. Marcie paced around the roof, praying God that Laura hadn't killed herself. Beebo came over after a while and talked to Jack.

They talked, they drank, the phone rang. Terry wandered around the apartment in a pet because nobody was paying any attention to *him*. In another part of town Burr cursed silently because Marcie would pay no attention to *him*. And still elsewhere Merrill Landon lay with an aching head and heart and peppered the detective agency he had hired with evil-tempered calls while they labored to locate his daughter.

Finally Terry exploded at Jack, "If you don't talk to me I'm going to get out of here!" He gave the nearest chair a petulant kick. "I don't have to hang around here till I drop dead from boredom."

"Go," said Jack. "You're driving me nuts anyway with that damn pacing the floor."

"I wish I *was* driving you nuts," Terry retorted. "I just seem to be in your way."

"You are, lover. Shut up and eat something. You'll feel better."

"I just ate!"

"Then just shut up."

"God! This place is a mausoleum. I've had enough!" He went to the bedroom and grabbed a sweater, but when he reached the front door he turned and found that Jack wasn't even looking at him. He was talking to Beebo. He was saying, "By God, it's worth a try. I'm going over there. Nothing could be worse than sitting here wondering if she's drowned in the damn river or swinging from a rope somewhere."

"Oh, for Chrissake, Jack!" Beebo snapped. "Have mercy. I'm not made of stone."

Jack got up and headed for the door. Terry stood uncertainly and watched him approach. "Make up your mind," Jack said to him. "In or out?" His anxiety over Laura made this attitude of impatience with Terry perfectly genuine. Yet Jack was not without a small sudden pleasure at Terry's reactions.

"How about you?" Terry said.

"Out."

"I'll go with you."

"I'll be back in an hour."

"I want to go with you."

Jack stared at him, again pleased and surprised. "You can't," was all he said, putting his cigarette in his mouth while he pulled his jacket on.

"Why the hell not?"

Jack took him by the shoulders. "Terry, you want to do something for me?"

Terry eyed him like a suspicious five-year-old. "I don't know. You're so bitchy tonight." He sighed. "All right, all right. What do I have to do?"

"Stay here. And if she shows up, hang on to her. I'll be back at—" He looked at his watch. "—at ten. No later."

Terry threw himself in an armchair with a huge sigh of disgust. "Oh, this Laura!" he groaned. "She must be the most fabulous female in the whole goddam world."

"She is," Beebo said briefly. She dinched her cigarette and walked out ahead of Jack. "I'll be at home, Terry," she called back. "If she shows up."

"Yeah, yeah, I know. I'll hogtie her and call all the newspapers. I'll notify the President. Christ!"

Jack and Beebo went down the stairs together and out into the lowering night. The first drops were coming down. "What'd you give him, Jackson?" Beebo smiled. "He's learning how to mind. He doesn't like it very much, but he's learning."

Jack shrugged. "He does like it, doll. That's the secret. He likes to be shoved around a little. I wish to hell I'd known before I bought all those stinking oysters."

Chapter Sixteen

It was five past ten and the rain was fairly heavy outside. Terry was curled up in the armchair watching television, eating peanuts and drinking a beer. He was irritated with Jack for being late. He tried to get interested in the film and sat for a quarter of an hour with his eyes on the set, wiggling restlessly, like a child in need of a comfort station. He jumped when a knock on the door disturbed him.

"Come in, you know it's not locked," he said without looking up. "Where the hell were you? At least I tell you where I'm going. Well talk, damn it." And he turned around to see a tall slim girl standing five feet from him, her long hair streaming wet and her clothes clinging to her body. He was conscious of nothing in her face but her eyes; huge, blue and heavy, dominating, agonized.

Terry stood up suddenly, stammering a little. "You must be Laura," he said finally. "I was beginning to think you weren't real." He took another look at her, pale as a wraith, her eyes the only warmth in the cold oval of her face. "Are you?" he asked. And then smiled a little sheepishly. "Well, don't just stand there. Come in and sit down."

She moved as if she were dreaming, one hand to her forehead, and he guided her to the sofa where she half sat and half collapsed, letting her head fall back against the cushions. She looked utterly exhausted.

Terry stood hovering uncertainly over her, staring at her. At last he said, "Jack says I've got to keep you here." She shut her eyes. "He's supposed to be home at ten. He should be right along. I'm Terry. Terry Fleming. Jack says he told you about me. He certainly talks a lot about you. He thinks the world of you." She gave no sign that she had heard or cared to hear.

At last in some consternation he said, "Would you like something to eat, Laura? You look like you could do with something." No answer. He went out to the kitchen and opened a can of soup. He fixed up the plate with crackers and cheese and, as a second thought, smoked oysters, and poured a glass of milk. Every two or three minutes he interrupted his task to go to the doorway and check on her. He thought she might vanish, like a ghost. But she didn't move. She looked dead. She scared him.

He put the food on a tray and brought it into the living room and sat down on the sofa next to her. He put the soup and milk on the coffee table in front of her and then he said, "Wake up. Wake up, Laura." She didn't stir. Terry put an oyster on a cracker. "Here," he said, shaking her a little. "Here, for God's sake, eat it. It's your oyster."

Laura stirred and opened her eyes, took one look at the smoked oyster, and turned away with a grimace. Terry was offended. "So what's wrong with smoked oysters?" he said. "Here. It's yours."

She looked at him then. Really saw him. And then sat up a little, rubbing her eyes. "Mine?" she repeated dimly.

"Jack says you bought 'em." Terry looked at her with bright eyes, curious now. "You might as well enjoy them."

Laura sighed and then saw the soup. Terry handed her a spoon and she ate it all without a pause or a word. It seemed to give her strength, to bring her back to life. "I haven't eaten," she apologized. "I can't remember…"

"Want some more?" he asked quickly.

"No. No thanks. Maybe later." She looked around the apartment, recognition and sense coming back to her face. "Where's Jack?" she said, and suddenly clutched Terry's sleeve. "Where's Jack?" She sounded frightened.

"He'll be back any minute," Terry said.

Laura stared at him then. "Oh, you're Terry," she said.

"You're Laura." He grinned. "I saw you first."

She blinked at him, unable to joke with him. Dead serious, she asked, "Did the oysters help?"

"Help?" he said. "Oh. You mean Jack and me."

"He says you love them."

Terry studied her, frowning over his smile, and then looked away in embarrassment. "Not the oysters so much," he said. "But *you* helped, in a roundabout way. By getting lost."

"I'm glad," she said, confused. "He loves you terribly." She seemed to have no sense that this might startle him or be the wrong thing to say. She hadn't the physical strength to censor herself. She spoke the necessary truths and no more. But Terry was strongly affected. He walked to the other side of the room and refused to look at her for a while, letting his feelings whirl around inside him. When he did look back, she was stretched out on the sofa, sleeping the sleep of complete exhaustion.

Laura woke up to find Jack sitting in the armchair sipping gingerly at a steaming cup of coffee. His eyes showed over the rim of the cup, heavy, anxious, and old. He lowered the cup when she wakened, putting it on the coffee table by the sofa and lighting a cigarette.

"It's a nice day," he said cautiously.

She sat up halfway. "What time is it?"

"Seven-thirty."

Laura dropped back and shut her eyes. She found a blanket over herself and her shoes were on the floor beside the sofa.

"Well," said Jack, "are you going to tell me where the hell you've been? Or am I going to ask?"

Laura turned her face suddenly to the back of the sofa and wept. "Oh, Jack," she moaned. "I killed him. I killed him. Oh, God help me." And she began to sob.

"Killed who?"

"My father."

"Your father," he said with friendly sharpness in his voice, "has a prize concussion. But he's very much alive."

She turned her head slowly to look at him, her eyes enormous and her heart stopped in her chest. "Alive?" Her voice was a startled whisper. She sat up suddenly and said it out loud. "Alive?" She grabbed Jack's arms with the strength of shock. "How do you know? How do you know? Tell me quickly."

"I will, give me half a chance." He pushed her back down and told her of his trip to the McAlton. "I just went up to the fourteenth floor," he said. "It was easy. There were a lot of people standing around outside his room and the elevator boy told me about it. Incidentally, you made a real friend. He thinks you're the original Goof Nut."

"But my father, Jack, my father?"

"There was a doctor with him. He's okay, Mother."

Laura half fainted and it was some minutes before Jack could bring her around. Terry sat on the floor by the sofa, watching her with interest while Jack propped her feet up on pillows. "That better?" he said.

"I hit him so hard," she murmured the moment she was able to talk. "I was sure I killed him. Maybe he died of the concussion." Her eyes went wide again with fear and she looked at Jack, but he shook his head with a little smile.

"No such luck," he said. "I talked to him last night."

She gasped. "What did you say? Is he all right? Did you tell him who you were?" The fears tumbled out of her.

"I called him on the house phone. Relax, Laura, you're among friends. I asked him if he knew where you were. He said no."

"What else?" Laura had clutched his arms with trembling hands.

"He was pretty curious about *me*, naturally. But I didn't give him my name and phone number. Now calm down, will you? You're giving me the screaming mimis."

"What did he say?" She was crying again. "What? Tell me!"

"He tried to get me to talk but I didn't tell him anything, except that I was your best friend. Finally he said he was afraid he had hurt you." Laura shut her eyes and covered her face with a groan. "He wanted a chance to explain. He said if I found you to tell him right away. He has an agency trying to track you down. He said to tell you he's sorry." Jack looked curiously at her.

"He's sorry," she repeated, staring. "He's sorry!"

"Did he hurt you, honey?" Jack said gently.

It was too enormous to describe, too torturous to explain; her own private agony. Not even Jack could share it with her. "Yes," she whispered. "He hurt me." She looked at Jack and he could see in her face how much more there was to it than the simple words told him.

Jack crushed out his cigarette angrily. "I wish I could break his head for him," he said.

"No, no," Laura said. "I thought I had killed him. I never meant to. I was sick. I've been so sick, Jack, you wouldn't believe—Oh, thank God he's alive. Thank God. I wanted to hurt him and I did. I never wanted anything more. Just a chance to get even with him."

"What the hell happened between you two?"

"I can't talk about it."

"You can to me."

"No. I can't. Not to anybody."

"Did he beat you?"

She shook her head. "Don't ask me, Jack," she said. "It's my own personal sickness. And his. It's between us, and nobody else."

Jack lighted a cigarette, watching her closely through the blue smoke. "Why did you go to him in the first place? Didn't you know it would be bad?"

"I had to," she said, her face drawn and intense. "I've been running away from him all my life. I had to quit running and save myself. I had to tell him face to face what I am."

Jack's brows drew together heavily. "You told him you were gay?" he asked.

"Yes. I told him."

"What did he do?"

She turned her deep eyes, accentuated by the thinness of her face, to Jack. "He hurt me, Jack. And I hurt him. But it's all over. Oh, my God, I'm so grateful I didn't kill him. Have you ever thought you killed somebody, and tried to go on living with it? It eats you up, it corrodes your brain and your body, it makes you sick, oh, so horribly sick Oh, Jack..." And he put his arms around her while she wept and Terry watched them in silence.

"That bastard," Jack murmured, comforting her. "That damn bastard. I think I hate him as much as you do, honey."

"No, no, I don't hate him," she whispered. "I can't anymore. I never will again. I understand now, so much. Nothing ever made sense before, but now I understand. He was weaker than I was, Jack." She spoke with wonderment. "He was more afraid of me than I was of him." It was a strange new feeling this knowledge gave her. "I don't know quite how I feel about him now. I won't know for a long time, I guess. But I still love him. I always loved him, even when I hated him the most. I only hope we never meet again. I can stand it if I never have to see him again."

Terry fixed her a breakfast, and she ate ravenously. She discovered they had stripped her wet clothes off and put a robe on her the night before while she slept. She pulled the robe close around her while Jack tried to make her tell him where she had been, but he got little satisfaction.

"I don't know," was all she would say, and when he protested, skeptically, she turned to him, her face earnest, and said, "I don't know."

"Ahhh, don't tell *me*," he said.

"I just walked, I guess. It all seems like a nightmare. The first thing I remember after I left Father is eating a bowl of soup. And then I fell asleep."

"Don't you remember me?" Terry said. "We had a nice little talk last night."

"We did?" She was surprised.

"Sure." He smiled, and made her blush with embarrassment. "I'll tell you all about it sometime." He grinned at Jack, who gave him a quizzical smile.

"So you don't know where you were?" he prodded Laura.

"I swear, Jack."

"Well, we didn't know either," he said. "And we damn near lost our minds. We pictured you—well, never mind what we pictured. You had us frantic, I can tell you."

Laura smiled at him a little. "Jack," she said, and put a hand on his arm. "You've been so good to me. I wouldn't have caused you any worry, only—only—oh, my God. Marcie! I forgot about Marcie. And Beebo." She turned to him, but he calmed her with a glance, holding her down in her chair.

"I called them," he said. "I called everybody. Even Papa Landon. I told them you were all right, and that's all. Your father doesn't know where you are."

Laura hung her head. "Jack, I didn't have a chance to tell you about Marcie."

"I know. You don't have to tell me. Marcie did."

"Marcie did?" She looked up amazed.

"Not in so many words, Mother. She just said you quarreled, and I got the idea. She sounds pretty unhappy about things."

Laura covered her face, her elbows resting on the table. "She knew, Jack. She knew all along that I was gay," she whispered brokenly. "She and Burr had a bet that she could make me make a pass at her."

After a long silence Jack squeezed her arm and said gently, "You had to learn. Now you know. We all go through it sooner or later." He looked up at Terry and found the boy staring at him, his eyes full. He looked away, confused, turning his attention back to Laura. "She wants to see you. She means it."

"I know. But I couldn't stand to see her. Even to talk to her. It would be hell."

"I know what you mean." Jack got up and poured himself another cup of coffee, saving himself a half inch in the cup for a jigger of whisky.

"It's not even ten o'clock yet," Terry reproached him.

"Shut up and drink your milk," Jack said and smiled at him.

"I'd better call the office," Laura ventured quietly.

"I did," Jack told her. "You're fired. They were damn nice about it, though. Dr. Hollingsworth wants you to come in and talk to him. Sarah gave me the pitch. It seems they admire your brains but they figure your nerves are loused up. I suggest, Mother, that you see my analyst."

"I can't afford it."

"Neither can I." Jack laughed. "Let's put Terry to work," he said to Laura. "It's time he earned his own way."

"Doing what?" Terry said.

"I don't know. What are you good for? Anything?"

"I can cook." Terry grinned.

"Good. I know a Greasy Spoon two blocks from here."

"Oh, hell!"

"Jack," Laura said suddenly. "Does Beth know I'm all right?"

"Beth?" Jack frowned at her. "You mean Beebo, doll?"

"I mean Beebo," Laura said quickly, growing hot.

"She knows."

"Did you tell her when I disappeared?"

"She looked all over the Village for you. She was worried."

"Do you think she'd talk to me?"

"No."

"Oh, Jack." She turned an unhappy face to him, pleading for a chance to hope.

"She might say 'good-bye' to you. Or 'go to hell.' Don't expect miracles."

"I guess I haven't any right to her friendship anymore." But it suddenly seemed terribly important; the most important thing in the world.

"Not as long as you get her mixed up with Beth."

"Oh, that was just a slip of the tongue."

Jack stood up and paced across the kitchen. He turned, resting his rump on the counter by the sink, and parked his coffee cup next to him. "Laura," he said seriously. "You fell in love with a girl named Beth once. You told me that. Then you and Beth broke up and Beth married somebody and quit school. And then you ran away from home. And you came to New York, and every damn female you met reminded you of Beth."

"Oh, no—" Laura began, but he held up a hand to silence her.

"Now listen to me, damn it! I'm beginning to wonder if you were running away from your father or from Beth."

"Jack!" Laura stood up and faced him, her temper rising.

"Marcie and Beebo look about as much alike as Laurel and Hardy. Yet they both remind you of Beth."

"But that doesn't mean—"

"And you fell for both of them. And don't tell me they were the only ones." His eyes were hard to meet. Laura looked down.

She shook her head. "No," she whispered, confused, rubbing her eyes. "No."

"Beth must have been a great girl, Mother. But you can't stay in love with her all of your life. Even if she *was* the first one." Laura's face flushed.

"I won't talk about this, Jack!" she exclaimed.

"You don't have to. I will."

"It's *my* private life."

"You've pulled me into it. What's the matter, are you afraid to hear me talk about it?"

She sat down, angry. "No," she said sharply. "I'm not afraid."

Jack took a sip of his café royale. "Okay," he said in a business-like voice. "I'm going to tell you something you won't like. But I think you ought to know it. You were never in love with Marcie, Laura."

They looked at each other and finally Laura exploded, "You're cracked! I thought you understood. I thought—*you*, of all people—understood how I felt about her!"

"I did."

"I don't want to hear any more!"

"I don't doubt it," he said. She rose again and faced him, defiant and hurt. "You loved Beth," he said, more gently. "You loved love. It showed in all you said to me, when we first met. You needed love and you went looking for it. You went looking for another Beth. You were bound to find her. You found her in every female face that appealed to you.

"Laura," Jack said slowly. "Marcie doesn't look like Beth. Neither does Beebo. Nobody looks like Beth but Beth. And Beth is gone. She isn't yours anymore. She belongs to a man."

Laura covered her face suddenly with a groan. "Jack, don't! Please," she whimpered. Then, gathering her anger around her, she said, "They *do* look like her! I swear they do!"

Jack shook his head. "They just looked like love, Mother."

Laura gave a little sob. "Jack, don't torture me."

"You know why I'm doing it. You know I don't want to hurt you. Now listen to me, Laura. You can't stay in love with Beth all your life."

Laura put her hands down and looked at him again. "Jack, you don't know how wonderful she was. You never knew her, you can't talk about her. She was so beautiful, she was so good to me. She made me understand what I was, when I was so ignorant and scared that you wouldn't believe it! And she made me understand without hurting me. She made it beautiful. I owe her so much. I loved her so."

"But she's married, Laura. You told me that yourself. You'll never even see her again. No matter how good she was."

"She never hurt me!" Laura flared. "Marcie hurt me, Beebo hurt me, but never Beth."

"Oh, balls!" Jack said. "Never hurt you, hell! She left you, didn't she! She slept with a guy and married him. What do you want, Mother, a silk-lined accident-proof guaranteed romance? Good for six months with lotsa kicks and no pain? Or your money back?

228

They don't come that way. Ask anybody. Ask me. Ask Terry." And then his face softened. "She's gone, Laura," he said quietly, significantly. "And you can't go back to Marcie."

Laura sat down and let the tears roll down her face, and her mouth trembled. "And I can't go back to Beebo," she whispered.

Jack walked over to her and leaned on the table, one arm on either side of her. He put his head against hers and said into her ear, almost in a whisper, "Beebo loves you, honey. She's no Beth. No Marcie. She's herself, and for all you know, that may be even better."

Laura covered her face then and cried.

Fifteen minutes later Jack, who had gone into the bedroom to dress, came back to the kitchen and said, "I'm going to the office for the rest of the day. Somebody has to pay the rent." He looked at Terry with a wry smile.

Laura looked up quickly. "I've *got* to talk to her, Jack. Where can I find her?"

"Beebo? She's working. Stick around till I get home, Mother. Sleep. You look like hell. Get Terry to read you a story or something. You can see her tonight."

"Thanks." She looked at him with wet eyes and then she smiled. "Thanks, Jack. For everything."

He grinned. "It's those damn oysters," he said. "I'm a new man." He winked at Terry and left.

Chapter Seventeen

The Cellar was not very crowded when Laura walked in at eight o'clock. By a quarter to nine, when Beebo got there, the place had filled up a little and the jukebox was going. Dutton, the sketch artist, was making a few bucks with the tourists. There was a table-ful of them in one corner that he was working on. Beebo sat down at the bar and began to josh the bartender. She didn't see Laura, and Laura's heart was pounding so high in her chest that she was afraid to go near Beebo. She didn't know what to say. She was sickeningly afraid of a rebuff, and she hung back in a sweat. She deserved a rebuttal, but she was afraid she couldn't take it.

She watched Beebo for a while, her face shaded slightly as she leaned away from the bar lights. She let the heads of the people next to her serve as a sort of cover behind which she could dodge when Beebo glanced her way.

For a while she was tortured to see Beebo chatting with other women; young pretty girls, like the two high-schoolers Laura had met with her one night.

Beebo was tired. She had two drinks and then she meant to go home. But she was detained by a boy who ran an antique shop a block from her apartment, who was a friend. They talked about nothing in particular, just glad to talk with somebody for a while. Beebo was slightly surprised when Dutton came up and handed her one of his sheets of drawing paper. Beebo took it with a wry little grin. "I knew you'd get around to me sooner or later, Dutton," she said. "I'm part of the decor in this joint. Let's see." She studied the caricature. "I hate to admit it, but it's good. Does my chin stick out like that?"

Dutton grinned. "Take it from me," he said.

Beebo eyed him. "You don't think you're going to get a buck out of me for this, do you?" she said, waving it under his nose.

"I've got my buck, friend," Dutton said, holding a folded bill up between his thumb and index finger. He smiled and pushed the sketch back at her. "It's yours," he said. "Keep it."

Beebo studied him a moment, frowning, and then she looked up and down the bar.

"If you don't like it," Laura said softly in her ear, "just tear it up. I can't complain."

Beebo turned on the bar stool to find Laura standing close behind her. They gazed at each other in silence for a moment. Then Beebo tore the sketch once across the long way and once the short, still watching Laura. And dropped the pieces on the floor. Laura looked at her, trembling. Beebo turned back to the bar and finished her drink in one swallow. Then she said to the boy beside her, "See you, Daisy." And she got up and left the bar.

For a moment, Laura thought she would die where she stood. And then she followed Beebo, walking twenty feet behind her, her heart working hard and making her gasp a little. Beebo walked out into the night, and Laura followed her, coming just a little closer, until she was about five feet behind her. Beebo walked on, slowly, without glancing back, without hurrying her pace. They walked for two full blocks like this, and across the street into a third.

And then Beebo stopped. Startled and scared, Laura stopped where she was, on the curb, with the street light illuminating her silver blonde hair and leaving her face in the shadow.

Slowly Beebo turned around. She looked at Laura. She dropped the cigarette in her hand and crushed it under her heel. For some moments they just stood there and gazed at each other. A man walked by, and then a couple. Then the street was empty.

Finally Laura said, in a whisper that carried dearly to Beebo's heart, "I love you, Beebo. Darling, I love you."

Beebo walked over to her, still moving very slowly, until they stood together in the pool of light just inches from each other. The dawn of a smile showed on her face.

"Little bitch," she said softly. "Laura...Laura..." She leaned down then, tipping Laura's face up to hers. "I can't hate you anymore," she said. "I've given up. There's nothing left but love." And she kissed her. Their arms went around each other suddenly, hard, and they stood there in the lamplight, kissing.

Then they turned and walked into the night toward Cordelia Street.